M. A. ROBINSON

IT ATE US

THE HAUNTING OF BURROW ESTATE

ISBNs:
eBook: 979-8-9992196-0-2
Paperback: 979-8-9992196-1-9
Hardcover: 979-8-9992196-2-6

Legal Notice & Disclaimer:
This literary work is intended for mature audiences. It contains language, themes, and subject matter that may be inappropriate for minors. Reader discretion is strongly advised.

This is a work of fiction. Names, characters, organizations, institutions, and incidents are either the product of the author's imagination or are used fictitiously. Any resemblance to actual persons, living or dead, or to real events is entirely coincidental—unless specifically acknowledged for narrative purposes. Any inclusion of real people, places, or events is used in a fictional context for storytelling and should not be construed as factual or as an endorsement of the depicted events.

References to real entities—including but not limited to businesses, brands, trademarks, films, songs, products, or public figures—are used solely for narrative and atmospheric purposes. All such references remain the property of their respective owners. Their appearance does not imply sponsorship, endorsement, or affiliation.

Any quoted lyrics, song titles, or musical references are used in accordance with the doctrine of fair use for artistic expression, commentary, or context. No commercial claim is made to copyrighted material.

The depiction of the Federal Bureau of Investigation (FBI) in this work is entirely fictional. No representation is made regarding the agency's actual policies, procedures, operations, or personnel. Any portrayals of the FBI or its agents are dramatized for fictional effect. Additionally, any FBI seal or insignia used within this book is an AI-generated fabrication and not an official emblem. It is not intended to replicate or impersonate any government seal, agency, or authority.

Author: M. A. Robinson
Line & Copy Edited by: Leslie Mott
Formatted by: Leslie Mott
Cover Designed by: GetCovers

WARNING

This book contains mature content, including strong language, graphic violence, death, gore, psychological distress, and disturbing themes. It is intended for adult audiences only (18+). Reader discretion is strongly advised.

This is a work of fiction. The events, dialogue, beliefs, and behaviors depicted do not represent the views, values, or beliefs of the author. Any opinions expressed by characters are not to be interpreted as endorsements by the author. The inclusion of controversial, offensive, or violent material is solely for the purpose of storytelling within the fictional narrative.

The author does not condone or promote any acts of violence, discrimination, abuse, or illegal behavior described in the book.

For a detailed list of potential content warnings (which may include spoilers), please refer to pages 362-363 at the back of the book

Dedication

To those who have endured abuse or trauma at the hands of another. Your strength, survival, and voice matter. This story is for you.

(Except you, Kyle. You know what you did.)

M. A. ROBINSON

IT
ATE
US

THE HAUNTING
OF BURROW
ESTATE

Chapter One

Burrow Estate

"Welcome to the Burrow Estate!" Amy enthusiastically points as we pull into the driveway.

Stepping out of Amy's run-down, red Chevy Caprice, I feel the crunch of the brittle, dead grass underneath my pumps. The gray, Victorian estate is fairly large, with bay windows that are hugged by dull, black shutters. The long, cracked driveway running along the side of the estate has dried-up weeds sprouting out of lifted cracks. A narrow, stone path outlines the house as it leads to the front steps of the home's slender front patio. When she told us on the drive over that we'd be seeing a luxurious estate, I wasn't expecting this.

"Sarah, what are you doing?! Get Emelia out of the back seat already – not like we have all day." Kyle snaps as he texts on his recently purchased BlackBerry. He said he bought it as a business phone for his new pharmaceutical sales position, though I have a feeling that is not all he is using it for.

1

"Okay, honey, can you help me get the wheelchair out of the trunk?" I ask, as I begin to gather our nine-year-old daughter's to-go bag.

"No way, I'm not getting my suit dirty. Unlike you, I work for our income. Just get the wheelchair out first, then wheel it to the side door so it is easier to put our daughter into it. This isn't rocket science, Sarah." Kyle continues to text without even so much as a glance. I roll my eyes.

Okay yeah, just show off in front of the realtor. Very classy Kyle. I think to myself as I struggle to get the wheelchair out of the trunk.

"Mom, I can wait in the car if it is easier. I know the wheelchair is heavy," Emelia yells from the back seat of Amy's sedan. I really do have the sweetest daughter.

"No, that's very kind of you to offer, sweetheart, but I want you to see the house, too. Who knows, maybe it could be our new home." I smile as I continue to struggle with the wheelchair. Finally, I'm able to get it loose and carry Emelia to the wheelchair.

"Are you done already?" Kyle huffs as he starts to walk ahead on the pathway. I feel anger boiling up inside of me, but I bite my tongue. I'm not going to make a scene in front of our daughter and the realtor. Silently, I push Emelia up the path.

Following from behind, I watch Kyle flirt with Amy, who starts twirling her hair. She's wearing a musty, muddy brown pantsuit that is at least two sizes too large for her frail figure. Her dirty-blonde hair is frizzy, yet stringy, hanging just past the shoulder pads of her worn-out blazer. Her faux-leather wedges make a hollow clack with each step up the stone path. The whole outfit looks like it came from a thrift store's donation pile.

Seriously Kyle, you are flirting with Ms. Goodwill reject? I think as we approach the front steps. They've been flirting with each other all day, and it has been nothing short of infuriating. I'm used to it from Kyle, but when a woman dares to flirt back in front of me, that's where I lose respect.

The wooden floorboards of the poorly made built-in ramp give a loud squeak as I push Emelia up. It feels like we could fall through at any moment.

"Wow, Mom, this house is huge!" Emelia exclaims as we approach the front door.

A horrible disaster, you mean. I think as I begin to notice the imperfections.

Up close, I can see the gray paint chipping off the siding and the black shutters hanging by what seems like webs that encompass the siding and front spiral pillars.

"All right, now to find the key..." Amy mumbles under her breath as she sorts through her pocket full of house keys.

The front door's frame is painted dark gray and has a unique, worn-out knocker on it. It's black cast-iron and it's shaped like a screaming woman's face with what appears to be spider legs coming out of her mouth. Two long, slender legs curve around the cheeks while the rest spread out, with two eventually coming together at the end to form the knocker's handle. Just looking at it gives me the creeps.

Well, that's definitely going to be removed if we get this place. I hate spiders.

"Ah yes, found it." Amy turns the key, and the door slowly opens with a long, deep screech.

Walking in, there is an open foyer that leads to the living room; a dark, solitary, spiral cast-iron staircase stands towards the back. The staircase leads to the upper level, which has a metal rail overlooking the open living room and front entrance. To the right of the foyer, is a wrap-around kitchen and attached dining room. The kitchen has polished wood counters with black painted cabinets and updated appliances including a plug-in microwave. The dining room is an open space adjacent to the kitchen and has a bay window facing the front of the home. To the left of the foyer, are open, carved wooden French doors that lead to a great room.

"Let's go check out the great room, Emmie. Maybe this could be a bedroom for you," I whisper as I start to roll Emelia through the French doors.

The room is bright considering the dark, hardwood floors. There is a beautiful stained-glass skylight, creating splashes of beautiful reds and purples along the cathedral ceiling and over the center of the room in the mid-daylight. Along the right side of the room, there is an enormous built-in armoire with flowers and trees carved into its cherry wood doors.

This would be perfect for all of Emmie's clothes and medical equipment. I think as I open the doors and visually measure the inside of the first armoire.

"Look at the window, Mom!" Emelia says excitedly as she rolls herself to the bay window facing the front of the house. "Maybe if we put pillows here, I can read while looking outside. You know I love watching birds." Emelia's eyes begin to twinkle.

I can tell she is envisioning herself living here happily, which is all that matters to me, especially with everything that has been taken away from my sweet angel's future.

"Watching birds is a waste of time, Emelia. You should continue to focus on your studies instead of daydreaming. Having a good education is what matters, not like softball's your scholarship-ride anymore." Kyle blurts out, interrupting our peaceful moment as he struts to the center of the room. I watch the twinkle leaving Emelia's face as she processes his remarks.

I lean forward and pull my daughter's long, beautiful strawberry-blonde hair behind her ear. "You will always be my beautiful songbird," I whisper to her. Her face slowly lights up again as she changes the topic.

"Hey Mom, is there a choir at the school here?" Emelia's cheerful spirit is back.

"I'm pretty sure they have one, Emmie. That reminds me," I turn to face Amy who is standing in the doorway. "Amy, can you tell us more about Aditville? I heard that this town was famous for underground mines or something?" I ask as I catch Amy gawking at my husband. This is not the first time I've caught her since we arrived at Burrow Estate.

"Hmm? What was that?" Amy jolts as if coming out of a trance.

Yep, just wipe off the drool while you are at it. I think as I roll my eyes.

"Sarah, just leave Amy alone. She's doing a great job," Kyle looks Amy up and down, "showcasing the home."

I would hate how much he's embarrassing me, except I am quite numb to it at this point. He's always had a thing for blondes, even pathetic ones.

Amy begins to blush, "Oh, Mr. Gallo-"

"Oh, Mr. Gallo was my father. Please, call me Kyle" he lets out a fake chuckle as he brushes Amy's elbow.

If you are going to flirt in front of me with another woman, at least have standards, Kyle. My thoughts are so loud I'm afraid Kyle may have heard them.

At this point in our marriage, his manslut behavior has become the norm. He's always flirting his way through any situation if he thinks it will benefit him. Kyle is that typical tall, handsome salesman with gray eyes and dark curly hair that he always styles just into place. He has a thing for the ladies.

Heck, it worked on me ten years ago when I got pregnant with Emelia. We got married because my father, who is an esteemed member of the Catholic church in Italy, threatened to disown me and strip all financial support, including paying for my nursing degree, if I had a child out of wedlock. Now I'm staying with Kyle because my father is about to pass away. The last thing I want is for my father's reputation at the Vatican to be tainted in his final moments all because I didn't wait an extra year to get divorced. However, in our current situation, I am not sure Emelia or I can afford a divorce, at least not without the inheritance from my father's will.

"It's quite okay, Kyle, I don't mind talking about the town you fine folks plan to move to." Amy begins to recompose herself. "Aditville was over a hundred years ago after settlers discovered underground mines scattered across the territory. Soon, word spread, and folks from everywhere began to move here hoping to strike gold in one of the mines. No gold was ever found, though some townsfolk whisper that these mines are thousands, if not millions, of years old! The Burrow Estate was one of the first homes built in this town and is one of the largest properties west of the Appalachian Mountains. It's listed as a historical estate and cannot be torn down, but you are welcome to do any interior remodeling to your heart's desire! What better way to start the Y2K than to purchase your very own Victorian estate?!" Amy's voice shrieks a little bit in excitement. I can tell the last part was rehearsed, probably in front of her bathroom mirror.

"I have to ask then, Amy, if it is one of the largest properties, why is it listed so cheap? The amount per square foot, without even considering the acreage, is well below market—"

"Excuse us for one moment, Amy." Kyle pulls me into the kitchen on the other side of the foyer, leaving our daughter and Amy in the great room.

"Are you stupid or something, Sarah? Do you want to lose this deal?!" Kyle aggressively whispers. He gives me the same bug-eyed look he makes any time I'm not doing something according to his master plan.

"It's too good to be true, hon. Something's off—"

"Just shut up and let me do the talking. You will not ruin this for me—I mean us." Kyle readjusts his suit coat and walks back into the room as I follow behind.

Once we are in the room, I walk back to Emilia who is near the bay window.

"Amy, we want to take the place, but we may need assistance with the down payment. Do you think the owners would be willing to cover the closing costs?" Kyle begins to use what he thinks is his suave voice. It takes every bit of my strength not to roll my eyes.

"The owners are eager to sell so I'm sure that won't be an issue. I'll confirm and then draw up the papers tonight." Amy has such a huge grin on her face I think her cheeks are going to split open.

"You are such a doll, Amy. Thank you," Kyle says in that stupid voice while winking at me. This time I do roll my eyes.

As we walk out of the room, a slight chill shoots down my spine — the same feeling I get whenever I feel someone staring at me.

Then—

A prolonged, intense creak of the wooden floor planks stretches out from inside the great room.

What the—

I turn around, but nothing's there. Just the same great room, but with an ominous feeling.

I could have sworn I heard something... I can't put my finger on it, but something isn't sitting right with me.

"What is it, Mom?"

I look down, completely forgetting for a moment that I'm still pushing Emelia's wheelchair.

"Oh, nothing. sweetheart, I just thought I heard something, but it turned out it was just my imagination,"

I reply as nonchalantly as possible. I don't want to worry my daughter for no reason.

I'm just glad Kyle isn't listening. He's been saying that I've 'gone nuts' since the car accident.

"Do you like the place, Emmie?" I ask. I need some reassurance that she will love living here. Her happiness is all that matters to me.

"Oh, I love it, Mom! The room is so beautiful. I will have the best sleepovers with all the new friends I'm going to make!"

"Just need those pillows, right?" I smirk. I can always tell what my daughter is thinking.

"Oh, you know it! And lots of stuffed animals. Maybe we could even paint the walls pink!" Emelia's eyes are sparkling with excitement. I can see she is planning out her next year in her new room—which is all the reassurance I need.

"All right, let's get back to the hotel, plan out your bedroom, and make a list. How does that sound?"

"Oh yes, yes, yes!" Emelia claps out of pure excitement as we start making our way back down the path toward Amy's car. There is still something bothering me about this house, but I just can't think of what.

Just shake it off, Sarah, you're just paranoid. Maybe Kyle is right, maybe I am going crazy.

Chapter Two
Moving Day

"Please be careful with that box, it's fragile." I point to the box near the edge of the moving van. It's moving day, and I can tell the movers Kyle hired are a little less than professional. Even so, I am not going to have them breaking my family's heirlooms.

"Yes, Mrs. Gallo, we'll move that box soon. Where do you want the piano?" The supervisor gasps as he readjusts the wooden baby grand-piano he and two crew members are carrying.

"Please place it in the great room, at the back, far-left corner facing outward. Thank you, George." I yell to them as they make their way through the front door.

The floorboards are extra creaky and make me nervous they're going to fall through the ramp along with my piano. Standing on the edge of the ramp, I hear something break from inside. *Yep, I'm just going to grab that box myself.* Picking up the box labeled *Family Heirlooms* I make my way inside, passing the creepy door knocker.

"I really need to ask them to get rid of that," I mumble as I begin the journey up the cast-iron staircase. Unlike the floorboards, the cast-iron steps make an almost echoing thud with each step I take. Up in the master bedroom, I start to unpack the box onto my king-sized bed. The sheets are not unpacked yet, but at least I find the protection cover to put on the mattress in the meantime.

Most of the heirlooms are from Italy, as my family is part of the Catholic Church at the Vatican. Within the box, I find the family crucifix that was passed to me by my father and his father before him. The crucifix is made of brass and rests on a dark, wooden cross. It is tradition to hang it up where all can see, which according to the church, includes the devil's eyes. The more visible it is, the more protection it will give against evil, or so my forefathers said. Most of the time, this means the crucifix hangs on the front door, which is perfect because then I have an excuse to get rid of that stupid door knocker that Kyle likes for some reason. Maybe it is because it's woman's face other than my own.

I better go check on Emelia, maybe she needs her bag changed. Leaving the crucifix on the bed, I make my way down to the great room. Coming down the staircase, I admire the candle chandelier hanging in the foyer, its iron frame draped in cobwebs. The worn cast-iron arms curve upward, each holding a dusty cream-colored candle. The wax has melted and dried in uneven rivulets down the holders. It seems that many of the fixtures in this estate are original cast-iron pieces dating back to when the house was first built.

12

"Hey, Mom, come check out my room!" I hear Emmelia yell from the great room, which will soon be her bedroom. Walking in, I notice the piano was put in wrong way, I sigh.

"Mom, check out the window! The pink and purple pillows we picked at the store are a perfect fit." Emelia pulls herself up onto the bay windowsill. "And super soft. I know my new friends at school are going to love it!" She scoots herself toward the inner edge, carefully making sure the drainage bag from her catheter is still covered by her pink dress.

"Yes, Emmie they work perfectly in this window! Were you able to unpack any of your clothes?"

"I was only able to do some because I couldn't reach the rod in the new closet. I'm sorry, Mom, I know you already have a lot to do."

"No sweetheart, you are fine! I don't mind helping you hang up your clothes at all." Just then, I hear yet another dish shatter from the kitchen. I feel my eyes twitching. If I don't get out of this house soon, I'll probably strangle the next crew member who breaks one of my dishes.

"You know what, let's go to the school and get enrolled. How does that sound?"

"Oh, that sounds fun!" Emelia pulls herself from the corner of the windowsill, being extra cautious in her new dress.

"How is your bag, do we need to drain it before we go?"

Emelia presses on the bag from over her dress. "Nope, all empty."

"Awesome let's get out of here." I help Emelia into the wheelchair, and we make our way to the front door. "Hey George, can you please remove this door knocker when you get the chance? I don't care what you do with it; I just want it gone." I yell into the kitchen, hoping to only hear his response and not another one of my dishes breaking.

"Yes, Mrs. Gallo, not a problem. I'll work on it after we get the medical bed in the room."

"Thank you, George."

CRASH.

A loud crash of what sounds like pots and pans emerges from the kitchen.

Yep, time to go.

We make our way down the ramp to the 1999 silver Honda Odyssey I bought shortly after the car accident last year. Before, I had a Mercedes that my father gave me when I graduated from nursing school. A whole year has passed, but I still miss it.

"Now to put this in the GPS..." I mutter as I fumble with the new navigation system installed in the van. I wish they had made it simpler. There are so many buttons, and the instruction manual might as well be written in Latin.

"Screw it, we'll just use the map. Emmie, do you mind giving directions?" Reaching into the glove compartment, I grab the Aditville town map we got when we purchased the house and pass it back to Emelia.

"Okay, Mom, the map says to turn right at the stop sign."

We drive for about fifteen minutes, finally arriving at Aditville Elementary School, the only elementary school in this small town. It isn't the smallest I've seen, but it definitely isn't the biggest either. The building is solid concrete, and I can tell it's three stories by the small, barred windows on each floor. It feels like we're about to walk into a prison. I don't know why this town loves the depressing color gray so much.

"All right, Emmie let's get you signed up! You can also ask them if they have a choir."

"Yay! I can't wait. It's going to be so much fun singing and making new friends!" Emelia's voice shrieks with excitement. I guess we're not looking at the same building. But that's something I love about my daughter; she is always smiling, no matter the situation.

Getting Emelia into the wheelchair, we head down the covered pathway to the front glass doors. Reaching the entrance, I try to open it, but the door is locked. Suddenly, I hear what sounds like someone clearing their throat through an intercom.

"What do you want?"

Huh? I look toward the sound of the voice and there on the cement wall next to the door is a little black camera attached to a speaker with a push button. The voice sounds agitated like I interrupted their spa day or something.

"Umm, we are trying to—"

I hear a sigh, "Ma'am, I cannot hear a word you are saying unless you hold down the button."

I hold down the button. "I'm sorry. Yes, we are trying to register my daughter for classes. We just moved into town."

15

"Well, I'm sorry to hear that. Fine. Wait for the buzz, then come in and wait in the lobby. The principal will come get you both."

A loud, obnoxious buzz emits from the speaker, signaling us to come in.

BUZZ.

I open the door with one hand and push Emelia inside with the other. The floors inside are also concrete, making it easy to roll Emelia into the lobby. The room is narrow with several glass doors and cameras on both sides. In the center of the room are black chairs, the older, curved kind you would see at the DMV. The walls are empty except for a few announcements and 'Do Not' signs. *What a pleasant place to foster a child's imagination.* I chuckle at my sarcastic thought. I am convinced this building was a prison at some point, if not currently.

One of the glass doors opens, and an older man looks directly at us. I can only assume this is the principal.

"You both can follow me." The older man steps aside and holds the door open for us. Probably the nicest thing to happen since we got here.

Following behind, we walk down a long hallway with several office doors on each side. The depressing gray theme continues as we pass bare walls with occasional award plaques. The man directs us to the very last office at the end of the hallway, shutting the door behind us.

"Have a seat." The man points to the two black leather chairs in front of his dark gray desk.

His office is the definition of minimalistic, there is nothing on his desk except for a notebook, a computer, and a single pen pointing straight ahead toward the only item on the wall—a classic white wall clock with a black rim. I move one of the chairs back so Emelia could take that spot with her wheelchair. From his large, black-leather executive chair, I can tell the man doesn't approve of the change. I don't care though; I'm not going to have my daughter sit in the back of the office. Sitting down, I lock eyes with him. The man's eyes were as lifeless as his pinstriped dress shirt. The bald man is short and stumpy, with gray hairs growing from a large mole protruding from his pointy chin.

TICK. TICK. TICK.

The ambiance of the wall clock ticks really sets the mood. It's a waiting game of who is going to speak first, and I'm not going to lose.

"Hi, I am Emelia, sir! Are you the principal? What's your name, sir? Oh, and is there a choir?!"

And just like that, I've lost.

"Well, aren't you the talkative one? Hopefully, that will change. But to answer your many questions, my name is Mr. Huso, and yes, I am the principal of this fine *private* elementary school." The man replies arrogantly. He has this stupid smirk on his face like he knows he's won.

What an awfully high-pitched voice for a man so rude and arrogant.

I already hate him.

"Now that I have introduced myself, why doesn't your mother introduce herself and tell me what she wants." Mr. Huso leans back in his chair and places his feet up on his desk. I'm surprised they reach.

"Hello, Mr. Huso, my name is Sarah Gallo, and we just moved into the area. We need to get Emelia enrolled in school. I was hoping she would be able to start next month for the fall semester." I smile and grit my teeth. I don't know why guys assume just because I'm blonde that they can be snarky and condescending. I'm already having a bad day, and his ill-mannered comments are not helping.

"Well, that depends on several factors, Mrs. Gallo." Mr. Huso turns his gaze to Emelia's wheelchair, examining it. "What's wrong with her?"

"Excuse me!?" I'm fuming. How dare he ask such a boorish question, especially in front of Emelia?

"I asked a simple question, Mrs. Gallo, or do I need to be more politically correct with you? To see if we can accommodate your daughter, I need to know why she is in a wheelchair."

"Well, since you must know, she is paraplegic, which means she is paralyzed from the waist down and needs the wheelchair because of it."

"Has she always been paralyzed, or is it temporary?" Mr. Huso's gaze never shifts from Emelia. It's irritating that he won't look at me while he's talking.

"Neither. Though I don't remember it, we were in a car accident about a year ago when our car was t- boned while running a red light. The impact was on Emelia's side of the car. She's lucky to be alive." I look at Emelia, who seems like she's handling the interrogation by Mr. Huso well. "She's a smart girl, Mr.

Huso. She has always been an A student and loves extracurriculars—"

"Who was driving?" Mr. Huso interrupts, this time looking directly at me.

"What? Why does that matter?"

"I'm just curious who I am dealing with, Mrs. Gallo. Or is it just *Ms. Gallo* now?" The devious look he makes as he tries to take a glimpse of my ring finger is disgusting. I'm losing my patience with him and struggling to keep my composure.

"It's Mrs. Gallo, and like I said, I don't remember. I suffered a brain injury in the accident, but I was told I was the one who ran the red light."

"Interesting. Pretty and dangerous. I'm surprised your husband stayed with you since you paralyzed your daughter."

Anger is boiling inside of me, and I can feel my face start to flush from rage. Who does this guy think he is, Napoleon?! I clinch my fists, trying to remain calm and stay focused on the task at hand.

Breathe, Sarah. Remember, Emelia needs to go to this school, and this jerk is the ticket in. "Mr. Huso, I must insist we get back on the topic of enrolling Emelia. We can have her prior school send over her transcripts— "

"Emelia will not be attending our school." Mr. Huso stands up and begins to walk around his desk and towards the door.

"Why not?!" I raise both of my hands in disbelief. I cannot believe what I'm hearing. What on earth could possibly be a reason to exclude a child from attending this school?

19

"We are not prepared to accommodate a student with her needs, nor is the school built that way. This used to be a prison."

I knew it.

Mr. Huso looks at Emelia like he pities her. This is the first time I've seen him express anything other than arrogance. "The building is not equipped, and the staff are not allowed to perform the necessary medical care for Emelia. Only a certified nurse would be allowed to. We only have one nurse and no funding to hire a second one specifically for your daughter. Being that we are a private school, unless you hire a nurse yourself, she will not be able to attend."

"I am a nurse. Why not allow me to attend with my daughter?"

"Is your license up to date and valid in the state?"

"It expired just a month ago because I was taking care of my daughter, but I am her mother—"

"Doesn't matter, Mrs. Gallo. Only certified nurses are allowed to provide medical services to students at this school. I will not bend the school rules for one child." Mr. Huso opens his door. "Now, when you have your valid license, we will get her enrolled, but for now, she cannot attend this school." Mr. Huso gestures for us to leave. I stand and turn Emelia's wheelchair around to head out of the office.

"Wait, what about choir? Can she at least go to choir here?" I'm almost begging. Singing in a choir is the only normal school activity Emelia has left. It means the world to her.

"Only students are allowed in the choir. I'm sorry, Mrs. Gallo." Placing his hand on my shoulder, Mr. Huso gently pushes us out of the office.

The walk down the hallway is silent except for the random squeaks from Emelia's wheelchair. Mr. Huso escorts us to the lobby, then outside where it is beginning to rain.

"Again, Mrs. Gallo, I'm sorry. I wish we were speaking under different circumstances. In the meantime, here are the 2000-01 school enrollment forms you'll need to fill out for Emelia once you get your license updated. And this is Mr. Gilbert's card. He's the local lunatic who also happens to be our town librarian. If you have any questions about our town, he will have the answers." Mr. Huso hands me the business card. Without looking, I shove it in the front pocket of my Levi jeans.

"Well, thank you anyway, Mr. Huso. You will be hearing from me soon. Goodbye." I wave as I begin rolling Emelia down the concrete sidewalk. The rain is now a downpour, the sound of raindrops banging like fast-paced drums on the steel sidewalk cover as we reach the minivan. I'm sad for my daughter. She's looking forward to attending school and making friends and not only is she not allowed to, but she had to hear it from an arrogant prick.

The ride home is silent except for the sound of windshield wipers swishing back and forth as the rain continues to pour. It is almost like the weather knows what kind of day we're having. Looking in my rearview mirror, I see Emelia staring out her window. Her smile has disappeared, a blank stare replacing the beautiful, happy air she had to her just this morning.

"Hey Emmie, why don't we order pizza tonight? We can get those cheese sticks I know you love."

"Yes Mom, that sounds good." Emelia continues to stare out the window without even the slightest change in her expression.

This is how I know she's truly heartbroken. The news is hitting her hard. It breaks my heart to see her like this. I can almost feel the pain that she is feeling. No mother wants to see their child like this.

I am definitely going to need a smoke later.

I promised Emelia I would quit, but for occasions such as these, I make an exception. These occasions seem to be happening more often recently. Once things settle down, I'll be able to stop smoking cold turkey. I need them now, though; even if I have to hide my smoking habit from Kyle, who finds smoking to be 'disgusting.' We arrive home as the movers are packing tools in their van to leave. The rain is finally subsiding, which is perfect because the last thing I want for my daughter is to be rained on after a day like this.

"Okay Emmie, when we get inside, I am going to order the pizza while you figure out what movie we're watching tonight. Hopefully, the movers set up the living room."

"Can we watch a romantic movie? I am in the mood for something sweet." Emelia smiles as she holds back tears. It is tearing me apart inside seeing her like this.

"Of course, sweetheart. Any movie you like, you deserve it after a day like today. We will get past it because after all, after a storm there is—"

"Sun!" Emelia chuckles.

It's an inside joke between us. When she was three years old, Kyle left for a week-long business trip. It rained each night, and when it did, Emelia would crawl into bed with me and cuddle up as I sang, 'You Are My Sunshine.' From then on, anytime there was a storm, Emelia would sing the song except, in her version, the only lyric was the word "sun." But heck, it was easy to remember the words! Ever since, Emelia has loved singing, and we always tell each other even when things are rough, there is always sun after a storm.

Walking through the front door, I notice the knocker is still there, staring at me with hairy legs coming out of its mouth. Whoever put it up in the first place had issues, without a doubt.

"George, can you please take this thing down before you leave?"

"I'm sorry, Mrs. Gallo, but it wouldn't budge. I tried several of my tools, even broke some of them trying to take it off. It won't move. Not even a smidge. I'm sorry." George shrugs, walking past me carrying his tool bag to his van. "Maybe just change the door out. But we are done moving everything in. Mr. Gallo said you would have our payment."

"Oh, how much do we owe you?"

"Two thousand dollars."

"What? How?!" I feel like my eyes are going to pop right out of their sockets. I cannot believe the price. I mean the number of dishes and who knows what else they broke is worth at least half that. Just when I thought the day couldn't get worse.

"You can ask Mr. Gallo, but that is what we agreed on." George is calm but insistent. I reach into my pocket, grab my flip phone, and call Kyle. To no surprise, it goes straight to voicemail.

I sigh, "Okay, I'll write you a check, but I'm going to post-date it to tomorrow. That will give me time to speak to my husband but guarantees you have your money if no changes need to be made." I write the check and hand it to George. Kyle seriously needs to stop relying on my funds.

"I understand. I apologize for any confusion. I must go now. Congratulations on the new house, ma'am."

"Thank you."

Just as he is walking to his work van, he turns back around.

"Oh, and ma'am? We couldn't find the wheels for the medical bed. I'm not sure if they are a box or something."

Great. "Okay, thank you for letting me know. Bye, George."

"Bye, ma'am!"

We wave to each other as he drives off with his crew.

"Now to go inside and see which dishes they broke," I mumble under my breath as I lock the front door.

Walking into the kitchen, I call and order the pizza. Hanging up, I notice there are several boxes still unpacked. The dining table is assembled, but placed off-center beneath the candle chandelier, which hangs in the center of the dining room. The cloth dining chairs are stacked alongside the dining room wall instead of at the table.

Two thousand dollars well spent. Thank you, Kyle. I roll my eyes and begin to pick up boxes and set them on our large, oval glass dining table.

Afterward, I begin picking up the chairs and placing them in their respective spots. As I push one of the chairs in, something catches my eye.

What the—

There, in the center of the table, is my family's crucifix standing straight up. Looking around the crucifix, I can see nothing holding it up. I have never seen it balance like this. In the past, I've always had to lean it on something or hang it by its hook, never has it been able to stand on its own.

I could have sworn I left you on the bed...

BANG!

The crucifix falls on the glass tabletop with a loud, sharp thud. "EEK!" I scream as I jump back.

"Are you okay, Mom?" Emelia yells from her room, she must have heard me scream.

"Yes, I am fine dear, I just got startled is all," I yell back, without taking my eyes off the crucifix.

How did you get here? I slowly pick up the crucifix and look it over. There is nothing different about it, except for a small crack on the back in the bottom corner of the wooden cross. It must have cracked when it fell over on the glass tabletop, but I can't help but wonder how it got onto the table in the first place. Maybe it was a crew member? Or maybe I am remembering wrong? Perhaps I left it in the kitchen before Emelia and I left for the school? *No... I would have remembered going into the kitchen... or would I?* Whatever it was, there is no point in stressing over it now, not when I have things like Emelia's education and getting my license renewed to worry about. *Now would absolutely be a great time for a smoke break.* I gently lay the crucifix back onto the table and I go into my purse, pulling out my secret stash of cigarettes. I always have my lighter in my pocket in case I need to bum one off somebody when I am away from my purse or trying to sneak one without Kyle seeing me.

"Hey Emelia, I'm going outside to wait for the pizza. When it gets here, we'll start our movie night. Do you need anything before I step outside?" I begin putting on my coat, I don't know if it will rain again, and I'm not taking any chances with my secret smoke break.

"I will be fine, Mom, and I already picked the movie. Prepare to cry happy tears!"

I chuckle. Emelia is just an amazingly sweet child, inside out.

"Okay, Emmie. When I come back, it will be with pizza."

"Yay!" I can hear Emelia laughing in her room. Despite everything that's happened, she is still such a joy to be around. I wish I could be brave like my daughter. Outside, I go around to the back west corner of the house and puff my first cigarette of the day.

"Ahh, yep, I needed that" I whisper as I inhale the next drag.

I still cannot get the image of the crucifix out of my head. I try but cannot figure out how it was standing

26

on the dining table, or how it got there. I keep thinking in circles, which drives me crazy. This is the opposite of the goal I'm trying to achieve with this smoke break.

Just as I'm putting out the butt of my cigarette, the pizza delivery driver pulls up to the house. What perfect timing. *Oh well, enough about this crucifix. Time for pizza and movie date with my daughter.*

Chapter Three
Emelia: Bedtime

L ying on the loveseat in the living room, I have the perfect view of the movie I picked out as it plays on our huge projection TV. The movie is finishing, and I'm proud it was just as good as I hoped it would be. "What a great movie! Are you crying yet, Mom?" I look over to see my mother curled up on the matching gray, linen reclining armchair, wiping away tears with her handkerchief.

My mother sniffs, "No, Emmie... I'm not crying." She replies while clearing her throat and straightening herself in the chair.

"Haha, I knew it!" I laugh. She's probably just upset I messed up her makeup by picking such a great romantic movie.

My mother is always super proud of how she looks. Even when she's sick or we aren't going anywhere, she always has her hair and makeup done. I can't remember the last time I saw her in sneakers. It must be an Italian thing, since that's where Grandpa's mansion is. I hope we can visit again soon. I overheard my mother talking to him about his health.

Getting out of the recliner, my mother walks over to the TV and ejects the DVD. "Now Emmie, movie's over. It's getting pretty late, let's get ready for bed."

"Aw, okay Mom." I don't really want to go to bed. It's way too fun staying up on our movie date night.

Lifting me off the loveseat, my mother helps me into the wheelchair, and I roll myself from the living room to the bathroom that's right next to my new bedroom. Inside, the bathroom is dark and musty with forest green pinstripe wallpaper that's starting to peel from the walls—it feels and smells old.

Hopefully, we can paint this bathroom pink and maybe add some flowers...

"Emmie, stop scheming over there and brush your teeth."

"Yes, Mom!" I don't know how my mother always knows when I'm planning something. She must be psychic.

Turning on the rusty brass faucet, the pipes make a hollow echoing noise as water begins to splatter out bits of brown specks before turning into a clear stream. "Eww," I whisper as I grab my hairbrush and toothbrush and start brushing my hair and teeth at the same time. I'm great at multitasking. I keep thinking about my remodel plans for this bathroom in my head.

Okay, the shower curtain can be sparkly purple and we can paint some daisies—

"Emmie, focus! It's bedtime and we still need to change your catheter bag and diaper after getting you into your pajamas," my mother yells from the living room.

"Okay, Mom!"

Seriously, how does she do that? How does she always know what I'm thinking? I can't get away with anything even if I wanted to. I finish up and roll to the French doors leading to my room.

"Mom, I'm ready for you!" Even though my mother is the only one who ever changes me, it's still super embarrassing. Like, what kid wants to be changed like a baby? I don't like it, but I know I'm lucky to have a great mom who takes such good care of me. She never makes me feel bad about myself, either.

"Okay sweetheart, I'm finishing cleaning up out here real quick. I'll meet you in your room."

"Sounds good, Mom." I roll myself through the cherry wood French doors into my room.

I love the doors and the cathedral ceiling—it makes me feel like I'm a princess going into my royal palace. The movers set most of my furniture up for me, which was super nice of them. My white dresser and mirror are put together next to my piano in the back of the room, near the French doors. The piano is still facing the wrong way, but it has wheels, so I know my mother can fix it.

Straight ahead is my medical bed, with my cute little white nightstands on either side. Most of my stuff is still in boxes, but my pink and purple lava lamp is set up on one of the nightstands, which makes me really happy. The lava lamp has glitter in it, making the prettiest colors dazzle over the room's cream and brown paisley wallpaper. I smile. While the room still needs more pink, it's looking great. I know my new friends will love it. Mr. Huso said I can't go to school until my mother has

renewed her license, but I know it won't take her too
long and I'll be able to go this year. I really do have the
best mother ever.

"Emmie, did you pick out your pajamas? I'm
almost done and will be in there in a minute or two."

"Not yet, Mom, I will now."

Rolling to the left armoire, I pull on the antique
brass handle to get to the boxes labeled *Clothes* on the
floor of the closet. I can tell the wardrobe is old because
of all the scratches on the floors and the inside of the
doors. Opening the first box that's just the right height
for me to reach from my wheelchair, I get lucky and find
my favorite pink pajamas. They're my favorite because
they have little white kitties on them. Every time I wear
them, I think about how much I want a pretty white cat.
If I had one, I would name it Belle.

"Found them, Emmie?" My mother walks into
the room with the diaper bag. She calls it my 'to-go' bag.
I think she does that because she doesn't want me to feel
embarrassed.

"Yep! I actually found my kitty ones!"

"That's wonderful, sweetheart. Let's get you
changed and ready for bed."

"Okay."

She lays a plastic, water-absorbent pad on the
end of the mattress and helps lift me into the bed as I try
to help by pulling on the bed's handlebars. We just got
this bed and even though it's not as pretty as my old one,
it does make it easier for my mother to help me get in
and out. Pressing the corded remote, I raise the bed. My
mother lifts off my dress and changes me into my
pajamas. She draws down my bottoms to my knees to

access my bag and diaper. I don't feel a thing while I watch her detach the catheter bag, place it on the hardwood floor, then start to unstrap the diaper. She pulls out the wipes and begins to clean the runny soil from my bottom.

"Not too much tonight, Emmie. Did you take your laxative today, sweetheart?"

"No, I forgot today. I'll make sure to remember tomorrow!"

"It's okay, sweetheart, today was a rough day." My mother finishes putting the new diaper on me and gets up to open the left armoire where my clothes are. She starts to dig through the boxes. I'm not sure what she's looking for.

"Found them!" She turns to show the fluffy, pink grippy socks she got me when we were shopping for the pillows we put in front of my window.

"Oh, I completely forgot about those! They're so soft. Thank you again for getting them for me, Mom."

"Of course, anything for my little songbird."

She goes to close the doors and pauses, shaking her head in disapproval. She sighs, "The movers really did a number on the doors and floors. What did they do, throw a raccoon in here?! There are scratches everywhere!"

"It's okay, Mom, I'm sure some of it is because it's old." I smile at her. I don't want her to be stressed.

She doesn't reply and closes the closet doors. She puts the socks on my feet and then pulls out a new catheter bag from the diaper bag. She gently twists the new one on and kisses my belly. Then she pulls down my pajama top and tucks me in with my baby-pink sheets and furry purple blanket.

"Now, get some sleep my songbird, we got a long day tomorrow." My mother whispers as she gives me another kiss, this time on the forehead.

Picking up the catheter bag off the floor, she walks to the French doors and flips the light switch. The room swirls as the pink and purples of my lava lamp mix with the red moonlight shining through the skylight.

"I love you, Emmie."

"I love you too, Mom."

My mother smiles and closes the doors behind her as she leaves the room. I adjust my pillow and stare at the ceiling, watching the warm colors from the lava lamp dance above me.

It reminds me of when I used to take ballet lessons before the accident. I used to love going on stage with my classmates and seeing my mom cheering me on in the crowd. It was fun to pirouette and feel the heat from the stage lights pass through my fingers. I would forget the audience was even there and just drift into the sound of the solo violin. It was the best feeling... a feeling I'll never have again.

I begin to cry. I try to be strong and grateful for what I have, but I miss being a normal kid. I miss playing softball and dancing to my favorite songs.

Sometimes I dream about running through the field of wildflowers at my grandfather's mansion in Italy. The field is filled with beautiful flowers of every color, and butterflies bounce from bud to bud as I twirl in the center. The sun is always warm and bright with not a cloud in the sky as I dance in my white tutu, slowly flapping my arms and starting to fly.

I know it's silly, but it's my dream, so I can! Flying up higher and higher, I pirouette above the field and laugh with the butterflies who join in the dance—the dance of the wildflower.

It's always at that moment, my alarm clock rings, bringing me back down to reality, where I am grounded, never to fly.

I'm still staring at the ceiling, deep in thought, when I'm suddenly interrupted by a deep scratching sound coming from the armoire.

SCRATCH...SCRATCH...

Huh?! My heart feels like it just stopped. I hold my breath and try to listen again. The noise gets louder.

SCRATCH...SCRATCH...

"MOM!!!" I scream as loud as I can.

There's something in my closet and without the use of my legs, I'm stuck. I can't run. I can't even scoot. Where's my softball bat when I need it?

I hear fast, heavy footsteps pounding down the spiral staircase from the foyer. The French doors fly open and my mom bursts into the room, holding a frying pan like she's ready to whack someone.

"What is it?! What happened?!" She flips the lights on and then starts to calm down when she realizes no one else is in the room.

"There's something in my closet! I heard scratching noises!" I point to the armoire, still panting.

My mom raises the frying pan and swings open the doors. But nothing's there. Just the same old boxes labeled *Clothes*.

She lowers the pan and comes to sit on the edge of my bed.

"I didn't see anything in there. Are you sure you heard something?"

"Yes, Mom. I'm not lying. I really did hear it!"

"I know you'd never lie to me, Emmie," she says gently. "I'm just saying... there could be a lot of reasons for the noise. This house is old, and old houses make weird sounds, especially at night. Plus, it's your first night sleeping in here, and that could make anyone feel nervous."

She takes my hand in hers and gives me a soft smile. "Would you like me to sleep here with you? Or we could both go sleep in the living room together, if you'd feel better out there."

Her voice is calm and sweet and suddenly I do feel better. Maybe she's right. Maybe I was just nervous.

"I think I'll be fine now. Sorry for scaring you, Mom."

"Don't you ever be sorry. I'm always here for you. After every storm, there is..."

"Sun!" I laugh a little. "Mom, you're so silly."

"Okay, sweetheart. I'm here. Call me if you need anything. I've got your panic button all set up, it's connected to the speakers in the kitchen and in my bedroom. Just press it and I'll come running."

She shows me where it is, even though I already know. It's a big red button right on top of the remote. Pretty hard to miss. She gets up, walks to the light switch, and pauses in the doorway to look at me one more time.

"You sure you don't want me to sleep in here with you?"

"I'm sure. Goodnight, Mom. I love you."

"I love you too, sweetheart. Goodnight."

She closes the door behind her and I'm back where I started, lying under my blankets and watching the lava lamp lights swirl around the ceiling. The colors make soft patterns, and my heart finally starts to slow down again. I let my eyelids drift shut.

Just as I'm starting to fall asleep, creepy, low clicking noises makes me wide awake.

CLICK...CLICK...CLICK

What was that?

I blink and glance over at my clock. It's almost 1 a.m. Then, the floorboards start to creak, and there is tapping, like quick footsteps

My eyes fly open. I don't move a muscle. I just stare up at the ceiling, where a huge shadow starts to stretch across the top of the room. The red glow from the skylight makes it hard to tell what it is, but it's definitely big—

And it's moving toward me.

Each step makes the floor moan. It's slow. Heavy. I feel frozen. My breath is caught in my throat. The shadow slides over the bed, then over me. My whole bed is covered in the black shape.

Then—

Silence.

Total, terrifying silence.

I shut my eyes tight and try to breathe, but I'm shaking. I whisper to myself, "It's just a nightmare. Wake up, Emmie."

Then I hear it—
The clicking.
Scary, low clicking.
CLICK...CLICK...
I open my eyes and turn my head. The armoire doors are open—and they're swaying. Back and forth. Like there's a breeze. But the air in the room is still and stale.

The squeaking keeps going. I press my hand over my mouth so I don't make a sound. I stare at the doors, trying not to blink.

Then I notice the lava lamp's light getting brighter. I glance up with just my eyes. The shadow on the ceiling is gone.

I exhale slowly and let myself relax. Maybe the nightmare is really over. I shift to get comfy again and reach over to grab the bed remote.

"Next time, I'll have this ready," I whisper, holding it close. "Even if it's just a dream."

The dancing lights on the ceiling make me feel a little better. I'm just starting to drift back off to sleep when—
BUMP.
My bed shakes. Something hit the bottom of my bed.

A low, growling hiss rises up from underneath.
HISS.
I jolt upright and go for the panic button—
And that's when I see him.
A boy.

He's peeking at me from the side of the bed. His face is pale and glowing red from the moonlight pouring through the stained-glass skylight. His black hair hangs over his eyes. His cheeks are sunken in, like he hasn't eaten in forever. His eyes look empty.

He tilts his head. His mouth hangs open, showing gross, dark teeth. We just stare at each other. The room is still and quiet.

He closes his mouth and leans his head sideways over the edge of the bed. The way he moves is weird. Like a puppet on strings.

Now that I get a better look at him, he seems around my age. And even though I should probably be totally scared—I'm not.

He doesn't seem mean.

Maybe he goes to the elementary school here? Or maybe he's homeless? He looks really hungry.

No. I'm dreaming. This has to be a dream. I sigh in relief. There is no way that any of this is real.

I use the bed's side bars to pull myself up and fix my pillow so I can sit upright.

"Hello," I say softly. "I'm Emelia. What's your name?"

Chapter Four
The Library

*R*ING...RING...
The classic black-and-white alarm clock on my nightstand goes off as I reach my arm out from under the covers to hit the *off* button.

"Ugh, I can't believe it is 6 a.m. already," I mutter under my breath as I leave my arm slumped over the alarm clock. I'm immediately regretting my decision to get an early start to the day.

Though I'm typically an early riser, waking up to Emelia screaming last night set me on edge and it was difficult to sleep after. I thought at some point in the middle of the night I would hear the alarm from Emelia's remote and would need to go charging in equipped for a fight. I would have been ready for it and this time I'd have my Louisville Slugger instead of a frying pan from the kitchen counter. It took a while, but I finally passed out around 3 a.m. Part of me wishes Emelia had taken my offer to have a slumber party on the couches. First nights can be scary for a nine-year-old, especially in an old house. Heck, the house gives me the creeps.

Finally gathering up the willpower to get out of bed, I head into the master bath to shower and get myself ready before I start the laundry. I make the effort to be presentable at all times—I feel it sets a good example for Emelia of how a classy woman should appear. Finishing the last touches of my makeup, I pull my hair up into a ponytail. With the July heat in this small town, I don't want my blonde curls to turn into a frizzy mess.

"Hello, gorgeous," I whisper to myself as I take a few last glances in the mirror before walking back to the bed, where I'd laid out my clothes the night before.

I picked out this adorable navy-blue A-line dress with white polka dots I bought at a local boutique right before we moved here. I also have the perfect white sandals to go along with the outfit. Cute, yet comfortable enough to walk through town later in the morning. My gold crucifix necklace completes the ensemble.

"All right, fun time is over, now to get to work." I say quietly to myself.

As I begin to gather dirty clothes, I realize situations like carrying laundry up and down steps is the reason why homes stopped having spiral staircases. I look over the railing to the floor of the foyer below. "Hmm, I know what I'm going to do." I smirk.

Grabbing as many dirty clothes as I can, I begin to launch them over the railing. Watching my masterpiece in action, it feels good to be improper for a moment. Handful after handful, I launch the clothes over the rail and watch them fall with amusement. On my last throw, I see a small piece of paper escape from the bundle in midair and flutter slowly as it gradually makes its way to the top of the mound of clothes.

Huh, what is that? I think as I make my way down the staircase, trying to be careful not to wake Emelia up.

Picking up the paper, I recognize it right away—Mr. Gilbert's business card. The one Principal Huso gave me yesterday. *Maybe Emelia and I should make a visit to the library while we are in town,* I think as I put the business card in my dress pocket and begin gathering laundry into the basket. With the last bit of clothes in my hand, I hear a familiar engine noise from outside of the house. I pick up the basket and carry it with me as I peer through the dining room window. There, parked along the curb in front of the house is Amy's red Chevy Caprice, engine still running. I see Kyle step out of the passenger's side and onto the sidewalk. He's still wearing the same classless ripped jeans and white t-shirt he had on yesterday.

"Why am I not surprised." I sigh and shake my head as I continue to watch from the window.

Seeing the side of his face, I can tell he's saying something, but I can't hear it from this distance. As the car drives off, Kyle blows a kiss towards it. Once it's out of sight, he turns around and begins to strut his way up the pathway to the front door.

"Shit." I whisper as I lightly jog to the laundry room at the back of the house.

I'm not in the mood for confrontation, and I don't want to wake Emelia if we start to argue. Just as I reach the laundry room, the door creaks open. Kyle's distinct footsteps echo through the house, the floorboards creaking beneath him. His steps lead toward the kitchen. A thud follows—I can only assume he's tossing his midsized tan leather duffle bag, full of god knows what, onto the counter.

"Wow, come home from working overnight and there isn't even any breakfast made for me. God, my wife is useless," I hear Kyle snark as the fridge opens with a creak.

This man buys his own lies. Unbelievable.

I shake my head as I quickly put the load into the washing machine. I then quietly make my way to the staircase, hoping Kyle won't notice me. I just want to be left alone. Just as I reach the staircase—

"Well, good morning, beautiful," Kyle says in his stupid suave voice.

Dammit.

Turning around, I see Kyle leaning up against the outer wall of the kitchen trying to do his *flirty* pose— one leg crossed over the other at the ankle, arms crossed, and leaning his shoulder against the wall. He looks ridiculous. It makes me want to vomit.

"Good morning. How was...work?" It takes every ounce of control not to let my expression slip. I do not want a repeat of last time.

A year and a half ago, I caught him cheating and confronted him about it. He lashed his anger out at Emelia and told her he was going to drop her out of the softball summer camp she was going to the following day. Emelia was so disappointed. I couldn't let Kyle pull her out, so I sweetly suggested he leave that night to go see a baseball game up in New York—just to get him out of the house so I could get Emelia to the camp. I think he knows Emelia is my Achilles heel.

44

"Work was good. I'm showing them who's boss and making an impression on my supervisor. I'll probably have to stay late a few times a week to keep my numbers up, but you know how pharmaceutical sales are—experimental drugs aren't going to sell themselves!" Kyle chuckles as he slowly starts walking toward me. He's giving me the 'I want you' eyes and I'm not about to let that happen.

"That's wonderful to hear but hon, you must be so tired from working all night long. Why don't you go upstairs and shower? I will bring up some sleepy-time tea to help you fall asleep quicker." I say as I start to walk to the kitchen to avoid any further advances. Kyle grabs my arm as I pass by.

"I don't think I want to sleep just yet. Why don't you come up with me?" Kyle whispers in my ear while holding my arm firmly. The thought of crawling into bed with him at this point is appalling.

"Oh, not right now, hon, I need to run into town to see about how to get my license renewed so I can be Emelia's nurse at school. Maybe after you had time to rest for a while—"

"Wait, you're going to try to get recertified after you caused an accident? What, are you going to write to the board, 'Please give me my license so I can be a nurse to the same child I paralyzed?' Sarah, are you stupid or something?" Kyle laughs mockingly as he lets go of my arm. "Even if they overlook the accident, do you really think they would even let you be certified with a traumatic brain injury? That alone must be a liability. I mean, you have been off the wagon recently. Have you looked into those psycho pills I told you to get on yet?

I'm sure I can get you some at work. I mean, whatever gets you back to normal." Kyle says with a smug, yet annoyed face, as he fidgets with his duffle bag.

"I am a fully qualified nurse and I didn't *lose* my license, it just expired. I think I only need to resend my credentials. I wish you weren't so condescending."

"Maybe I wouldn't have to be if you weren't out of your mind."

Just before I can respond, Kyle continues, "Speaking of which, I took the liberty of stopping at the pharmacy in town to pick up your medications." He puts the pharmacy bag on the counter and rolls his eyes. "And for the love of god, take them."

I reach into the bag and pull out the pill container. The label is the same, but the pills are a different color than usual—blue instead of the normal pink.

"These don't look the same, they're a different color...."

"Oh, the pharmacist said these pills are from a different manufacturer. They look different, but it's the same medication. Gosh Sarah, now you're questioning pharmacists? Let me go ahead and grab the tin foil so you can make yourself a hat." Kyle huffs as he starts to make his way up the stairs to the master bedroom. Probably to catch up on the sleep he didn't have last night with Amy.

"Maybe if you knew where the foil was..." I mumble under my breath as I walk into the kitchen. I grab a glass from the cabinet and take the pill. As I place the bottle into the medicine cabinet over the microwave,

I glance at the clock above the double farm-style brass sink. It's almost 8 a.m.

"Wow, where has the time gone? Guess we are going to have to eat Pop-Tarts on our way into town to stay on schedule. I'm sure Emmie won't object." I say to myself as I reach into the pantry and pull out a couple packets of strawberry Pop-Tarts.

"Hey Mom, I'm ready to get out of bed." I hear Emelia yell from her bedroom.

"Okay hon, I'll be right there." I yell back as I stuff our breakfast into my hot-pink satchel, still sitting on the kitchen counter from yesterday.

I start to march off toward the double French doors—and I see him. A tall, frail man stands in front of the door, his back turned to me. He holds up an old, rusty lantern, its dim candlelight flickering against his oversized brown trench coat. The style is old—almost like he stepped out of the 1800s. He's covered in dirt from the tip of his tattered top hat to his torn black leather boots. Cobwebs cling to his dusty gray pants as he stands there, absolutely motionless.

"Hello? Who are you and what are you doing in my house?" I say as I slowly start walking toward him. It's strange, he looks like he jumped right out of an old movie scene.

"Mom, are you okay?" Emelia yells from her room. I turn my head toward Emelia's voice.

"Yes hon, just a moment," I respond and as I turn my head back, the man is gone.

What the heck? Did I just imagine this? No, he was right in front of me. I think as I scan the rest of the room, but he is nowhere to be seen.

47

Confused and slightly freaking out, I shake it off to the best of my ability and head into Emelia's room.

"Good morning, Emmie. How did you sleep?" I say calmly as I head toward her bed.

"It was great, Mom, I met a new friend last night in my dreams. His name is Romeo. Well, actually I'm not sure what his name is. He didn't talk much... not at all. Actually, he moved kind of funny. Like a puppet." Emelia giggles as she starts to peel off her purple and pink covers.

"Oh? *He,* huh? This better not be a boyfriend I don't know about." I smirk as I start to open the armoire and pull out her folded wheelchair.

"No, Mom, that's gross! They've got cooties!" Emelia makes a puckered face like she just ate something sour. I laugh.

"Okay, just making sure. I don't want to have to scare any boys away from my beautiful songbird." I chuckle as I roll the wheelchair to the side of the bed. "I wish I had a great imagination like you, Emmie."

"Yeah, in my dream he stayed at the end of the bed and listened to my stories. He really is sweet. If he wasn't a dream, you would like him." Emelia smiles as she stares straight up at the cathedral ceiling. The lava lamp is still on and she's watching the sparkles dance.

"I'm sure I would have loved him, Emmie. but we'll get you in school soon and you can make lots of friends." Helping her into the wheelchair, I turn off her lava lamp. Now the dark wood floors are glistening with reds and purples from the morning sun shining through the stained-glass skylight. "And they all better be girls!"

"Ah! Mom, stop!" We both start to laugh as we get Emelia ready to head into town.

We are just finishing our last bites of Pop-Tarts as we pull into the small town of Aditville, rolling over its worn brick roads. The entire town is built from brick, which gives it a nostalgic, historical charm. Each small shop stands separately, a maple tree planted in front, roots pushing through the brick sidewalk.

Along the pathways are weathered wooden benches nailed into the brick sidewalk between businesses. Every building has an old wooden sign, seemingly repainted every few years, but still showing chipped paint through the cracks. The maple trees are overgrown, too large for the town, but I understand why no one wants to cut them down. Aditville has been here since the 1800s—no doubt the trees have, too.

"Emmie, keep an eye out for the library. That's where we are going first."

"Oh yay, the library! I want to find some animal books while we're there. I love learning about animals!" Emelia replies, excitement in her voice.

She loves to read, especially about nature. I wish I had been as bright as she is when I was her age.

"Oh, there it is Mom, on the right!" Emelia points to the small, light-tan brick building at the end of the road. A wooden sign out front reads 'Library.'

"Wow, you have some great eyes, Emmie!" I say as I pull into one of many empty parking spots in front of the building.

I step out of the minivan and hear a slight whistle in the air as a breeze passes through the leaves and brushes my cheeks. I pause for a moment. The town, though tranquil and quaint, leaves me with an unsettling feeling. I look around and realize there are no birds, no bugs, no people—nothing. Just the whistle of the wind and the creak of wooden signs swaying on rusty chains outside each store's entryway. I have never experienced such a hollow feeling in a town that wasn't abandoned. I get Emelia out of the van and into her wheelchair and we make our way inside the library.

Dust puffs all around us as we step inside the building—I can tell the library is not the most popular place in town. The room is poorly lit, but I can see rows of dark wooden shelves filled with books that most likely haven't been touched in years. The main source of light is a stained-glass window on the library's eastern wall, which paints the room with glowing reds and purples. "Emmie, why don't you look around? If you need anything just yell for me."

"Oh, sweet! Thank you, Mom!" Emelia whispers excitedly as she begins to roll herself to the aisle labeled *Biology and Nature*.

As she rolls away, I make my way to the stained-glass window. Something about it is familiar to me and I want to get a closer look. I pass several aisles of bookshelves and find myself standing in front of the massive window. The stained glass depicts a beautiful woman in a long, blood-red, empire-waisted gown with purple adornments and jewels. One of the woman's long sleeves is draped over her shoulder as she holds a bejeweled goblet above her head. The woman's face, accented by a cracked background of royal purples and blood reds, is looking down toward her other hand, where she appears to be holding a small, clear spider— the only part of the entire window transparent and unstained.

"She is quite beautiful, isn't she?" A quivering voice whispers from behind me. I turn around and see an old man. He looks like he jumped out of an old Western movie, wearing a red-and-blue long-sleeved paid collared shirt tucked into faded jeans and held up by a worn-out leather belt. The blue of his gentle eyes stands out from his pale complexion and scruffy white beard. Hunched over a black cane, shaking slightly, he offers me a kind smile.

"Why yes, she really is quite beautiful. Who is she?"

"Well, no one knows for sure. The man who commissioned the local artists at the time never disclosed it. But if you ask me, I think it's the Greek mortal Arachne," the man slowly lifts his cane and points it at the spider. "Peculiar, that's the only part of the glass not stained. Makes you wonder what John Burrow's intention was." The man lowers his cane.

"Did you say John Burrow? Was he the original owner of the Burrow Estate by any chance?"

"Why, yes, my dear. The very same."

"We just moved into the Burrow Estate a couple of days ago. There is a stained-glass skylight in my daughter's room. Now I'm wondering if the house originally had stained glass in every room."

The man begins to chuckle. "No, my dear, John Burrow just had the two windows created. In fact, the pair are identical, he wanted a spare in case the one in his house broke. Seems John Burrow was very protective over the windows, or at least that's what the pioneer journals say." The old man's voice crackles. I can tell he's enjoying our interaction just as much as I am. It's refreshing to have a genuine conversation. Besides my daughter, I haven't had a pleasant interaction with anyone since we arrived in this town.

"Oh, how rude of me, I'm Sarah. What's your name, sir?"

"Why, my name is Gilbert Hickok, but you can call me 'Mr. Gilbert.'"

"It's great to meet you, Mr. Gilbert. In fact, my daughter and I came to the library to talk with you—Mr. Huso over at the school told me you may be able to answer my questions about the town." I reach into my pocket and fish out the business card Huso gave me yesterday, I give it a once over and then pop it back into my dress pocket. "I was also wondering if I could get information about how to renew my nursing license here?"

"Oh, wonderful. Well, come. Step into my office and I will do my best to help you, my dear." Mr. Gilbert replies as he slowly hobbles toward a room at the end of the aisle.

I slowly walk alongside him as we make our way to his office. The room is packed—every table, every corner has books and papers stacked to the ceiling. Surrounded by walls of documents, books, and dusty cobwebs, I notice on the far side of the office there is a huge, old map that appears to be of an underground passageway of some kind. The map is stained a dark tan, its edges have deteriorated, and there are some random black smudges marring a few areas of the inked drawing. Laid atop the map are red strings that extend across held by thumb tacks, pinning aged article clippings to various locations on the map's passages. On the right side of the map is a large section where the passages stop, then reappear again on the other side, almost like there is a huge section unaccounted for. Next to this map is a desk with an old, bulky desktop computer and a black, rusted dial phone. An old, wooden chair sits next to the desk, facing the map—probably where Mr. Gilbert spends most of his day.

"What's all of this, Mr. Gilbert?"

"That my dear, is the map of underground mines right here in Aditville. Each passage drawn was verified by miners and written in their journals. My great-great-grandfather collected the journals from the miners and began creating this map. He wanted to uncover what secrets the mines had to offer, if there were any. Since then, my family has worked to complete the map— we've collected journals, newspaper articles, and maps from miners who have gone underground. Since I never married or had kids, this endeavor will probably end with me." Mr. Gilbert stumbles a bit as he plops into the chair facing the map.

"Why is this section not marked?" I ask as I point to the large open spot on the map.

"That is quite the eye you got there, Sarah." Mr. Gilbert smirks, a twinkle in his eye as he continues, "No miner was ever able to access that area because it's blocked off by rock and debris. There have been written accounts of miners finding black powder and barrel pieces in the blocked passageways. The best I can tell, John Burrow set off gunpowder barrels in the mines to block the area. I wonder what he was trying to hide..." Mr. Gilbert leans back into his chair and pulls out a cigar.

"John Burrow? How do you know it was him?"

"Well, the unmapped area is directly under the Burrow Estate."

"What?!" I gasp. I knew the town was known for its mines, but I never thought there'd be one directly under my house.

"Just like everyone else who moved to Aditville in the 1800s in search of gold, only John got there first. According to the journals, John ended up buying the whole land and started building the town from the ground up using his own funds. Though they couldn't prove it, the townsfolk believed that John had already found the mine, and he used the gold he found to purchase the land which he later called Aditville." Mr. Gilbert takes a deep inhale of his cigar, then slowly exhales a small ring of smoke into the stale air. "The first building he built though was his own home, which is the one you currently reside in. That's why its called the Burrow Estate. It belonged to the town's founder John Burrow"

"But why would he blow up the entrances to the part of the mine that was below his house? If he had already found the gold, what was the point in blocking it off?"

"Well, those are the million-dollar questions now, aren't they? And how he got into the mines is a whole 'nother mystery in and of itself." Mr. Gilbert puts out his cigar in the nearby ashtray. The last bit of cigar smoke fights to escape the cold brown glass. "There are no records of him accessing the mines through the main entrances and there have been no entryways found on his property, either. Quite mysterious, that John Burrow was." Just as Mr. Gilbert is about to continue, Emelia rolls up to the office's door.

"Hey Mom, I found an awesome book in the biology section. It's called *Animals in Plain Sight*. How cool is that?!" Emelia attempts to roll into the office and accidentally knocks a stack of old notebooks over. "Oh no, I'm so sorry, sir!"

"Don't you worry about it, sweetheart, they look better this way. And take the book—it's yours now." Mr. Gilbert smiles as he slowly gets up and hobbles toward Emelia.

"Thank you, sir!"

"*Sir* was my father, call me 'Mr. Gilbert,'" he replies as he reaches into his pocket and pulls out a candy wrapped in red and green foil. Hand shaking, he hands the candy to Emelia.

"Oh wow! Thank you, sir— I mean Mr. Gilbert." Emelia grabs the candy and immediately begins unwrapping it. I laugh. My daughter is no stranger to sweets.

"Mr. Gilbert, are you sure you want to give the book to my daughter? Won't other children want to check it out?"

"My dear, she is the first child to check out a book in years. I would have no better payment than the knowledge that the book will be loved and read by a fellow curious mind." Mr. Gilbert suddenly shifts the

55

conversation, "I completely forgot—you had questions for me. What are they?"

"Oh, no worries, Mr. Gilbert. We'll come back in a couple days. I know Emmie can't wait to start reading her new book." I smile at Emelia as she opens the book to glance through the pictures. I'm glad she found a book to enjoy while I figure out her school situation.

Walking us to the door, Mr. Gilbert reaches into his pocket and pulls out a pen.

"If you have any questions in the meantime, you can call my direct line in the library. I can write the number on the business card you got. Not that I don't enjoy the company, but I know you must have your hands full with the move and all." Mr. Gilbert says, his voice quivering. I see his hand shaking and gently grab the pen from him.

"Oh, thank you very much, Mr. Gilbert. Allow me to write it down." After I write down the number, Mr. Gilbert clears his throat.

"Please stop by anytime. It gets lonely and I quite enjoy the company of two wonderful, charming ladies such as you fine folks."

"You are too kind. Thank you. You will hear from me real soon. Bye-bye for now." I say to him as I push Emelia through the front doors and onto the brick sidewalk.

As we make our way to the minivan, I look up onto the sidewalk and stop suddenly. A woman sits on the bench next to the library crying and rocking as she holds herself. Her dark complexion is barely visible beneath the long sleeves and lace of the long black Victorian dress she wears. A black lace bonnet covers her head, its attached ebony veil obscuring her face. With each sway of her rocking, her vintage black buttoned boots click against the brick of the sidewalk.

"Ma'am, are you okay?" I raise my voice just loud enough for the woman to be able to hear. I don't want to leave Emelia alone, plus who knows who this lady is?

"Mom, who are you talking to?"

I look at Emelia who seems perplexed. "Why the lady on the bench, sweetheart."

"Mom, no one is sitting on the bench."

"Huh?" I look up again, except this time no one's there. The woman just...vanished. I look around, but there is no one nearby except for us and the subtle whistles in the breeze. Puzzled, I glance back at Emelia. "Well, I guess you are right, Emmie. I must have been seeing things. Don't tell Dad, okay?"

"No problem, Mom. I won't say a word. I promise."

"Thank you, hon," I say as I lift Emelia into the back seat. I do hope Emelia keeps her word and doesn't tell Kyle. God knows I wouldn't hear the end of it. He'd probably try to put me in the loony bin.

Chapter Five
Pet Store

I begin to drive away from the library when suddenly Emelia shouts from the backseat.

"Oh, Mom! Mom! There's a pet store. Can we stop and go look around, please?" Looking in the rearview mirror, I see Emelia giving her best pouty face as she places her hands in a prayer position. I sigh.

"I mean, how can I say 'no' to that adorable face? Fine, we'll stop at the pet store. Only for a moment, though. We have to get back in time to make dinner before your dad gets home."

"Oh, yay! Thank you, Mom, you're the best!" Emelia raises her hands in the air as she starts to chant. "Pet store! Pet store! Pet store!"

We pull into yet another empty parking lot in front of the rusty red-brick pet store. 'Puppies and Kittens Available' is written in alternating pink and blue letters on the store's front windows. I am not the only one who reads the sign.

"Oh, Mom, there are puppies and kittens available! Can we play with them? Please?"

"That is up to the shop owner, sweetheart. We'll ask though." I reply while stepping out of the minivan to get the wheelchair.

After getting Emelia into her wheelchair, we make our way to the front entrance. I take a look around and notice two empty benches outside the store, I stare at them intensely as we pass by to ensure a woman doesn't randomly appear on these benches, too. At this point I'm paranoid.

Opening the glass door, a loud *ding* echoes throughout the store. As expected from a small pet shop, aisles are lined with pet supplies, bags of kibble, cages, and a wall filled with collars in every color and style imaginable. The store would be silent if it weren't for the faint sounds of puppies and kittens whining from the far back end of the store.

"Hello, is anyone here?" I call out as we near the front counter. As soon as I speak, rustling sounds radiate from the back and a door swings open. A woman steps out, presumably the shopkeeper. She looks to be in her fifties, her tanned skin the texture of leather. A dirty red-and-white bandana covers her pulled-back stringy dark brown hair. She wears faded jean coveralls over nothing but a stained sports bra, paired with black work boots. As she moves behind the counter, I see some of her blackened teeth are missing—most likely from dipping wads like the one that's currently making her bottom lip stick out past her chin. If *White Trash* were a magazine, she would be on the cover.

"What do you want?" She says in a high raspy voice.

Trying to keep my composure, I reply as pleasantly as possible.

"Well good afternoon, ma'am. If it isn't any problem, my daughter wishes to play with the puppies and kittens you have available."

"Well, ma'am, you are right they are available— but for purchase, not for playing." The shopkeeper snarks in a mocking tone as she leans over the counter to look at my daughter. My daughter's wheelchair always has a way of grabbing rude individuals' attention.

"Right, but before purchasing, I think it's important my daughter plays with them to see if they are a good fit, don't you think?" I cock my head and give a fake grin as I stare the shopkeeper in the eyes. I'm not about to have her ruin a perfectly good day.

The shopkeeper rolls her eyes. "I suppose that would be proper. Come on, follow me." She says as she grudgingly starts walking to the back of the store, Emelia and I following right behind.

The puppies and kittens are separated into their own play yards with toddler gates keeping them from escaping. Inside, they have ragged toys—clearly reused with each litter—along with the bare necessities. Only a few puppies and kittens are left to choose from. Leaning over the gate, I notice all the kittens appear to be from different fathers, as none of them share the same coloration.

"Hey Emmie, look! There's a fluffy white one just like your pajamas."

"Really?! Let me see!" Emelia shrieks as I reach over the gate and pick up the white kitten.

It's fluffy with green eyes and a little pink nose. I place the kitten on Emelia's lap and it immediately begins to purr and knead on Emelia's stomach. Emelia starts to giggle, then abruptly stops as she stares straight into the kitten play yard.

"Mom, please put this kitten back, I want to see the orange one." She says sternly as she points to a kitten in the far corner of the enclosure. It's scruffy and a part of its left ear is missing. It looks to be in really bad shape.

"Are you sure, hon? You always said you wanted a white kitty."

"Yes, Mom, please let me see the orange kitten."

I can tell Emelia isn't going to budge. I put the white kitten back and then reach to the far corner and gently pick up the orange kitten who lays limp in my hands. I place the kitten onto Emelia's lap. She smiles and begins to pet the kitten. It purrs while keeping its eyes closed. The way Emelia is looking at it makes me feel like she relates to its pain.

The shopkeeper shakes her head with disapproval.

"You sure you want that one? Its leg will probably never heal and who knows how long it'll last? Besides, don't you want a kitten that can play around and jump on your lap from time to time? You won't have that with this one. I was actually planning to give it to Reggie at the end of the day."

Without taking her eyes off of the kitten, Emelia cries out.

"No don't say that...you'll hurt his feelings! He might be different, but that doesn't make him better or worse than any other kitten. He wouldn't want to be made fun of or looked at differently just because he's hurt. How would you like it if someone didn't like you because you got hurt? That's not very nice at all, lady." Emelia begins to tear up, she must be comparing her life to that of this orange kitten. Emelia looks up at the lady, "He is the most beautiful kitty in the whole wide world. He's perfect because we understand each other, unlike this *Reggie* person. Who is Reggie, anyways?"

"My pet python. He eats kittens and puppies we don't think will make it."

Emelia's face is struck with horror. She lifts the kitten and holds it against her chest.

"NO! You cannot kill him. Mom, please can we take him? Can we save him, please?" Emelia looks up at me with tears in her eyes. She sees herself in this cat, and the shopkeeper's comments hit my sweetheart hard. I can't let her down, especially right now.

"Sure, Emmie, let's get him. We'll buy all the supplies he'll need, too. Do you have a problem with that, ma'am?" I direct my question at the shopkeeper who shrugs.

"Nope, no problems here but he'll come with no warranties."

"That is fine, ma'am," I reply as I reach to hold Emelia's hand.

Emelia smiles at me, still holding the kitten against her chest. The shopkeeper rolls her eyes.

"Alrighty then, I'll ring you up at the front when you are ready." She scuffs as she heads toward the front of the store.

Walking out of the store with plastic bags of kitten supplies up my forearm, I roll Emelia, still holding onto her new kitten, to the van. I look over my shoulder to see if the woman I saw earlier is sitting on the bench, but no one is there. *Maybe I really am just seeing things...*

"Hey Mom, what are you looking for?" Emelia asks, looking directly up at me. She is more observant than I give her credit for.

"Nothing, sweetheart. Let's get your new kitten home." I reply, lifting her and the kitten into the back seat.

Heading home, I periodically look in my rearview mirror to check up on Emelia. She is smiling ear to ear as she cuddles her new kitten—who has not stopped purring since being placed in her hands. It has been a while since I have seen her this happy after the accident.

"So, Emelia, what are you going to name it? I know you've always wanted to have a cat named Bella."

"No, Bella is a girl's name. I was thinking Oliver. Like from that one orphan movie."

"That's a very fitting name, Emmie. I am sure he's going to love it, isn't that right, Oliver?" I look in the rearview mirror again and my heart drops.

There in the back seat next to Emelia, is a little boy staring directly at me through the mirror, grinning. He looks about ten years old, dressed in a dirt-stained, ruffled long-sleeve shirt and tight black trousers. His grayish-blond hair is unkempt, and his whole body looks anemic—his sunken cheeks making his lifeless eyes seem to bulge from their sockets. I look at Emelia, but she seems completely oblivious to the boy sitting next to her. I need to be sure I'm the only one who sees him.

"Hey, Emmie, can you hand me the map that's on the seat next to you?"

"Sure, Mom." Emelia says as she grabs the map and hands it to me which gives me my answer—I'm the only one who can see him.

Am I hallucinating? What's going on?

As if he can hear my thoughts, the boy frowns, still staring at me through the rearview mirror.

Ok, I'll try again...maybe I'm seeing dead people? The boy smiles, showing all of his crooked teeth. *Yep, I am officially going insane. I mean ghosts aren't real. They can't be... can they?*

"Mom, what are you thinking about? You've been pretty quiet." Emelia asks, interrupting my train of thought. I look back again, and to my relief, the boy is gone. "I am just thinking about where to put all of Oliver's stuff. We need to make sure he feels welcome—but look, we're home!" I say as I pull up to the house. As I park, Kyle walks out and heads toward the minivan. I step out, and suddenly he's right next to me.

"Hey, what took you so long? It is almost five o'clock, you should already be making dinner. Wait, what the heck is that thing?" Kyle makes a disgusted face and points to the kitten in Emelia's lap. I'm not surprised. If I wasn't distracted by my own delusions, I would have been mentally preparing for this fight on the drive home.

"Emelia needs a friend, and Oliver needs a loving parent. They're perfect for each other and she loves him. Don't worry, we'll take care of it. Won't we, Emelia?"

"Yes, yes, yes! Please, Dad, I love him so much!" Emelia lifts the kitten toward Kyle, who steps back, repulsed.

"Oh god, it looks horrible! Are you guys sure it's even alive? What did you guys do, pick it up off the side of the road?" Kyle shakes his head, "Fine, you can keep it. Doubt it will live long anyway. Probably won't even make it past the night." Kyle turns around and heads back to the house, ignoring the bags in the car.

A faint rumbling growl fills the awkward moment.

I look down to see Oliver growling, his eyes locked on Kyle as he walks away. I smirk.

Maybe this cat is smarter than I thought.

Chapter Six
Dinner

"Here we are, *bon appétit*," I say as I place plates of spaghetti in front of Kyle and Emelia, who has Oliver in her lap. Kyle looks down at the spaghetti, then digs around in it with his fork. He lifts a few strings of pasta, as a look of disapproval spreads across his face.

"Where is the protein? Where are the meatballs?" Kyle grumbles, aggressively stirring up the spaghetti as if one will magically appear. "We didn't have time to run to the grocery store today, so I made what we already had. I thought you would have preferred that over takeout."

"What do you mean you didn't have time? You have been out all day—you just didn't think about it. Every meal needs protein in it, Sarah. This isn't new." Kyle shoves a big bite into his mouth, sauce painting his chin as he loudly slurps the noodles. He talks with his mouth full, "Stop making excuses, Sarah. Just say I'm right, like always." Kyle smacks his lips as I watch mushed spaghetti bounce on his tongue with every word protruding from his unbearable mouth. I grit my teeth.

"Yes hon, you're right. I didn't think about stopping at the grocery store. I'm sorry." I'm not in the mood for an argument, especially a senseless one. "How is your spaghetti, Emmie?"

"Oh, it's delicious! Thanks, Mom!" Emmie replies as she attempts to sneak a piece to Oliver, who gladly starts to chomp down the spaghetti noodle. Kyle looks over with a face of disgust.

"Oh my god, what is that dirt rag doing at the dinner table?! Emmie, I do not want to see that *thing* anywhere near this table!" Kyle's condescending tone enrages me. It takes everything not to smash his pretty face into the plate of spaghetti in front of him.

"Kyle, Emmie just got Oliver today and needs to form a bond. Studies show a strong bond makes for a well-behaved cat in the long run. You won't have to worry about the cat peeing outside the litter box or scratching the furniture. You wouldn't want your favorite armchair to get ruined, would you?" I lie through my teeth. Facts are the only thing Kyle somewhat listens to. I cross my fingers, hoping he buys it.

"I wouldn't have to worry about it if you didn't get her the dirt rag in the first place, but fine. When that thing is older it will not be allowed at the table, okay Emmie?"

"Yes, Dad." Emmie smiles as she looks down at Oliver, now asleep in her lap, the fur around his lips stained red from spaghetti sauce. We sit in silence, the only sounds are the soft clink of forks against plates and the occasional scrape as spaghetti is twirled. I'm just beginning to enjoy the calm when it's interrupted.

"By the way Sarah, how's Antonio doing?" Kyle asks as he continues to dig into his plate. He's already gotten seconds, which isn't surprising.

"My father's doing all right. Why do you ask?" I respond without looking up from my plate. There always seems to be some kind of ulterior motive when he asks seemingly innocent questions.

"I was just asking. I know he has been pretty sick with his recent chemo treatments. What kind of cancer does he have again? I forgot."

"He has lung cancer."

"Oh yeah, that's right. Too bad, really. This is why I get on your case about smoking, Sarah. It's not healthy, aside from it being a disgusting habit in general." Kyle continues with his mouth full. "You're still in his will, right? Not saying I want him to kick the bucket, but he is getting close. We should really think about what we are going to do when he does pass. I mean, he has that huge estate in Italy. Would you want to sell it?"

I look up at Kyle who seems so nonchalant about the topic as a whole.

"I am not really comfortable planning my father's death, Kyle." I'm livid. How long has Kyle been daydreaming about my father passing for him to be this casual about the topic? Kyle is a jerk, but even this is more than I would expect from him.

"We'll need to have this conversation at some point, Sarah. I'd rather be prepared than be caught with our pants down when it happens." Kyle takes another huge bite. I watch him silently as he continues to stuff his face. Kyle finally notices my disapproval.

"Okay, maybe this can wait for another time. But we'll need to talk about it at some point." Kyle wipes his face with a napkin. Getting up from the table, he goes over to Emelia and rubs her head aggressively. "Emmie, make sure to clean up that cat. It stinks."

"Yes, Dad, I will."

"Good." Kyle leaves, walking up the spiral staircase.

After cleaning up the dining table and kitchen, I turn to my bag on the counter. *I need a smoke break after that conversation.* As I grab the cigarette pack, I hear three slow knocks at the door.

THUD... THUD... THUD...

I look at the clock on the microwave—6:43 p.m. Who would knock on our door at this hour? I quickly shove the pack into my skirt pocket and walk to the door. I reach to grab onto the handle when I hear the knocks again, but the sound isn't coming from the other side of the door—it's right next to my ear.

Where is that coming from? I look up and on the back of the door is a rod knob with a small ring. "This must be the other end of the creepy door knocker," I murmur as I feel over the top of the cast-iron bolt and ring. It's securely mounted. No wonder George couldn't remove it when we moved in—the knocker's bolted straight through the thick, solid gray oak door. George was right, the whole door would have to be destroyed to remove it. Looking closer, I notice the hinges are made of the same thick cast iron.

"John Burrow did *not* want this door to go anywhere…" I whisper, as a sudden chill crawls down my spine.

*THUD… THUD… THUD… **THUD!***

The ring on the back of the front door starts knocking with increased speed and intensity. Out of pure instinct, I grab it. The ring immediately stops moving in my hand. Holding it in silence for what seems like hours, I feel something unusual. Opening my hand, I take a closer look at the ring. Distinct scratches mark the inside of the ring. The hair-thin grooves curve along the inner part of the ring, never reaching the outer edge.

How odd for there to be scratches in such strong cast iron. It must have taken a lot of abuse—

"Hey Mom, how do you wash a cat?" Emmie yells out from her bathroom, breaking my train of thought.

"You use a wet rag and wipe him. Be gentle, though, we haven't gotten his leg checked out yet." I yell sweetly. I look back to the door.

What were you up to, John Burrow?

There are mysteries in this house, and I want to solve them. But for now, a smoke break and then a much-needed relaxing bubble bath.

Chapter Seven
Bathtime

I sneak back inside from my smoke break and go check on Emelia's progress washing Oliver. I peer through the doorway, not surprised by the atrocity unfolding in an already ugly and outdated bathroom. Water covers the floor, and soap suds—speckled with tufts of orange fur—splatter across the wallpaper like some art deco piece. In front of the sink, Emelia sings a made-up song while Oliver fights for his life against the wash rag. "Clean kitty-kitty, Pretty kitty-kitty—"

MEOWWWW!

I can't help but chuckle at the sight, but at the same time, I am not looking forward to cleaning this up. I really need to hurry up and take that bath while I can.

"Hey Emmie, how is it going in here?"

"Oh, hi Mom! It's going great. Oliver was very dirty, but he is almost clean now! Just need to get his ears." Emelia's face is determined as she battles with Oliver. Though he puts up a fight, he finally allows Emelia to wipe the inside of his ears.

"All clean!" Emelia lifts Oliver in the air as if he were Simba from *The Lion King*. It'd be an almost perfect imitation of the scene if it weren't for Oliver's disapproving face and slanted ears. Oliver begins to make a low, angry, rumble.

"Now none of that, Oliver, you be a good kitty." Emelia places him onto a clean towel in her lap, tucking it around him like a blanket. Oliver begins to purr and I smile. It's great seeing Emelia so happy, especially after the last few days.

"Now that Oliver got his bath, I think it's time I take one. Emmie, will you do your best to clean up in here? I know you're not able to get everything. Just do what you can, and I will take care of the rest later. Okay, my songbird?"

"Yes, Mom! Don't worry, Oliver and I will do a great job. Right, Oliver?" Emelia says as she starts to pet the kitten—who is now asleep in her lap curled up in the dry towel.

"All right Emmie, if you need anything just let me or your father know. He should also be upstairs."

"Okay, Mom."

I leave the bathroom door wide open and head upstairs. With each hollow step echoing, I can't help but hope Kyle won't hear me coming. I just want to start my bubble bath in peace. At the top of the stairs, I look over and see Kyle sitting up in bed, his Sony VAIO laptop open in front of him. I try to walk quickly to the master bathroom—

"Did Emmie wash that dirt rag?" Kyle asks without taking his eyes off his screen.

I sigh. "Yes hon, Emmie cleaned up Oliver. She did a great job, too."

"Good. What are you doing?"

"I'm about to take a bubble bath."

"What?!" Kyle looks up from his laptop, his face perplexed, as if the thought of me taking a bath is absurd. "Why would you take a bath now when Emmie isn't even in bed yet? What if she needs help and you can't because you are naked, soaking in a tub? How selfish of you, Sarah, and you call yourself a nurse." Kyle shakes his head in disappointment.

"Emmie is nine, almost ten in a couple of weeks. Also, *you're* home. If something comes up, can you watch her for the next thirty minutes? I just need to relax."

"You need to relax?! Do you not see I am working here?!" Kyle says aggressively pointing at his laptop. "I have been working ever since we moved in, while you've had the luxury of being home with our daughter. I should be the one relaxing, not you."

Oh yeah, you have been working so hard at Amy's place. Hope you pulled a muscle, asshole. I'm fuming. The nerve of this man to pretend to be working nonstop when all he's been doing since we arrived is chasing the easiest tail. My anger must be obvious at this point because Kyle changes his demeanor. Closing his laptop, he sets it aside and walks up to me. He cups my face in his hands gently.

"But I can see how much stress this move must have caused you. All I want is your happiness. I'll watch Emmie while you take a bath. Do you need anything before I leave you to it?" Kyle whispers.

Kyle's gray eyes stare into mine with a level of kindness I haven't seen in weeks. These are the eyes that seduced me when we first met. I wish I hadn't been so

75

gullible back then. Maybe I would have seen through his facade before getting pregnant with Emelia and being forced into a marriage by my father for the sake of his religious convictions. If I wasn't so financially dependent on my father back then, would I have gone through with the wedding? And if it wasn't for threats of being removed from the will, would I be divorced by now? My mind keeps racing until it is interrupted—

"Well, my love?"

Oh, that's right, he's right in front of me. I swallow. "No, I don't need anything hon. Thanks for watching Emmie."

"Okay, sweetheart. Love you." Kyle kisses my forehead and walks down the staircase.

I walk into our master bathroom. To the right of the remodeled shower stands the original soaking tub. Its hammered copper exterior catches the light from the bathroom's dangling crystal chandelier. The interior is cast iron with an off-white enamel overlay. One end rises higher than the other, and the tub rests on four cast-iron claw feet, molded into lion paws with talons digging into the black-and-white tiled floor. At the end of the tub, an updated brass faucet curves over the rim. "I will give it to you, John Burrow, you sure had style," I say quietly as I start the bath and squeeze my favorite Japanese blossom-scented body wash under the faucet, creating thick, lush bubbles.

Seeing steam rising from the tub, I turn off the faucet, pull my hair into a messy bun, slip off my navy-blue dress, and step into the warm, bubbly bath. I sink into the hot water and lean against the higher end, my feet peeking out from the bubbles, almost touching the faucet.

"Oh, yeah… that's nice." I sigh in relief as I sink further into the tub and close my eyes.

It's been a while since I've been able to take a nice, long relaxing bath. Honestly, I can't even remember the last time I had one. Even before the accident a year ago, I was either working at the hospital or home taking care of Emelia. Kyle would always be away on some trip and even when he was home, most of the time I would wish he wasn't. There are many things I regret about this marriage, but Emelia isn't one of them. Emelia has been the one constant good in my life, I don't know what I would do without my sweet angel.

Moments pass before I notice the light flickering. I open my eyes and look up at the chandelier. The bulbs flicker intermittently, their glow refracting off the dusty crystals.

"I wonder what that is about—AH!"

I look down and staring at me over my toes is a boy's face. His complexion is grayish pale and his medium-length, greasy black hair hovers over his sunken cheeks. He appears to be naked, and his hallow, soulless eyes are fixated directly on my chest. Realizing this, I cover myself. The boy's gaze trails up my neck, to my face, and then finally straight into my eyes, as if peering into my soul. His blackened fingers creep over the edge of the tub and the lights flicker, then go out completely. Now in total darkness for what feels like eternity, my heart pounds through my chest as I struggle to breathe through the panic. The lights turn back on.

The boy is gone.

"Where did he go?!" I dare not say louder than a whisper.

I wait a few moments and look around.

Everything seems to be back to normal. The lights aren't flickering. and I can hear Emelia singing *You are My Sunshine* to Oliver. I sigh in relief as I shift higher up against the tub lining, laying my head back over the edge with my eyes closed.

The lights suddenly shut off. Then back on.

"What is wrong with those—"

I open my eyes and the boy is standing over me. He grabs my hair and violently slams my head back over the tub's rim. With his other hand, he yanks down on my jaw and holds my mouth open. I want to scream. I want to call for help, but nothing comes out. I'm frozen, terrified. Forcing my head still and mouth open, he leans his face over mine until our mouths align.

A spider's leg splits open his lips as the boy slowly opens his mouth. A large, slender-legged black spider cautiously crawls out of his mouth and dangles on its thin silken thread. I watch in panic as the spider slowly lowers itself toward my open mouth. It's so close I can see its fangs twitch with each hyperventilated breath that escapes my frozen lungs. The spider slides into my mouth. I gag as it tickles my uvula on its way into my throat. I start to thrash but the boy holds me firm, watching my agony in delight; a smile creeping across his face with every cough I make. Only after the spider passes my throat canal, does the boy release me. I lurch forward, shaking uncontrollably, grabbing at my throat and grasping for air.

I look up—the boy has disappeared. I close my eyes and start to exhale a sigh of relief when I feel a sudden burning in my chest. I look down. There—just below my sternum—I see the outline of the spider as it crawls just below my skin, making it stretch and micro-cut as it gradually makes its way down to my stomach. I scream in pain and horror. Just as it reaches my belly button, it stops and begins to dig back into my stomach. There is an instant of respite and seconds later a sharp, burning pain pulsates from my belly button. I see a small hole forming from the side of my umbilical knot as a single spider leg emerges. I look on in horror as a second leg squeezes through—the skin ripping, blood from the micro-cuts creating a pool in my naval

The spider's head peaks through the blood, grabbing the skin above and dragging itself out. As it pulls, the torn flesh rips wide, launching the spider halfway up my stomach. Blood sprays over my face, filling my mouth with the taste of iron as I continue to scream. I lie motionless in water now dyed red from my own blood. The spider stands tall, lifting its two front legs at me, hissing. It crouches down, backing up to jump—

"What is wrong!?" Kyle swings the door open.

"Spider! Spider! Get it off! I'm bleeding! Take me to the hospital I need stitches and an x-ray and a, and a—"

"What spider? Where are you bleeding? I don't see any blood." Kyle walks in, looking under the tub as he searches the bathroom. "Huh?"

I look down and the spider is gone. There are no micro-cuts, no gaping hole in my belly button. The water in the tub is still warm, though it has less bubbles. It's as if nothing happened.

How?

Kyle walks around the bathroom trying to find the spider. He makes it back to the doorway and stops, face no longer concerned, just annoyed. He sighs.

"You need to get a hold of yourself. There is no spider. I checked the whole damn bathroom. Do we need to get you on a different medication, Sarah? We just got to this town, I can't afford a bad reputation."

"I'm not crazy."

"Whatever, Sarah. Emmie is going to need help getting ready for bed soon anyway. Are you ready to be a mom again?" Kyle says, shaking his head as he walks out.

I step out of the tub and walk to the mirror, I stare at myself, water dripping off my naked body. Aside from my half-pulled-out bun, nothing is out of place.

Maybe I am going crazy...

Chapter Eight

Kyle: One Year Ago

"Why, Kyle Angelo Gallo, you are a lady killer if I've ever seen one." I cockily say to my mirrored reflection in our modern master bathroom.

The marble floors and cream walls create the perfect backdrop as I study myself in the extra-wide mirror over the marble counter and silver faucet. Everything must be in its place, no matter the occasion.

Getting ready for my daughter's ballet recital is tedious. I wish Emmie was more into softball. At least softball is during the warmer months, and she could get a scholarship for it. It's not like I want to pay for her college, especially since I couldn't go myself. No, everyone must make their own way in the Gallo house, including my daughter. To be honest, I wouldn't even be going to this stupid recital if it weren't for the smoking-hot Latina ballet instructor at Emmie's school. She's one of the few bitches left in this town I haven't been able to score—*yet*. With how fly I am tonight though—black slacks and button-up, paired with my brown Calvin Klein belt and matching shoes? I'll have no problem getting Ms. Catalina's number this go around. But you know what they say, the harder the catch the more satisfying the reward.

Grabbing my favorite styling gel with a 'classic' scent, I squeeze a glob into the palm of my hand and spread it throughout my scruffy black hair. As I comb it back, I see perfect lines form.

"Classic scent for a classic guy. Damn, I am one good-looking dude." I bite at my reflection.

"Hey, Dad, when is Mom going to be home?" Emelia, standing in the bathroom doorway in her white tutu and pink tennis shoes, catches me by surprise. She can be real quiet when she wants to be. It's quite annoying.

"Emmie, you know better than to sneak up on me."

"Sorry, Dad. When is Mom going to be home? Oh, and what do you think of my tutu? Isn't it so fluffy!?" Emmie twirls in front of me, as if I'm supposed to be impressed. I'm not.

"Yes, hon, very nice. Now run along. Mom should be home anytime now."

"Okay, Dad!" Emmie replies as she excitedly runs off.

That reminds me, I look at my watch—4:45 p.m.

Where is that bitch? I think as I continue to fix my hair.

She really did catch herself a good-looking man. Strong, successful, sexy, what more could she have wished for? It does help that she's coming up on her father's inheritance soon—or at least I thought it would be soon. But that bastard keeps chugging along. God, it feels like he has been in and out of remission for forever now. The old man just needs to kick the bucket already. It wasn't supposed to take this long. There's a lot of money just sitting there, not being put to good use. I look at my watch again—5:04 p.m.

Seriously what is taking her so long? There is no way I'm taking Emmie to the recital by myself.

The more I think about it, Sarah really is lucky to have a man like me. It's a dangerous world out there, and there are plenty of men who would prey upon a dainty, Catholic blonde like her. She is cute enough, but the moment they hear of her future inheritance? They'd marry her for the money alone, offer no protection and leave her high and dry as a single mother. Not me, I'm strong, I would never leave her alone with a child. That would be just cruel. In fact, when Sarah got pregnant, I graciously proposed to her with a ring I could afford at the time because that is the type of man I am. No, I will protect them. I'll make sure the money is used to build our family up.

I glance at my reflection in the mirror one more time to make sure my hair is perfect.

"Plus, who wouldn't want my babies?" I say in my most seductive voice followed by my killer smirk.

"MOM!" I hear Emmie yell from downstairs, followed by the sound of the front door closing.

Welp, guess it's that time. I think as I make my way out of the room and stand at the top of the stairs, watching Sarah and Emmie interact below.

"Hi, sweetie! Your tutu is so cute! Do a twirl for me." Sarah beams as Emmie twirls. It's cute and all, but we don't have time for this.

83

"Hey, Sarah, it's almost time to leave, hurry up and get ready." I yell down from the top of the stairs. Sarah looks up at me from below, just now realizing I'm up here. She should be more aware of her surroundings.

"Oh, sorry hon, the hospital was crazy today. Barely made it out of there. I'll come up and get ready. It won't take me long." Sarah replies as she starts making her way upstairs. As she tries to pass me, I grab her by the arm and pull her in.

"*Mmm*, the things I will do to you tonight," I seductively whisper in her ear. Sarah pulls away.

"Kyle, I've got to get ready so we can leave on time. We'll see how things go tonight. Please make sure Emmie doesn't forget her ballet shoes." She instructs as she walks past me into the bedroom.

Her pushing me off like that enrages me. I look *this good*, and she doesn't give me the time of day? Bosses me around like I am a kid or something? Honestly, it's no wonder I have to get affection from other women. She isn't giving it to me. Seriously, I deserve better than this treatment. I mean, look at me. Who wouldn't want to jump my bones? Even I am attracted to myself. Withholding love from me is just cruel. Selfish. Maybe she's cheating on me. What else could explain why she's holding out on her own husband? If that is the case, the bitch will seriously regret it.

I make my way downstairs and grab Emmie's ballet shoes. I look at my watch again—5:23 p.m. We need to leave soon. Even though I hate the idea of going to this stupid recital, I hate the idea of being late even more. I hear the door shut upstairs and watch as Sarah comes around the corner. Her red sweater dress daintily hugs her curves and skims her mid-calves. Her black leather ankle boots make dull clicks on the wooden stairs as her curly, blonde locks bounce in rhythm. She looks cute enough, though I wish she wouldn't wear something so tight. Who else does she need to look good for? I don't want other men gawking at her. It pisses me off when other men look at my wife like a piece of steak. It enrages me. Maybe she does it on purpose...

"Are you ready to go?" I say, reaching out my hand. Sarah places hers in mine.

"Yes, hon, I'm ready."

The ballet recital is as boring as I thought it'd be. Trying to act excited while watching my daughter spin in circles is a chore, but I guess this is what fathers are supposed to do when their eight-year-old daughter is frolicking on stage. Though I do have to admit the violin soloist is pretty talented—and cute. I wonder where she's from.

I look over at Sarah who is fixated in amazement at our daughter's dance solo. I look back at Emmie dancing on stage to the violin's melody. I'll admit, it is cool she was picked out of all the kids to do a solo. It is not surprising, however—I mean, she is a Gallo after all. She gets her talents from her father. I smirk as Emmie's solo finishes. Emmie bows and everyone in the audience stands and cheers. On stage, an out-of-breath Emmie beams. I stand up.

"Ya, that's my girl!" I scream and blow a whistle. I glance over at Ms. Catalina. She notices me, smiles, and then turns her attention back to the stage and Emmie. I grin.

Yep, that number is as good as mine tonight, I think as I continue to clap.

The recital concluded, I and all the other parents are ushered to the after-party meet-and-greet in the school cafeteria. A few white and blue balloons float along the top of the metal-rimmed ceiling, and a banner hangs over the tables of finger food that reads: *Congratulations Ballerinas!* As Sarah and I enter the cafeteria, I see Emmie running toward us.

"Congratulations, sweetheart! You looked so beautiful up on that stage!" Sarah yells as she crouches down, arms wide open. Emmie runs into Sarah's hug.

"Thank you, Mom! Did you like it, Dad?" Emmie asks looking up at me from Sarah's arms.

"Yes, you did great, hon. I'm proud of you." I reply while scanning the room. With all the kids coming back from the recital, Ms. Catalina can't be far behind. As we make our way to the finger food, a gentleman and his daughter approach us.

"Great job out there, kiddo! Hey Sarah, how are you doing? Is this your husband?" The guy says enthusiastically while giving Emmie a high-five.

The man is a little shorter than me, with straggly, dirty-blond hair and round wire-wrapped glasses. He's wearing a wrinkly, cream button-up with an outdated maroon blazer and some faded blue jeans. His attire screams *nerd.*

Who the fuck is this guy and how does he know my wife's name? Are they screwing or something? The thought alone makes my skin bubble.

"Hello, Dan! Yes, this is my husband, Kyle. Kyle, this is Dan. His daughter, Becky, is in the same dance class as Emmie." Sarah explains. Dan reaches his hand out to shake mine.

"It's wonderful meeting you, Kyle, I've heard so much about you."

"Oh, you have, huh? Interesting because Sarah's never mentioned you." I reply as I give Dan's hand a firm squeeze, he grimaces and pulls his hand back.

"Wow, you got yourself quite a grip there." He chuckles as he shakes his hand out.

What a little bitch, can't even handle a real man's handshake. The more I think about it, there is no way Sarah is cheating on me with this poor excuse of a man. I mean, just look at him! I think as I watch Sarah laugh at god knows what that jackass is saying. *Or maybe she is. Never mind that. Now is my opportunity to go find Ms. Catalina.*

I scour the room; it only takes seconds to find Ms. Catalina talking with some parents in the far corner of the cafeteria. I straighten my slacks and unbutton the top button of my shirt—it always makes the ladies go crazy, and Ms. Catalina will be no exception. I start to walk over—

"Hon, can we leave now? Emmie's very tired. I think she might actually fall asleep in the car on the way home. She exerted herself on that performance." I hear Sarah say from behind me.

I feel my eyebrow twitch. Of course she wants to leave when *she* is done flirting with her boy toy. But I'm a good father and husband, so I'll make the sacrifice and get her number some other time.

"Of course. Can you pass me the keys? I'll drive."

"Oh, really? Thanks, hon." Sarah reaches into her satchel, pulls out the keys, and tosses them to me. Sarah's father purchased the Mercedes-Benz E-class for her as a graduation present—one of the few financial choices her father has ever made that I actually agree with. Luxury cars are an investment. Not only are they reliable, but this cherry-red Mercedes looks great when pulling up to a client's house. The sales industry is dog-eat-dog, and every advantage helps. Plus, it doesn't hurt that it works on the ladies.

Driving home, my knuckles turn white from squeezing the wheel. I'm furious. After everything I have done for this family, Sarah repays me by flirting with another man? That alone is bad enough—but him? He's such a downgrade compared to me. I mean, is she blind? My thoughts spiral as my foot presses harder on the gas pedal. Sarah looks over from the passenger seat, face etched with concern.

"Kyle, don't you think you are going a bit fast? We are in a 35 and you're doing 55—"

"Just shut up and look out the window. I'm the one who should be concerned about the road, not you."

"Woah, where did this come from? And keep your voice down. Emmie's sleeping."

"You don't get to tell me what to do after that little stunt you pulled back in the cafeteria."

"What stunt? What are you talking about?"

"*Oh, Dan, you are so funny. He-he-he.*" I say in a high-pitched mockery of her voice. Sarah's jaw drops.

"What are you talking about? Do you think I was flirting with Dan or something? You were there the whole time. And seriously, keep your voice down!"

Sarah loudly whispers, her face red. Her face always turns red when she's upset. That's all the proof I need—only a guilty person would be this upset over a mere accusation.

"Oh, you don't want Emmie to know what a cheating whore her mother is?" I snap back in sarcastic astonishment.

"I am not cheating on you, Kyle. And how dare you accuse me of cheating when *you've* cheated on me with god knows how many women by now? I saw how you were gawking at Emmie's ballet instructor. Have you slept with her too, or is she still just another one of your targets?" Sarah crosses her arms and stares at me, waiting for a reply. She's not turning this around on me that easily.

"Oh, go ahead and make yourself the victim Sarah. I'm always the bad guy. Why don't you take a look in the mirror."

"*Look in the mirror?!* What are you talking about, Kyle?!"

"You are going to regret cheating on me, slut."

"I am not cheating on you!"

At this point, we are pushing 70mph. The light up ahead turns red but it's late and no one's on the road at this hour. Sarah looks at the speedometer and then at the light.

"Kyle, slow down, we're going to run the light!"

"Do not tell me what to do, woman! I know what I'm doing."

We reach the intersection, the power and rebellion coursing through me as I keep my foot on the accelerator.

"Kyle, please stop—"

As Sarah utters those words, I see lights behind her—then, in an instant, those lights crash into us. Time stops as the Mercedes spins end-over-end across the entirety of the intersection, finally coming to rest upside down. I crawl out through the shattered driver's-side window. A drop of blood drips onto my hand.

Panicking, I reach up to my forehead to find the cut. *Oh, thank god—it's in my hairline. I won't have a scar on my face...* I think as I look back at the almost unrecognizable Mercedes. Farther down the road, I can see the other vehicle engulfed in flames, but it doesn't look like anyone's inside.

"Oh no, Sarah and Emmie!" I panic as I limp to the passenger's side of the vehicle. Emmie's door is completely caved in, her lower half pinned between the door and her seat. In the front, Sarah hangs upside down, unconscious, her head resting against the window as blood trickles down. From somewhere behind me, I hear police sirens. Knowing the fire department will have to cut Emmie out, I pull on the front passenger door to try to get to Sarah. It takes all my strength, but I finally get the door open—just enough to fit Sarah through. I release her seatbelt and struggle to wiggle her out, dragging her a few yards from the car.

The sirens get louder, I look up and police lights about a block away. I put my ear on Sarah's chest, listening for a heartbeat. Listening for any sign that she's okay. I hear a wheeze.

I close my eyes. *Oh, thank God, she's alive.*

"Sir, are you okay?!"

90

My eyes fly open—I didn't even realize a police officer had walked up on us. I tear up.

"No, my daughter is stuck in the back seat and my wife needs to get to a hospital. Please help, officer!" I beg. The officer walks over to the vehicle, shining his flashlight into the backseat where Emmie is. He reaches up to his radio—

"Dispatch, we need EMS and Fire on scene immediately. Have Fire bring the jaws of life—juvenile is trapped in the backseat of a crashed motor vehicle.

"10-4. EMS and Fire en route to your location now" the radio barks back. I feel myself starting to calm down. The officer turns to me and takes out his notepad.

"Now sir, I'm going to ask a few questions to understand what happened here. Who was driving?"

I look down at Sarah lying there, unconscious, but alive. I look from her face to her tight red dress, and a flood of emotions overwhelms me. I think about how she humiliated me back at the cafeteria, and what she must have been doing behind my back with Dan at all those ballet practices...

I said were going to regret it, Sarah.

"Sir? Can you answer the question? Who was driving when the accident occurred?" The officer repeats. I look down again and kiss Sarah gently on the forehead.

"My wife, officer."

Chapter Nine
Mirror

I lay in bed, still shaken up from last night. It felt so real. The boy holding my mouth open. The tingling, scraping feeling of the spider crawling down my throat. The burning sensation of my skin stretching. The horrific pain of my belly button ripping open as the spider's leg pierced through it—I can still taste my own blood in my mouth. Breathy, gargling snores ring in my ear.

SNORE.

I turn over and see Kyle lying on his back, spread eagle, snoring obnoxiously. Between the living nightmare I experienced last night and Kyle's obtrusive snores, I knew there was little chance I was going to get any sleep. I even smoked a whole pack before I came to bed to try and calm my nerves, and I was still shaken up. My alarm clock goes off.

BEEP BEEP BEEP.

Is it 7 already!?

Slapping the *off* button, I begrudgingly roll out of bed and walk into the master bathroom. I cautiously peer inside, then walk towards the full-length mirror. I lift my pajama shirt to look at my stomach, which is perfectly smooth with no visible marks, as if nothing happened last night.

"But it just disappeared the moment Kyle came in. How? It doesn't make any sense..." I whisper as I start getting ready.

Something isn't sitting right with me. Since we moved in, strange occurrences keep happening—but only to me. Why am I the only one experiencing this? I know I've been struggling mentally since the accident, but even I find this to be excessive. My thoughts jump to the tall man I saw standing at the front door yesterday morning. There was something peculiar about him. Though I never saw his face, his clothes were strange. Even covered in dirt, I could tell his long coat and top hat were of high quality, how I would imagine a rich gentleman would have dressed in the 1800s. *Was that John Burrow's spirit? And if so, what was he trying to tell me?*

There is a mystery here, and I am going to solve it—if only to prove I'm not losing my mind.

I turn on the sink and allow the water to heat up as I scrub my face with my washcloth. The room begins to steam as I lean over and splash the facewash off. Just then, I hear a drawn-out glass squeak.

SQUEAK.

I look up and see something being drawn on the fogged bathroom mirror. I gasp and jump back as an invisible hand continues to draw on the steamy mirror. With each slow, squeaky stroke, a letter begins to form. The air, now thick with the weight of steam, makes it hard to see—but I squint and see a large, backward S taking shape.

S... What does that mean?

The invisible hand continues to draw the next letter until—

"Sarah, stop wasting the hot water! I don't want a cold shower." Kyle yells. This man has horrible timing. I doubt he's even out of bed.

"No, you need to see this! Something's writing on the mirror!" I yell back, keeping my eyes on the mirror as steam thickens around me. The second letter starts to take the shape of a J.

SJ? No, it's still writing...

"What are you talking about, Sarah? Nothing's on the mirror."

I look back at Kyle, who is now standing in the doorway.

"How can you not see it!? It is right—" I look back and it's gone. The steam's cleared and only the sound of the running faucet remains. "But, how?"

Kyle sighs. "Sarah, did you forget to take your pills again?"

"I'm not crazy."

"Whatever, Sarah." Kyle rolls his eyes and walks back to the bedroom. I stand there, staring at a mirror that is now completely clear, my mind racing. I know what I saw, someone or something, was writing on that mirror but as soon as Kyle walks in—it's gone. Like nothing happened. Even if my mind were playing tricks on me, why would I imagine that?

I continue to get ready for the day, mind spinning. *What was it writing? SJ... S.. I? U?* Whatever it was writing, it has to mean something.

I walk back into the room and head to the laundry basket filled with yesterday's freshly washed clothes. I pick out a pair of dark Levi's and a lavender button-up blouse. Kyle watches from the bed as I get dressed.

"Wow, I haven't seen you wear jeans in quite a while. What are you doing, yard work or something?" Kyle smirks and stretches out his arms like he already had a big day.

I sigh, irritated. "No, I'm just exhausted and don't feel like getting all dolled up today. I'm going to the grocery store. Will you keep an eye on Emelia and make her breakfast while I'm gone? I won't be long." As I say this, the smug look on Kyle's face slowly turns into one of annoyance.

"Why can't you take her with you?"

"Because I need the trunk for groceries and can't put her wheelchair back there."

"Well, can't she wait in the car?"

"Kyle..."

He sighs, "All right, fine. Just don't take forever."

"Thank you," I say without even looking at him, as I make my way down the spiral staircase. Even from here, I can hear Emelia talking to Oliver. When I reach her room and open the doors, I see her in bed holding Oliver up in the air.

96

"Good morning, Oliver!" Emelia says in a baby voice. Oliver lets out a faint meow and flicks his tail in irritation.

"Good morning, sweetheart! And morning to you too, Oliver." I say with a smile. "I'm heading to the grocery store. Do you want or need anything while I'm there?"

"Ooh can you get some Nerds?!" Emelia asks, eyes beaming as she puts Oliver on her lap. I guess it has been a while since she's had any.

I chuckle and smile. "Sure, hon. Anything else?"

"Nope! That's it. Thanks, Mom!"

"No problem. I won't be gone too long. Make sure to keep an eye on Oliver."

"I will, Mom! I'm going to read him the new book I got. When you get back, I'll tell you all about it!" Emelia pets Oliver who starts to purr and knead the fluffy purple blanket gently.

"I can't wait! Bye, sweetheart."

"Bye, Mom."

I grab my purse off the counter, turn toward the door—and trip over something, falling hard to my knees.

"Ow! What the heck?" I look back and see the crucifix on the ground—the same one I know I put back on my nightstand after it mysteriously appeared on the dining table. As I reach back to pick it up, I notice that the bottom wood is splintered. *What are you doing here?*

"Is everything okay, Mom?" Emelia yells from her room.

"Yes, sweetheart, I'm fine. I just tripped is all!" I yell back as I get up, quickly putting the cross on the counter. As I walk toward the door, I feel someone staring at me. I turn and look up to see Kyle leaning on the upstairs railing, watching me.

He saw me trip. Great. I think as I open the door to leave.

"Leaving now, love you!" I yell and wave goodbye to Emelia through her open doors.

"Love you too, Mom!" Emelia lifts Oliver's paw and waves it back to me. Oliver's face seems to scowl as he makes a low growl. I chuckle and walk out the door.

Chapter Ten
The Market

I follow the map laid out on the van's passenger seat, driving past the library and pet store as I make my way to the edge of town, where the road transitions from brick to gravel. I pull into the grocery store's parking lot, my back tires kicking up clouds of dust. The crunching of gravel is the only sound as I park in front of the store. I notice a few other cars in the lot, though they look to be abandoned as several have windows smashed and tires removed.

Stepping onto the uneven gravel, I notice several large nail holes and long, splintering cracks running down the storefront's wooden pillars. Patches of white paint cling to the remaining splinters. Several rusted gas tanks are scattered across the porch, their dull surfaces streaked with stains from the nozzles. Cobwebs cling to them as they lean up against each other in piles. Overhead, the low roof sags slightly in places, a few loose shingles hang off the edge, movingly rigidly in the wind. The parking lot is eerily silent, except for the rhythmic creaks of the wooden store sign swaying from its rusty chains. In faded red letters, it reads: JB Market.

"Well, this looks like it passed inspection recently," I mumble sarcastically as I walk through the heavy glass door.

DING.

The overhead bell chimes as the door slams behind me with a loud thud, making me jump. The sound echoes throughout the small store and I'm instantly overwhelmed by the lingering smell of musty air. Flickering panel lights showcase narrow aisles with crammed shelves. At the back, I can just make out a refrigerator, empty except for a few cartons of eggs and milk. I'm not sure what I expected from the town's grocery store, but it isn't this. A deep, monotone voice interrupts the stillness.

"Welcome to JB Market where we carry the best produce in town."

Behind the only checkout counter is a lanky teenage boy leaning back in a chair. I can barely see his freckled face behind the curtain of his unruly ginger hair. His mouth is gaping open like a bass fish as he plays on a Game Boy. I look around the whole store—not a single fresh fruit or vegetable in sight.

"Excuse me young man, where is the produce?"

"Huh?" The boy glances up, as if surprised I asked him a question. He looks around the store, slightly confused, then tilts his head back to peer up at me from beneath his stringy hair. "Oh, I guess we're out, ma'am. Sorry." He looks back down and continues playing his Game Boy.

I sigh. I'll just have to make it into the city sometime next week when Kyle can watch Emelia for longer than a few hours. I'll get what I can for now. I grab one of the store's two shopping carts and make my way to the canned food section. The off-brand cans are caked in dust, some with labels ripped clear off. On the top shelf, a few bags of flour have what looks like mouse holes chewed through them, spilling white powder onto pickled jars below that hold some of the strangest concoctions I've ever seen. As I sift through the mess trying to find a single usable item, the bell dings as someone walks into the store. The door slams shut, and I catch a whiff of a familiar scent. I can't quite pinpoint it, but then I hear her obnoxious, Southern belle voice.

"Well good morning, Billy, how is your Ma doing at the pet store?" Amy asks, flipping her hair back. I almost don't recognize her with this new makeover. Her now-curled hair bounces off the tan leather jacket she wears over a white tank top and faded bell bottom jeans. Her brown suede belt has a "CK" buckle—Calvin Klein; Kyle's favorite brand. He must've taken her shopping the other day when he was "working all night."

I really hope she doesn't see me. I try to turn around and face away from her, but I'm too late.

"Oh hello, Mrs. Gallo!" She yells walking up to me, her perfume more overwhelming than the musty air. Now in front of me, I notice she's wearing pearl earrings—pearl earrings that look identical to the missing set my mother gave me. *Did that asshole really give my mother's earrings to this bitch?*

"We're about the same age, Amy. You can call me Sarah. Though, I am glad you remember that I'm married. By the way, nice earrings. Where did you get them, if you don't mind me asking?" I reply in a snarky yet sophisticated way. I want it to be clear that I know what she's been up to, but I don't need to stoop to her level. Amy grabs one of her ears as if she'd forgotten what she's wearing.

"Oh! These old things? I've had them for a while now." She replies, then attempts to change the topic. "But enough about me. How are you enjoying your new home?"

"Well, those *old things* look very similar to the ones my late mother passed down to me. Unfortunately, they've gone missing." I say with a straight face, staring Amy down. I can tell I'm making her nervous by the way she starts to fidget with her jacket pockets.

"Well, I am very sorry to hear that." Amy clears her throat and straightens her posture as if to find a new sense of confidence. "But anyhow, I need to get some ground beef. I'm making my family's secret spaghetti and meatball recipe. It's to die for! You know what the secret ingredient is?" She leans in to whisper before I can reply. "Love." Amy giggles. "See you around, Sarah." She bumps her shoulder into mine as she walks past me toward the refrigerators.

Bitch.

I feel my blood boiling. Kyle's always been an asshole, but I never thought he would go as far as giving away my family heirlooms to his sluts. This is a new low, even for him. "Breathe, Sarah, Breathe." I whisper under my breath as I continue to search for salvageable food. Gathering what I can, I head to the checkout counter where Billy is still playing his Game Boy. I loudly clear my throat a few times until he leans back to look up at me. He slowly stands up and starts scanning my items and placing them into a paper bag.

"That'll be $34.92, ma'am." He states almost resentfully. He must hate when his job gets in the way of his game time. I reach into my purse and pull out two twenty-dollar bills.

"Here you go." I hand Billy the money. He opens the cash register and starts counting how much change he owes me with his fingers. I roll my eyes.

"Uh, ma'am? I only have bills. Is that okay?" He asks as he holds out four one-dollar bills. I'm annoyed at this point, but I can't really blame the boy. I mean, look who his mother is.

"I guess five dollars back will be fine. I don't need the eight cents."

"Five dollars? Oh, yes. Sorry, ma'am." Billy apologizes, grabbing another dollar out of the till and handing it to me. I take my bag of groceries and open the door to leave—

A man and a woman hang from the front pillars, facing each other. Flies buzz around them as their bodies sway in the wind. They're suspended by rusted spikes impaled through their open mouths. Blood drips down their clothes. A gust of wind carries the stench of rotting flesh to my nose.

I freeze in the doorway.

"Ma'am, are you all right?" I hear Billy ask from behind me as I try to process what I'm seeing.

This isn't real, Sarah. This is all in your head...

"Ma'am?"

"Yes, Billy. Everything's okay. I, um... was just looking for my keys," I say, pretending to rummage through my purse. "Found them! Silly of me. Have a good day!"

I quickly close the door behind me and slowly start walking toward the bodies.

They appear to be a couple. Both wear matching brown aprons with *O'Brien Market* stitched across the front in blue thread.

The woman—frail and in a light-blue cotton dress with a fitted bodice and full skirt—looks like she stepped out of a different time. Her dress is torn, stained with dirt and her own blood—which drips from her mouth, down the frills of her dress, and onto the wooden porch. Her face is bruised, and her upper teeth appear to be splitting in half from the weight of her body hanging on the spike. Her hollow eyes peer through red curls, still locked in a look of frozen fear as she stares at the man impaled on the opposite pillar.

The man is muscular, wearing a bloodstained button-up shirt and thick brown trousers with patched knees. A few strands of hair from his long, grizzly-red beard twist around the rusted spike jutting from his mouth. His battered face stares directly back at the woman.

I begin to tear up at the sight. The pain and torture they must have endured is beyond comprehension.

What are you doing, Sarah? They're not real. Stop crying...

I sniffle, wiping away my tears. As I begin to walk past them, the woman grabs my arm.

I scream.

I try to pull away from her strong grip, but she's not attacking me—she's trying to say something.

"Mmmmph. MMMMPH!" she mumbles through her impaled mouth, saliva and blood dripping onto my blouse.

I stop struggling and try to steady my breathing. She's not trying to hurt me. I glance around to make sure no one is watching, then cautiously lean in.

"What are you trying to tell me?" I whisper.

Still mumbling, her eyes drift off mine and into the distance. She raises my arm with her hand, pointing toward the far edge of town.

I follow her gaze—past the parking lot, beyond a tree line in the distance. Just past the trees, I see it: a small, grass-covered hill rising up near the edge of the woods.

"Is it the hill?" I ask gently.

She stops mumbling and locks eyes with mine. Slowly, she reaches into her apron and pulls out a blue ribbon. She presses it into my palm and folds my fingers over it.

"I'm not sure what you need from me... but I'll do my best—"

"Sarah, are you all right? I heard a scream. Who are you talking to?" Amy asks with concern. I was so distracted I didn't even hear the bell when she opened the door. I have to think of something quick. It's not like I can tell her I was talking to a corpse.

"I screamed because a wasp flew in my face."

"Where!?" Amy ducks, panicking as she scours the area.

"Oh, I think it's gone now, thank goodness. Anyways, I wanted to ask you something, Amy. What's on that hill? This place is so flat and wooded, I never thought I'd see a hill around here."

Amy's worried expression turns serious. She stares at me in silence for what feels like minutes.

"Oh, don't you worry about that hill, Sarah. Nothing's over there. Just a pile of dirt teens like to sneak off to when their folks aren't looking. I've got to go—this spaghetti isn't going to make itself!" Amy hurries past me, gets into her Chevy Caprice, and drives off.

Amy was definitely lying—but what could there possibly be to hide about a hill? Why would she lie about it? Is it connected to that couple or the blue ribbon? I'll investigate it later this week, but for now, I need to get home to Emelia. I'm sure Kyle is just itching to leave the house for Amy's spaghetti.

Chapter Eleven

Father

S itting in the parking lot, my knuckles whiten as I squeeze the steering wheel, trying to force myself to leave. It's hitting me what just happened—what I saw. It doesn't make any sense. Am I just imagining all of this? Why would my mind create such vivid and realistic details? I'm not even a fan of horror movies, let alone thinking about grotesque corpses.

My heart races in my chest and a cold sweat drips down my spine. What if these ghosts *are* real? And if they are, why are they coming to me? What could they possibly want from me? It's not like I can perform an exorcism or say a blessing—I'm barely even Catholic, just by baptism and association through my father. I don't even pray anymore. What could I even offer ghosts older than my late grandfather?

I turn on the engine and put my minivan in reverse. I back up, half-expecting to see a ghost, but nothing's there. I let out a breath and began to relax. What am I even thinking, ghosts aren't real... right?

"All right, let's change the vibe in here," I say with a grin, twisting the knob on the radio. I keep turning until the static clears and a deep voice fills the car.

"You're listening to Top Hits Radio on 103.5. Up next is your favorite color and French building—*Blue* by Eiffel 65!"

"Now that's what I'm talking about!" I shout as I make my minivan a stand-alone karaoke joint. "I'm blue Da ba dee da ba di!" I scream-sing as I drive through the old town. If there were ever any people around, I know they'd be staring at the crazy blonde in a mom-van screaming about how blue she is. Just as I get to the last chorus—

RING...RING...RING...

I hear my phone ring in my purse. I sigh aggressively. Of course I get a call right in the middle of my jam. I pull out my phone, glance at the caller ID, and see it's my father. *Why is he calling?* I flip it open to answer.

"Hello Father, are you doing all right?"

"Oh, Sarah, how many times do I have to tell you? Call me 'Papi.'" His raspy voice echoes in my ear, followed by a cough. He definitely sounds worse than the last time we spoke.

"I'm sorry Papi, but answer my question—are you all right?"

"Always straight to business. You haven't changed a bit. Even when you were little, you were always so serious."

"Papi..."

"Can't a father just call his daughter to talk? I haven't seen you or Emmie in years. How's she doing? I still remember when she'd play in the field out back, bringing home baskets full of wildflowers. You remember that? The gardener used to get so mad, but I'd slip extra euros into his paycheck to keep him quiet!"

My father chuckles, but the laughter quickly turns into a fit of coughing. It sounds like he's struggling to catch his breath. "Emmie always had the purest little heart. I miss that little rascal," my father wheezes.

"Papi... what's wrong?"

"Sarah, please! Let me have a normal conversation with my only daughter. Please, Sarah—"

His words are cut off by another fit of coughing.

I pull into the driveway and leave the engine running, my free hand tightly gripping the steering wheel. I feel tears welling up. Deep down, I know what this phone call means, and I can't hold it back anymore. I struggle to keep my voice steady.

"You're right. I'm sorry, Papi. You won't believe this, but Emmie got a cat."

"She got a cat!? Oh, wow! How'd you convince Kyle on that one?"

"Oh, I didn't. We just brought him home after Emmie begged me to stop at a pet store. Kyle calls the cat 'dirt rag.'"

"*Dirt rag!?* What a cleverly horrible nickname!" He laughs, and I can't help but join in.

It feels good to laugh with him, something I haven't done in so long. It's been years, really—too many, and I know I'm mostly to blame. Since the forced marriage, I've carried anger toward my father, avoiding his calls and making excuses not to visit, only showing up on holidays. But now I feel the weight of my absence.

109

Emmie deserved to have him more in her life. At least, I tell myself, her memories of him are all good ones.

"Hey Sarah, do you know why your mother and I used to call you Honey Bear?"

"No, Papi. Why?"

"When you were just a toddler, you were obsessed with the book *Winne-the-Pooh*. One day, your mother heard something strange coming from the kitchen. When she walked in, what did she find? There you were, sitting on the floor with jars of honey from the neighbor's bee farm, shoving both your little hands into the jars and shouting, 'Pooh, Pooh!' as honey poured everywhere! I was so mad at the mess, but your mother just laughed and laughed. And that's how you got your nickname—Honey Bear."

I hear my father sniffling in the background, and for a moment, there's a long pause.

"You know, Sarah, your mother would be so proud of the woman you've become. You and Emmie, you're both spitting images of her."

"Oh, Papi..." The tears come then, uncontrollably, as a deep ache fills my chest. I miss my mother more than words can say. My father has never said anything like this before, and it hits me harder than I expected. I can hear my father beginning to cry.

"I love you, Sarah."

"I love you too, Papi!" I choke out, tears streaming down my cheeks like a waterfall. A heaviness presses down on me, as sadness begins to consume every part of me.

"Oh, and hon? One last thing." I hear a faint crinkling in my ear, like he is removing a piece of paper from an envelope. "I got your letter in the mail and I can have my attorneys change it like you requested, but are you sure this is what you want?"

"Yes, Papi. I'm sure."

My father lets out a heavy sigh. "All right. I will do as you have asked. I'm going to go get some rest. Tell Emmie that I love her. I don't have the strength to talk to her right now. Will you do that for me please, Honey Bear? Will you tell her that I love her?"

"Of course I'll tell her. I love you, Papi."

My father sniffles. "Bye, my Honey Bear."

"Bye."

I hear the quiet click as the phone line is disconnected. I turn off the van and sit there, wrapped in silence. My heart aches, the thought gnawing at me—this might have been his goodbye call. I knew the cancer was spreading, but I thought I had more time. I guess that's what we all think—there's always more time. Until there isn't. I wipe away my tears and step out of the minivan, grabbing the single bag of groceries from the back seat.

As I open the front door, I find Kyle leaning against the counter, suitcase by his side, tapping his foot impatiently while texting on his Blackberry. He looks over at me.

"Finally! What took you so long? I got a call about a business conference for the rest of the week, and I don't want to miss my flight," Kyle says, striding toward me. He stops and eyes me closely. "What happened to your makeup? Were you crying?"

His stupid, judgmental tone makes my blood boil. Every bone in my body wants to strangle him.

111

Maybe he could be another ghost that haunts me. *He's not worth it*, I remind myself, taking a deep breath to calm down just enough so I can reply.

"I just got off the phone with my... Papi."

"Oh? How is he doing?" Kyle's tone changes drastically. He seems very interested in how my father is, a little *too* interested. My gut is telling me not to trust him.

"He's doing okay. The treatments seem to be keeping his cancer from spreading more." I lie. Kyle looks slightly annoyed by my answer.

"Oh, that's...great." He grabs my hand, the one holding the grocery bag. "That's it? Are there more groceries in the trunk?"

"Yes, that's it. The store didn't have much to choose from."

"Pfft. You could've taken Emmie then. What a waste."

Just then, a horn blares outside our house. I turn to see Amy's Chevy Caprice parked at the curb. Kyle lets go of my hand.

"Well, there's my ride. Try not to get jealous," he says, picking up his suitcase. As he walks toward the door, he pauses and turns around. "Oh, and call someone to fix that stupid railing. It wiggles."

With that, he walks out and gets into Amy's car without a second glance. I stand there, watching him go. Once the car drives off, I close the door and set the bag of groceries on the kitchen counter. I hear Emelia's wheelchair squeak as she rolls into the room.

"Hey, Mom! Did you bring lunch? Dad said you were bringing home food."

I glance at the clock—it's just past 1 p.m. I sigh. The jerk couldn't even be bothered to feed our daughter. All this stress calls for a smoke break.

"I have some food with me. How about this," I say, starting to unpack the random mix of groceries. "You eat while I step outside for a bit. Then, after you're done eating, you start your piano lessons? I'll come back in shortly after you begin. How does that sound?"

"Sounds great, Mom! But after piano, can I tell you about some of the cool animals from the book Mr. Gilbert gave me?"

"Of course, sweetheart." I smile through my exhaustion. I can't wait to go take a much needed smoke break.

Chapter Twelve

Piano

"It's not real, Sarah. It's all your imagination." I whisper to myself as I finally manage to light the cigarette in my vibrating hand. I take a deep, shaky drag. The smoke fills my lungs like a hot air balloon, lifting my mood just slightly. With an almost forceful exhale, my body began to loosen, and tingles ran down my face to my lips.

"Ahhh…that's much better."

Leaning on the side of the manor, I allow the weight of my head to fall back against the house, my hair getting entangled in the splintered wood panels and uneven grooves. Slight stings shoot through my scalp as the splinters pull at my curls. The pain oddly gives me a sense of comfort. With my mind questioning everything, it's nice to know this slightly uncomfortable moment is real. I take a few more drags and enjoy the slight breeze that kisses my cheeks through the cigarette smoke. Just as I'm beginning to fully succumb to relaxation, the peace of the moment is broken by the discordant sound of a piano playing *If You're Happy and You Know It.*

"*Ugh*. I told Emmie to practice her lessons, not goof around. Oh well, it was time to go back in anyway." I put out my cigarette against the side of the house and save the remainder of it back in my half-smoked pack.

I walk up the stairs, the jarring piano notes growing more annoying the closer I get to the front door. *I'm going to have a talking-to with Emmie. This is unacceptable. She knows to take her lessons seriously.* Maybe it's because of the day I am having, but I'm definitely in no mood for any more shenanigans. I am not happy, and I do know it.

I swing the front door open, the door knocker making a slight rap as I storm through the foyer and into Emelia's room.

"Emelia Rose Gallo, you are supposed to be practicing—"

No one is there.

If You're Happy and You Know It continues to play, but no keys are moving. The room is empty except for the unsettling melody echoing off the cathedral ceiling from an untouched piano.

I stand there puzzled. I know what I'm hearing, but my eyes don't believe it. I slowly walk up to the piano, still covered in dust from the move. I look closer, some of the keys have faint smudges in the dust, like someone has touched them. I sit down at the piano bench, hunching over the keys. I hesitantly press the lowest of the smudged keys and start playing in ascending order.

I play the first note twice, then the next highest key, after the third key, it dawns on me: I'm playing *If You're Happy and You Know It*. The air falls silent as the melody fades. I feel like time's stopped as I stare at the imprinted keys. For some reason, I succumb to the uncanny urge to play it again, this time singing along with each slowly pressed key.

"If...you're...happy...and you know it, clap your hands—"

Out of nowhere, two small, decaying hands flash into my peripheral view, mere inches away from my cheekbone. The hands are lacerated, with maggots crawling out of every crevasse and pushing off the fingernails from underneath. The wriggling parasites are so fat, pus is starting to sweat out of them. Their stench fills the inside of my nostrils. The disgusting sound of their chewing of rotten skin is only superseded by the sound of the hands clapping along with the song.

CLAP. CLAP.

I jolt and collapse to the ground, my elbow scraping the piano keys with a discordant vibrato as the weight of my body knocks over the bench sending it crashing to the cold, hard floor. The lid of the bench flies open, lesson books scattering and sliding all over the hardwood floor. One tattered book flies open as it glides in front of me, its yellowed pages showing a colorful watercolor illustration of smiling puppet-like children holding hands. Beneath the image in alternating rainbow colors, is the cheerful title: "If You're Happy and You Know It."

I open my mouth to scream, but only wheezes escape. I kick my legs as hard as I can, scraping my heels against the floor and slithering my body backwards until my back presses against the paisley brown wall. I squeeze my gold crucifix pendant against my chest, as

117

the room seems to tilt to the side, a heavy pressure weighing my head down as I desperately scan the room for any sign of the hands. The boy. The Spider. The ghosts. The bodies. Anything.

But there is nothing.

I start to zone out, staring at the floor as I feel the internal vibrations of panic being replaced by the pressure of my heartbeat, the sound echoing in my ear as it pulsates in my throat. I sit in this moment for what feels like eternity, when it is suddenly interrupted.

"Mom, are you okay?! What happened?!" I slowly look up to see Emelia a couple of feet away in her wheelchair with Oliver in her lap. I snap out of it.

"Oh, I umm... I just fell by accident. I'm fine, Emmie." I start to stand up, and as I do, blood drips from my elbow.

"Mom, you're bleeding!"

I look down and sure enough, my left elbow is bleeding. I must have scraped it pretty badly against the piano keys when I fell. I try to bend it, and a shock of pain shoots down my arm.

"Ouch! Yeah, you're right, Emmie. I'm going to have to get this checked out." I look over at Emelia, her eyes filling with tears about to spill over to her cheeks. I walk over and lean against her in an awkward half-hug while keeping pressure on my elbow.

"I'm so sorry, Emmie. I didn't mean to scare you. Don't worry, I'll get it checked out. Do you want to help me wrap it up? You can be my doctor. Dr. Songbird has a good ring to it!"

"Nah, I'm Dr. Emmie." Emelia starts to smile, then makes a playful serious expression. "Now, young lady, you will take it easy on your elbow and get lots of sunshine. That's an order."

"Yes, ma'am!" I reply with a salute. We both start to laugh as we make our way into the living room. I look over at a stack of unpacked boxes piled in the corner, "You know, I think the first-aid kit may be in one of those boxes. Will you check the first one? I'm going to look in the Yellow Pages to see if there's a doctor in town."

"Okay, Mom! Oliver and I will look in the boxes, maybe we can do some unpacking at the same time."

"What a wonderful idea, sweetheart. Let's do it." I smile as I look at Emelia, who is now hard at work unpacking a box with Oliver quietly meowing, as if to cheer her on.

A few moments later, I hear Emelia shout, "Found the first-aid kit, Mom!" I look up and see her waving the small box in the air. Good thing, because holding my elbow makes it difficult to dig through these boxes for the Yellow Pages.

"Thank goodness! All right, Dr. Emmie, I'm ready for the procedure."

"Yes, young lady, hold still!"

I stretch my arm out as far as it will let me against her wheelchair's armrest. I can't extend it fully without sharp pain shooting down my arm. Emelia begins to wrap the cut.

I must have sprained it. This week is not going to be easy without Kyle's help. I sigh.

"Are you okay, Mom? Is it too tight?"

"No, no hon. I was just thinking about where the Yellow Pages could be."

"Oh, do you mean that huge phone book? I just saw it in the same box the first-aid kit was in."

"That's perfect. Now I can call a doctor and hopefully get an appointment." I look down at my bent elbow—even the slightest movement stings. "Emmie, I might have sprained my elbow when it hit the piano. It may take me longer to do daily activities. I'm going to call your dad, too, and see if he can come home to help out while my elbow heals. I'm sorry, hon, hopefully it doesn't interfere with anything."

"It's okay, Mom. Even if Dad can't come home, we'll figure it out." Emelia doesn't look up as she meticulously wraps the bandage, making sure there is not a single crease. She attaches the bandage clips, then pats it to signal she has completed the task. "Now remember, young lady, lots of water and sunshine, 'cause after every storm there is..." Emelia playfully draws out her *s,* waiting for me to finish the phrase. I chuckle.

"Sun." I really do have an angel for a daughter. How did I get so lucky?

Chapter Thirteen
Doctor

"**B**oy, I'm glad I got this county's Yellow Pages before we moved here. I would be shit out of luck if I didn't." Using my good arm, I plop the bulky paperback phone book on the kitchen counter.

"Was that a bad word I heard, Mom?"

Shit, how did she hear me all the way from her room? Damn, she has good ears!

"Uh, no sweetheart, I said *shoot* out of luck. Yep. That's what I said."

"Uh-huh, suuuuuurrre."

"Don't you have some piano lessons you should be practicing right about now, Ms. Sassy-Pants?" I hear Emelia groan and mumble.

"Aw, man."

"What was that?"

"I said okay, Mom!"

"That's what I thought." I chuckle. She reminds me of when I was her age. I was also very sassy and would whine when my father told me to practice my lessons. Thinking about it, I hope he's as okay as he claims. I really should try to visit him soon. Maybe I can arrange that when Kyle comes back from his 'business trip' with Amy. God, I hate that bitch, but if it's not her, it would be some other pathetic floozy.

Flipping through the book, I find the county's single doctors' office.

"Would you look at that, it's right next to the library, that's convenient." I pull my flip phone from my purse on the counter and dial the doctor's number. The line rings for a while until an older woman's voice finally answers.

"Hello, thank you for calling Gold's Medical Office. How can I help you?"

"Hello, yes, I would like to schedule an appointment for a possible sprained elbow. Are there any openings this week?"

"I'll check. Please hold." The line clicks, and the most annoying elevator music starts to play with periodic advertisements. After what feels like an hour, the woman comes back on the line. "Doctor Gold has an opening this Thursday at 9 a.m. Would you be available?"

"Yes, that should work." I hear the woman typing.

"Name?"

"Sarah Gallo."

"Okay, Ms. Gallo, we have you scheduled."

"Thank yo—"

CLICK.

She hung up on me. I would be bothered, except it seems that everyone in this town, except Mr. Gilbert, has a stick so far up their ass, they should be choking on it. It really is quite annoying. Speaking of annoying, now to call Kyle.

I click the speed dial on my phone for Kyle. The line rings, but then quickly goes straight to voicemail.

"You have reached the one and only Kyle, I must be very busy to miss your call. Please leave a message after the beep."

BEEP.

"Hey, I think I may have sprained my elbow, and it's going to be hard taking care of Emmie by myself. Any chance you can leave your business trip early? Call me back." I snap my phone closed. Of course he won't answer my call, he's 'busy.' I sigh. I seriously have the worst luck right now.

I hear the lid to the piano bench creaking open and Emelia shuffling through the lesson books. Even though she can't press the piano pedals, playing the piano is one of the few consistencies still in her life after the accident. The more normal I can make her life, the better. Emelia strikes and holds a note, a deep tone echoes throughout the room as she continues to play, *You Are My Sunshine.*, It sounds like she's holding the notes to overlap one another, something she hasn't done before. I walk over to her room.

"What a creative way to play without pedals, sweetheart!"

"What do you mean, Mom?"

"I mean how you're holding—" I look around the corner. There, sitting next to Emelia, is the woman from outside the library.

Her black, satin skirt flows over the bench next to Emelia's wheelchair, the lace trim grazing the hardwood floor slightly with each movement she makes. An embroidered bodice binds her waist and highlights her slender curves as the embroidery trails up gold buttons to her high-cinched turtleneck. Only her red lips against her dark complexion are seen under her black-laced veil. The woman looks at my daughter's hands and smiles, following Emmie's lead, her long, sheer black lace sleeves lightly touching the keys as she delicately plays a low note next to Emelia. The haunting yet soulful melody resonates throughout the manor as they play together.

"I'm sorry, what were you saying, Mom?"

"Oh, uh...nothing. Nothing, sweetheart. Just sounds beautiful." My voice shakes a bit as I try not to blink. Emelia looks back at the piano keys and starts to sing *You Are My Sunshine*. The woman softly hums a low harmony with my daughter's light tone, their voices filling the room. Tears begin to form in the corners of my eyes. It is both transcending and horrifying. The thought of a ghost playing with my daughter should terrify me, but there is something about the spirit of this woman that's beautiful. I lean against the doorway as I continue to watch and listen to the spectacle. The last note is finally struck, and Emilia turns to me.

"Did you like it?"

"Did I like it—" I look at the woman sitting motionless, like a statue. "I loved it! You're getting better by the day, my little songbird." Joy washes over Emelia's face as she starts to wheel past me.

"I'm hungry. What's for dinner?" I look down at my phone, which is still in my hand. It's now a little past 5 p.m.

"You're right, Emmie, it's getting pretty late. Are you okay with pizza again?"

"Duh! I love pizza!" As I am about the turn to the living room, I look back at the piano—the woman's gone. A cold sweat starts to trickle down my forehead as my feet feel planted into the ground. Emelia looks up at me.

"Are you okay? Is it your elbow?"

Oh, no. Emelia is starting to notice. Snap out of it, Sarah.

"Yes, dear I'm fine, just zoned out is all. I'll call and order a pizza. By the way, where's Oliver?"

"Yay!" Emelia cheers as she shoots her hands straight into the air. "Oh, and Oliver's sleeping on the bed. He needed his catnap." Emelia mischievously smirks at her joke. I let out a forced giggle.

"Good one, Emmie!"

"Thank you, I thought so, too! Want to watch something while we wait for the pizza?"

"That's a wonderful idea. Why don't you pick out the movie?"

"Sweet! I'm going to make you cry again!" Emelia says as she rolls vigorously to the bin of movies next to the box TV.

I glance over at her bed before following behind. Oliver is lying down, but he's not sleeping. His eyes are narrowed in disapproval, ears pinned flat against his head as he lets out a low, rumbling growl.

He is not a happy boy right now. I wonder if he can see what I see?

Chapter Fourteen
Movie Time

Sinking into my recliner, I hopelessly try to watch the movie as I stare blankly at our big box TV. My mind has not stopped thinking about all that has happened today and not even watching a heartfelt movie like *Free Willy* is keeping my attention. Heck, I wouldn't know we were watching *Free Willy* if it wasn't for the killer whale and the fact that Emelia insists we watch it at least once a year.

All the "ghosts" I have seen today, scary as they were... none of them tried to hurt me. Hell, one of them played the piano with Emelia! So, if they are not here to hurt us, what do they want?

I look over to Emelia who is lying on the couch, a paper plate with a half-eaten slice of pizza resting on her chest. Eyes glued to the screen, she slides the pizza slice across the plate and into her mouth, unaware that Oliver, sprawled out on her stomach, is dragging himself stealthily inch by inch toward the leftover pizza crust hanging slightly over the edge of the plate. I crack a smile. As the movie plays, my mind starts to drift.

And why can't anyone else see them? Did my brain injury open up some kind of third eye shit and that's how I can see them? Well, no, then I would have been seeing ghosts before we moved here...

"Hey Mom, are you crying yet?"

Huh? I look up, and the credits are rolling. *Did we watch the whole movie already?!* I rub my eyes and shift to an upright position.

"No, Emmie, not tonight anyways. You might get me on the next movie."

"Aw, man!" Emelia makes a pouty face, then looks down at Oliver snoring, his large belly sticking up as he uses the mostly eaten pizza crust as a pillow. "Oliver! Did you eat my crust?!" Oliver's eyes squint open for a moment, then shut again as he continues to lightly snore. I hold my mouth as I try to control my snickering.

"Not funny, Mom!"

I burst into uncontrollable laughter. I laugh so hard it brings me to tears. Emelia can't help but join in.

"Well, there you go, hon. You got your tears!"

"Yep! I told you I'd make you cry tonight." Emelia's giggles wake up Oliver, who stretches out his little paws. "Wakey-wakey, Oliver."

"Speaking of which, it's getting late. We need to start getting ready for bed."

"Aw, okay." Emelia gently pouts as she holds up her arms, ready for me to help her into the wheelchair. I push the wheelchair next to her and lock the wheels.

"Emmie, since I am doing this one-handed, I'm going to need you to wrap your arms around my neck tightly while I try to get you into the chair." I squat down to her level and wrap my single arm tightly around her waist. Putting her on the couch was easy, as all I had to do was essentially dump her onto the couch and adjust her legs after. Getting her into the wheelchair, however, wasn't going to be easy. I brace myself.

"Okay, on the count of three. Ready?"

"Ready."

"One…two…three!" My body strains as I struggle to lift her. It takes every ounce of my strength, but I manage to get her safely seated. Emelia starts to wipe off her hands on her pants as a drip of sweat rolls down the back of my neck. I look at the couch. Oliver is perched on a cushion, his tail slightly twitching as his purr rumbles from his tiny fury body. *Enjoyed the show, Oliver? What a little turd.* I laugh.

"Are you okay, Mom?" Emelia looks at me with concern in her eyes. I give her a reassuring smile.

"Yes, hon, I'm fine. Now let's get ready for bed."

Chapter Fifteen
Railing

"Goodnight my little songbird, sleep well. I love you."

"Love you too, Mom! Night."

"Night."

I gently close the French doors to Emelia's room. I sigh as I make my way to the kitchen to pour myself a much-needed drink. Yet another thing I have to hide from Kyle.

He calls me an alcoholic, but I don't consider someone who drinks an occasional glass of wine to be an alcoholic; probably just another way Kyle likes to get on my case about something. Either way, my hidden stash is going to come in handy tonight. Balancing my body against the cabinets, I squat down and without looking, reach into the far back of the bottom cabinet.

"Come on, where are you...?" I mumble as I continue to fumble around for the bottle of Barolo—until I feel something furry.

"EEK!" I jerk back my arm and fall on my ass.

A small set of whiskers emerges from the wooden cabinet door. Eventually, a rat pokes its head out. Its beady black eyes stare at me before it scurries back into the cabinet. I lay back onto the floor in hysterical laughter. I stay like this for a moment, crying and laughing maniacally, staring up at the kitchen lights until I see colorful dots floating around. Finally, the laughter stops, and I lie there, listening only to the faint sounds of the rat scampering in the cabinets. Strangely, this moment feels peaceful as I allow my mind to escape even for this mere moment—until it is interrupted.

THUD.

I don't flinch. I am too mentally drained and exhausted to react to anything right now. I continue to lie there until my curiosity won't allow it anymore. I slowly get up and walk around to see where the sound could have come from. As I step around the counter, and there it is. The crucifix, back on the floor, but this time, the wood pieces from the bottom of the cross are scattered on the floor. I shake my head.

"*Tsk. Tsk.* The rat is at it again, knocking my crucifix over. At least that is one mystery solved." I pick up the crucifix. The bottom has splintered into a sharp point, similar to a wooden stake in old vampire movies.

"Well, this will come in handy whenever a vampire comes around—or a *rat* vampire. That cute little rat did have extra beady-looking eyes!" I hold the stake up as if I am about to stab something. "My god, did I *really* just say that? Yep. It's official. I'm delirious. Time to go to bed." I mumble. I'm about to put the crucifix back on the counter when I pause. *You know what, I'm going to take you with me upstairs. Just in case.*

After turning off the lights, I make my way up the spiral staircase, crucifix in hand. Each step feels heavier than the next as the deep creaks echo across the living room. The loft-style master bedroom is luxurious, but it's times like these that make me wish we lived in a one-level home. Once in the room, I place the crucifix on the bed as I awkwardly change one-handed into my light-pink nightgown and finish my nightly bedtime routine. My eyes feel weighed down, and by the time I'm done, I'm hardly able to keep them open. I walk, dragging my feet until my knees hit the edge of my bed, at which point I face-plant into the soft, blue comforter. My eyes instinctively close as I pull myself fully onto the bed, not even bothering to get under the covers. My thoughts begin to fade as I am about to drift off to sleep—until I hear something.

Whispering.

"Suh-tay-tih"

My eyes snap open as my body tenses, my senses hyperaware.

"Suh-tay-tih"

I shoot into an upright position. Grabbing the crucifix, I punch it straight out in front of me like a shield, scanning the room.

I see a tall, dark shadow in the corner. I dare not blink as I start to hear my heartbeat in my throat. I open my mouth to speak, and a whisper comes from behind me.

"Suh-tay-tih"

I jump up into a fighting position and turn to face behind me, the crucifix shaking vigorously in my hand above my head, ready to strike. Another dark, but shorter shadow peaks from behind the bedframe, its shadowy hand slowly grabbing the bed's post.

"Suh-tay-tih"

I turn to look, another shadow to my left.

"Suh-tay-tih"

Another to my right.

"Suh-tay-tih"

"Suh-tay-tih"

Turning in circles on my bed, my heart drops to my gut as I come to a horrific realization.

The shadows.

The whispers.

"Suh-tay-tih"

"suh-tay-tih"

"suh-tay-tih"

Have me surrounded.

"Suh-tay-tih"

"suh-tay-tih"

"suh-tay-tih"

And they are closing in on me.

The group of voices repeating the same gibberish. Some of them sound like children, their giggling dissonates as the whispers grow louder. The shadows have surrounded the bed, and dark hands start to grab at the comforter's edges.

Reaching towards me.

"suh-tay-ti suh-tay-tih suh-tay-tih suh-tay-tih"

"suh-tay-tih suh-tay-tih suh-tay-tih"

"Suh-Tay-tih Suh-Tay-ti Suh-Tay-tih"

"SuH-TAY-tIh SuH-TAY-tIh SuH-TAY-tIh "

"SUH-TAY-TIH SUH-TAY-TI SUH-TAY-TIH SUH-TAY-TIH!

"NOO!!!" I scream as I jump over the hands off the bed and run to the staircase.

Small, girl-shaped shadows giggle as they block my path. More shadows start to drag themselves on the floor towards me. I back up and my back touches the cold loft railing. The whispering shadows are getting closer.

And closer.

And CLOSER.

My face tingles as I feel the blood drain from my face. I press myself harder against the cast-iron railing.

I have nowhere to run.

I turn to look over the edge and the long fall to the living room floor beneath.

Sarah, you might have to jump.

Just as the thought crosses my mind, one side of the railing snaps, revealing rusted, sharp spikes protruding from the edge. It bends back over, launching me towards the opening below. I grab onto the other side to steady myself, dropping the crucifix. I watch it fall.

CRACK.

As the crucifix stabs into a crack in the hardwood, the whispering stops. I hesitantly turn and look behind me to where the shadows were about to consume me moments ago—nothing. Not a whisper, not a sound— I'm left alone, standing against a partially broken railing. I let go of it, my hand still pulsating from squeezing so hard.

I slowly make my way down the staircase to the crucifix, which is lodged upside down, Jesus's head wedged in a crack in the floor, the sharp stake pointed to the ceiling. I lean over and try to pull it out. No luck. I blankly stare at the crucifix, my body stiff and heavy. After a while, I exhale a long, deep breath.

"Nothing says cursed like an upside-down crucifix in the middle of the living room. I think it's time for that bottle of Barolo."

Chapter Sixteen
Sheriff Ashford

"
There has to be a hotel open somewhere nearby. I don't think I can stay in this manor much longer." Flipping through the Yellow Pages on the counter, intermittently taking long gulps of wine, I find the hotel we stayed at last week and call them. The line is directed to voicemail.

"Hello guests, we are temporarily shut down for fumigations. The re-opening date is unknown. We apologize for the inconvenience and hope you consider us for your future visits to Aditville."

CLICK.

Just what I want to hear. The place we stayed at last week is infested. *What if we slept with bed bugs or worse, cockroaches... eww.* I shudder at the thought and quickly chug what's left in my glass. I go to pour more, but the bottle is empty. I sigh as I glance over at the clock. It's now 4:23 a.m. I gently rest my head against the cold, granite counter. My body is so exhausted but my mind is wired. I've already had a few smoke breaks, and it seems nothing can relax me enough to go to sleep.

I mumble only what I can understand. "It can't get any worse than this—"

BZZZZ... BZZZZ... BZZZZ...

I feel buzzing vibrations against my cheek. My phone is ringing, but who would call me at this god-awful hour?

"*Ugh*, I'm going to be so pissed if it is a scam caller." My cheek still against the counter, I grab my phone out of my purse and look at the caller ID. It's Kyle.

Great.

I flip open the phone and hold it against my exposed ear, "Good morning."

"What are you doing up so early, Sarah?!"

"You called me?" I say with slight confusion in my voice until it dawns on me—he's trying to leave a voicemail instead of talking to me. In hindsight, I probably should've let him. I'm not in the mood to listen to his lying ass either.

Kyle scoffs. "Oh whatever, Sarah. Anyways, what the hell did you do to your elbow? You know it's going to cost money to go to the doctor, right? We don't have those kinds of funds, at least not yet anyway."

"What do you mean *not yet*?" I can hear Kyle hemming and hawing, trying to figure out what to say. I can also hear a woman tittering in the background. He clears his throat.

"When I get my first paycheck, obviously. But I guess it doesn't matter how you hurt yourself. I'm calling to let you know I'll be home Friday afternoon. That's the earliest I can get back. The boss has me working overtime on these pharmaceutical sales." The tittering continues in the background. At this point, I am almost certain it's Amy. What a fucking cunt. The both of them.

"Yeah, you definitely sound busy all right. Thanks for calling." I am about to hang up when I hear Kyle continue.

"One more thing, I called Sheriff Ashford and told him you hurt your elbow. He said he would keep an eye on you while I'm gone. Just to make sure you and Emelia are safe."

"You what?! And who is this sheriff?!" My body jolts up like someone gave me a pinch of Adderall. While Kyle talks, I walk to the dining room window.

"He's the sheriff of the town. I met him while I was down there a month ago for the job interview." I peek behind the curtain. A cop car is parked across the street. "We hit it off right away and I now consider him a friend. He'll take care of you while I'm away, but I've got to run. These drugs ain't going to sell themselves! Love you."

"Okay, bye—"

CLICK.

The line disconnects before I can finish. I look down at my phone and roll my eyes. *What is up with everyone hanging up on me recently?!* I glance back out at the cop car, my eyes squinting and aggravation intensifying as I try to make out what the driver looks like, but between the tinted windows and the impending sunrise, it's impossible to see anything.

"Okay, that's it. I'm too tired for this bullshit," I growl between my teeth. I shove my feet into the sandals by the door and storm out of the house, their soles slapping the pavement as I charge the cop car. Standing in front of the driver's door, I tap the window aggressively. A moment later, the glass slowly rolls down.

The first thing I see is a dark brown cowboy hat, followed by scruffy brown eyebrows and a pale face hidden behind aviator sunglasses perched on a large, pointed nose. The awkward moment is silent, except for the squeaking of the window pressing against the rubber seal as it slowly reveals the sheriff, who gives me a creepy smile through his brown-and-gray-speckled five-o'clock shadow.

"Why you must be Mrs. Gallo. Good morning." The sheriff grins through his southern twang, showing his gold canine tooth.

"Nice tooth," I reply sarcastically. He seems amused by my comment.

"Why thank you, my wife sure does love it. If you know what I mean." He winks at me, which gives me the creeps. "But how rude of me? I am Sheriff William Ashford. But you, *Mrs. Gallo*, you can call me Bob."

"Thank you, *Sheriff Ashford*. Why are you outside of my house?"

"Why I am here to watch over you and your sweet daughter, Mrs. Gallo, by Mr. Gallo's request. Also," Sheriff Ashford pauses for a moment as he takes off his sunglasses. "I've been hearing that you have some questions about this here town and its folks."

Huh? What is he talking about? He notices my perplexed look.

140

"You were asking the town realtor about the hills outside of the country store? Ring any bells?" The sheriff's grin fades as he stares into my eyes. It feels like I'm being interrogated. But why does it even matter? I clear my throat.

"Oh, yes. I noticed the hill, the *only* hill, and just asked Amy about it since she was walking past me by chance. Did she tell you about it?"

"Oh no, my son Billy did. You remember the hard-working young lad at the store?"

Pfft. Hard-working?! Yeah, maybe his thumbs are from all those video games! Sheriff Ashford frowns. I must have made a face when he said that. This lack of sleep is catching up to me and it's getting harder to control my facial expressions. He continues.

"Well anyhow, that hill is where all the rascals go to 'do the deed.' It would be best to stay away from there if you don't want to step on condoms or see any pizza-faced brats doing it."

"What brats? The only kid I have seen in this town since we arrived is your son, unless he is one of those 'brats' you are referring to?" I step back as Sheriff Ashford opens the door and steps out of his car. He is a lot taller than I expected him to be. At least six-five. Standing uncomfortably close, he looks down at me.

"The Ashford's have been protecting this town and its people since the day it was established, and I'll be damned if anything, or anyone, changes that."

I feel uneasy. Between the indirect threat and overpowering cologne, I am not in the right state of mind to deal with this. I remain motionless, nonetheless. I don't need to give him an excuse to act irrationally right now. He leans down, his mouth right next to my ear, and deeply inhales a whiff of my sweaty, unwashed hair into his oversized nostrils. A chill runs down my spine. I can feel his warm coffee breath in my ear canal as he whispers, "Do we understand each other, Sarah?"

I control the shaking in my voice as I reply, "Yes, Sheriff, I understand."

He pulls back up into an upright position, still looking down at me, only this time his eyes linger on my nightgown. I suddenly remember I'm not wearing a bra. I blush with embarrassment, as my body tenses up with an overwhelming sense of yuck that makes me want to gag. It takes a moment and then I feel my confidence building back up, and I shake off the feeling.

"I think it's about time I go check on my daughter. Anything else you need, Sheriff?" Sheriff Ashford grins, his tooth shining as sunrise begins to creep over the horizon.

"No, I think we're good for now. I'll be around for any more questions you may have." He turns and gets back into his car, leaving the window down. I start to walk away.

"Oh, and Mrs. Gallo," I look back at him as he settles back into the black leather seats. "I will be keeping a good eye on you, you know, to make sure you are okay and all. Wouldn't want to disappoint that *husband* of yours." I scoff and continue to walk back to the house. Sheriff Ashford raises his voice for me to hear him, "If you need any help with anything, and I mean anything, Sarah, I will be right here."

I don't even need to look back to know he has that creepy grin again. He's probably undressing me in his mind with each step I take toward the house. *Shake it off, Sarah, just another creep to ignore.* After what feels like way too long, I'm finally back inside. I have an almost uncontrollable urge to smoke, but I don't want to go back outside and have Mr. Creep watching me. Kind of negates the whole purpose of de-stressing. I go back upstairs to get ready for the day before it's time to wake Emelia up. As I step into the room, my alarm clock goes off.

BEEP. BEEP. BEEP.

I snicker and shake my head as I press the *off* button. *Yep, today is going to be one of those days.*

Chapter Seventeen
The Hill

"Hey Mom, what's for breakfast?" Emelia asks as she rolls up to the table. Oliver curled up in her lap.

Breakfast? Shit, I'm lucky to even be functioning right now with the night I had, though meeting Sheriff Douchebag this morning was no better.

"Let me see what we got, hon. The store didn't have much to choose from yesterday…" I reply as I start to pull food out the cabinets and list them under my breath. "Okay we got peanut butter, bread, chicken ramen… And of course, strawberry Pop-Tarts—"

"Ooh, ooh! Let's have Pop-Tarts!"

"Are you sure? We've have had Pop-Tarts for the past couple of days."

"Yes-yes-yes! I LOVE Pop-Tarts!" I laugh. She is so easy to please. I open up two packs and we sit at the table.

What's the deal with that hill? What is there some Hills Have Eyes *shit going on that they don't want newcomers to know about?* Just then, a low but loud rumble emits from outside. I go to the window and peek out from behind the curtain—Sheriff Ashford has started his patrol car. I watch as he drives off and the rumbling engine fades.

I need to go check out that hill, and now is my chance... I walk back to the kitchen counter and take my medication as I start gathering my things. Emelia is still at the dining table.

"Hey, Mom, can I tell you about one of the animals I read about in my book? You said I could yesterday, but we didn't have a chance."

"My goodness you're so right, Emmie. I'm sorry! I do need to run some errands this morning and since I can't fold and lift the wheelchair, I'm going to have to leave you here with Oliver. Once I get back, I would love to hear all about those animals. Is that okay, Emmie?" Emelia frowns as her eyebrows furrow.

"Are you going to see Mr. Gilbert to get your license renewed so I can go to school?"

Crap, how could I forget about that?! I can stop by on the way back from investigating the hill. Damn I feel like a horrible mother right now.

"Yep, that's on my list!"

"Okay. But you promise when you get back, you'll listen?"

"Yes, I promise. Are you going to be all right by yourself?" I ask as I walk to the front door. Emelia turns her wheelchair to face me.

"We'll be fine. Right, Oliver?" Oliver's head and whiskers are dusted with Pop-Tart crumbs from Emelia eating above him. He shakes his fur and gives a faint meow as if he is agreeing with her. I smile. They really are so adorable together.

146

"Okay, you two be safe. I'll be back before lunch. Love you!"

"Love you too, Mom."

Walking out the door, I feel an overwhelming sense of guilt. How could I forget about getting my license renewed? Unless I can figure out homeschooling, this is the only way Emelia can attend school. In order to be the mother Emelia deserves, I need to figure all of this out, or else I am going to go insane. I get into the minivan and rest my head on the cold leather steering wheel. Even with my eyes shut, they throb from the strain of being held open for so long. I sit here like this for a moment, tiredly trying to gather my brain cells together to formulate a plan for the day.

"All right, I'm going to find the hill at the edge of town and look around for clues. After, go see Mr. Gilbert and ask about getting my license renewed, and maybe see if he knows something about this hill, depending on what I find. I got this." I encourage myself as I start the engine with my good hand and head into town.

The town is livelier this morning than on my prior visits. People are scattered outside of the shops, huddled together, gossiping like chickens circling their prey, pecking at whatever bug seems the juiciest. That bug, currently, is me. As I'm driving through, townsfolk stop talking mid-sentence and stare at me, followed by whispers. Though I try not to make eye contact, I can't help but notice my past suspicions are correct—there are no children in this town, or at least none that I can see. Only a few backwoods teenagers, reluctantly hanging out with their parents.

147

How strange. Why are there no children? I think as I continue to drive.

I make it to the edge of town, where I find a tall line of trees, their roots gripping the edge of the gravel road, it's as though Mother Nature placed a gate of trees to guard her forest. It takes a while, but I finally spot a narrow dirt path that heads in the same direction as the hill I'd seen from the storefront. I park the minivan and walk up to the beginning of the path. It's muddy and overgrown with weeds; if it weren't for there being bare dirt from foot tractions, there would be no way to tell there even was a path here. I look down at my white Adidas sneakers and back at the muddy path, then back at my sneakers.

Sigh. "Welp, here goes nothing." I roll up my jeans and take my first steps onto the path.

I wince as my perfectly white shoes sink into the mud and dirtied water seeps through to my ankle socks. The further I travel along the path, the more the brush and tall grass act like barbed wire, scraping against my calves and leaving behind an itch that burns through my nerves. The mud weighs me down, and I begin to wonder if I'm crazy for even trying to investigate a hill. I mean, it's just a hill, what could I possibly find on a mound of dirt? Just when I am about to give up, I see a glimmer of light peeking out from the trees.

I'm almost there.

With renewed energy, I pick up the pace.

"This better be worth sacrificing my Adidas for!" I growl under my breath as I angrily clomp off the path and into the clearing.

The hill stands in the middle of an opening as the morning sun glints on the wildflowers' dewy petals, like they are the forest's crowning jewels. The sight takes my breath away. Maybe it *is* worth sacrificing my sneakers for. I begin my ascent up the hill, the dew on the flowers cleans the scrapes on my legs. It's not long until I reach the top, where a large, lonely tree stump rests solemnly.

I look around the stump for any clues, but there's nothing. Not even the typical "I Heart You" carvings that love-sick teenagers do when they lose their virginity. Nothing.

I sit down on the stump. Hunched over, elbows dug into my knees, as I cradle my head using my good arm. Have I really wasted all this time, and my shoes, for nothing? Maybe I read too much into Amy's and Sheriff Ashford's reaction to my question. Maybe I was just hoping there was something to all of this, so I did not have to believe the truth—I'm going crazy.

"God Sarah, you are so stupid!" I scold myself, tears trickling down my cheeks.

In anger, I thrust my leg forward and kick the ground, stubbing my toe on something hard.

"Ow! What the-?" I look down where I stubbed my toe, there is a piece of concrete peeking out from the grass that had grown over it.

I immediately get down on my knees and start digging and pulling out the grass with my hands. Soil pushes under my fingernails and cuticles as my fingers claw into the earth. I keep going until the concrete is fully uncovered, and I am shocked at what's revealed—

It's a tombstone.

My hands shake both from the digging and the disturbance of it all. I wanted to find something, but I didn't expect to find something so grave. Now with more caution, I gently wipe away the soil enough to read the engraving:

Here Lies Ada Marie Burrow Freeman.
God has taken back one of His angels too soon.
November 17, 1825 – March 30, 1826.

Burrow? Could this deceased four-month-old baby be John Burrow's? I don't remember anyone mentioning that he had a child. Is that what everyone is so hush-hush about? I need to talk to Mr. Gilbert...

I pause, the wind brushing against my cheeks, sending my curls dancing in the air as I stare at the grave. I begin to think about how horrible it would be to lose a child so young, and how I couldn't imagine what I would do if anything happened to my sweet Emelia.

I'm overwhelmed with emotion, my already burning eyes sting and hair sticks to my wet cheeks, as drops of tears fall on the grave, slowly washing the soil away with each drip. Moments pass, and I wipe my tears away, then pluck a nearby wildflower and place it on the grave and whisper.

"I will find out what happened to you."

Chapter Eighteen
Newspaper

It doesn't take long to get to my minivan and drive back into town to see Mr. Gilbert. Hopefully the library's open, though I doubt Mr. Gilbert has anywhere else to be. Just as I am stepping out of the van, a patrol vehicle pulls up between me and the library entrance. I keep walking forward, avoiding eye contact when the vehicle's door squeaks from being swung open. I look from my peripheral: emerging from overtop the hood is a cowboy hat, followed by sunglasses, and then finally a smug face with a gold tooth. Sheriff Ashford slams the car door and walks quickly to block my path.

"Why hello, Mrs. Gallo. What a coincidence seeing you again this morning. We really shouldn't be meeting like this, might make my wife a bit jealous." He smirks sideways, allowing his gold tooth to peek through his chapped lips. I try to walk past him.

"Good morning to you too, Sheriff, now if you don't mind—" He shifts his weight to further block me from passing and puts his hand on my shoulder.

"What's the hurry, darling? The day has only just started." Smiling, he slowly looks down at my face, then my chest. His smile fades when he sees my muddy sneakers. "Went on a little hike did we? You didn't go see that hill I told you not to, right?"

"And if I did?"

"Well, we might have a little problem." He pauses as he glances over at my minivan. My heart sinks into my gut.

Please don't ask about Emelia...

"Where's your daughter?"

Fuck.

My tongue feels stuck against my lower teeth as my jaw clenches. I can't respond. I don't know how to respond. Is it illegal in this state to leave a child home? *God, Sarah, what were you thinking?* Sheriff Ashford grins, then takes a small step closer to me, his beer gut almost grazing my chest.

"You know, child neglect is a serious crime. I can make it like it never happened. But I might need something in re—"

"Leave her alone, Billy!" An old but familiar gravelly voice yells from behind Sheriff Ashford.

"Stay out of this, you old loon. This is none of your concern." Sheriff Ashford barks back, never breaking eye contact with me.

"You're outside of my library, Billy, and there are no laws saying she can't leave her daughter home while she shops for a little while. Now if you don't mind," limping out from behind Sheriff Ashford comes Mr. Gilbert, his cane hitting the brick sidewalk in cadence with his heavy, raspy breaths. He gently hooks his arm around mine, "We have business matters we must attend to." There is a moment of tension, and even though Sheriff Ashford is wearing sunglasses, I can feel him glaring at Mr. Gilbert. The sheriff lets go of my shoulder and starts walking to his car.

"I have to be going now, anyway. I'll be seeing you around, Mrs. Gallo. Take care of yourself, old coot, would hate for anything to suddenly happen to you."

Mr. Gilbert gently pats my hand as he releases my arm. He takes a few teetering, but deliberate steps forward, then lifts his cane and points it at Sheriff Ashford like a rifle.

"You keep your empty threats out of my town."

"*Your* town!?" Sheriff Ashford rips off his glasses and storms toward Mr. Gilbert, who doesn't flinch.

"Yes, sonny, MY town. Now, unless you want me to tell your wife about your recent *real estate* inquiries, I suggest you scurry on out of here." The sheriff's face turns the color of a ripe tomato and is filled with so much rage, I'm half-expecting smoke to come out of his ears. I guess Amy gets around more than I realized.

Sheriff Ashford straightens his collar and carefully puts on his sunglasses back on "I'm leaving, but because I've got better things to be doing than arguing with you, old man." He opens his car door, and just before he gets in, he tips his hat at me. "I'll see you around, Mrs. Gallo."

"Get on, GET!!!" Mr. Gilbert yells, waving his cane while hobbling toward the patrol car. Sheriff Ashford gets into his car and peels out. Mr. Gilbert lowers his cane and straightens his shirt with a "humph" before slowly coming back to me. He holds out his arm. "Now, may I take you inside Sarah?" I smile and nod as I hook my arm in his and we walk into the library.

He guides me to his office, which hasn't changed since the last time I was here. It's still filled with the same piles of journals, notebooks, and paper bundles, some stacked almost to the ceiling. He points to an empty metal chair by the door and then makes his way to his office chair, promptly slumping deeply into the worn leather cushion.

"Now my dear, what brings you by today?"

"Well," I sit down in the offered chair and cross my ankles underneath me. Even though the place is dingy, I'm still self-conscious about my muddied sneakers.

"Oh, silly me! You were asking about getting your nursing license renewed! Yes, yes, I have that information right over here." Mr. Gilbert uses his cane to slowly pull himself out of his seat and walks over to the least dusty pile of papers and starts to flip through them.

"I wanted to ask, did John Burrow have any children?"

"Not that anyone knows for certain."

"Then who was Ada Marie Burrow Freeman?" Mr. Gilbert pauses mid-page turn, then continues to flip through the pile.

"You went to the hill, didn't you?"

"And if I did? Who was she, Mr. Gilbert? Who was that baby? And why does everyone in this town want to keep her a secret?"

154

"It's not necessarily *Ada* that the town is keeping as a secret. I suspect it is much more heinous than that, at least that's what my forefathers believed. Ada is most likely collateral damage, unfortunately." Mr. Gilbert's hand shakes as he grabs his coffee mug and takes a sip. He looks at me. I think he can tell I'm confused and trying to process what he told me. He lightly laughs.

"I'm sorry, you must be so perplexed! Well, let me start at the beginning. It all started when John Burrow started to build this town back in the 1800s." He starts to explain as he looks around his bundles of papers scattered in mini-towers. "John was wealthy. He gave shops to new owners for nothing but their cooperation. It gave people a fresh start—but on his terms. Many resented him for it."

"Why resent a man giving away free businesses?"

"Because his rules were considered radical at the time. John was an abolitionist, but not the kind who wanted to 'send them back.' He believed all people were equal—Black, Irish, Native. He banned discrimination. Many of the white settlers thought he betrayed his own kind, at least this is what they whispered and wrote in their journals."

"Then why not leave? Couldn't they just move away?"

"Most couldn't. They had sold everything to come here, hoping to strike gold. By the time they arrived, they had nothing left. They had no choice but to bite their tongue and secretly mine for gold at night."

155

"Why at night? I thought that was the whole purpose of coming here was to, as you say, 'strike gold?'"

"Another great question! You must remember, John owned all the land, so along with outlawing discrimination, he also put into place a 'no mining' rule, which is why those who opposed him would mine in the shadows, hoping to make it rich before getting caught. One of those families was the Ashfords."

I gasp. Mr. Gilbert smirks.

"Yes, Sheriff Ashford's family were early law keepers. They despised John, but tolerated him—until word of his forbidden love got out. There is not a single journal I've read from that time that didn't mention John's blasphemous love affair."

"Love affair? What could be so horrible about love?"

"It wasn't love that was the issue, but with who—ah yes, here we are!" Mr. Gilbert grabs a bundle of papers on top of a pile in the far back corner.

He drops yellow-tinted pages on his wooden desk, sending puffs of dust into the air. I get up and start walking over to the desk. "Rumors were that John had fallen in love with Mary Beth Freeman."

Freeman? That was Ada's last name...

"What's wrong with that?!"

"You must keep in mind, Sarah, back then, slavery was legal and even considered normal. A free colored woman was already frowned upon, let alone a white man being intimate with one. Heck, it was even illegal back then, but John Burrow didn't seem to care. He loved that woman. And even though they didn't

156

come right out and say it, everyone in town knew of their taboo love."

"So, what happened?"

"Well things were business as usual until Mary had a baby. That's when things started to take a turn for the worse. The townsfolk started convening in secret, conspiring to take over the town from John Burrow, whom they suspected had broken the law. The meetings were led by the sheriff of the town—"

"Sheriff Ashford."

"Right. Their plan was to take over the town and appoint the sheriff as the town's new leader on March 30, 1826, but then—"

"Something happened to the baby."

"Right again! Maybe you should be the one telling the story." Mr. Gilbert jokes as he starts taking newspaper articles from the bundle. "The baby died of sickness, and the townsfolk were invited to the burial at the top of the hill. During the funeral, John and Mary Beth were hand in hand for most of the service. This was all Sheriff Ashford needed to convince the town that John was not fit to run."

"So, what happened next?"

"Well, that's the kicker. I don't know."

"What?! How?!" I'm in shock. How could that part be a mystery, but the rest was in the journals and newspaper articles? Mr. Gilbert hobbles over to a stack of old journals and motions me to come over. He opens the top one.

"You see right here? March 30, 1826. The funeral is written about but..." He turns the page. The next entry is ripped out, only jagged fragments remain from where the paper was torn from the binding. The opposite page shows April 2, 1826. Mr. Gilbert sighs. "The rest of the day of the funeral and the following day were ripped out of the journals. The only thing we have to go off of are the newspaper articles, which are no doubt fabricated."

"Fabricated?"

"Yes, let me show you." Mr. Gilbert motions to follow him to the desk, where newspaper articles are already set aside. He points to newspaper that's yellow and curled on the edges, I dare not touch it out of fear it will disintegrate in my hands. The headline reads, *Free Woman Charged with Murder of Town's Founder Body Still Not Found.* In the center is a sketch of the murderer, Mary Beth. Something seems familiar about her and then it hits me—she's the ghost I saw outside of the library and the one playing the piano with Emelia.

No, no. This can't be real. Is it? I'm in complete disbelief. How is this even possible?

"This newspaper was printed on March 31, 1826, the day *after* the funeral. Now, even if it made sense that John's lover would murder him the day of their child's funeral, does she even look like she'd be strong enough to hide a man's body in a small country town? No, I don't believe it. Not one bit! But check this out..." Mr. Gilbert turns a few pages and stops on an article with a sketch of a family standing in front of a country store. The couple is standing next to each other, with a small girl who appears to be around eight or nine years of age standing between them, her curly hair pulled back by a ribbon. They are all wearing matching aprons and are smiling in the sketch.

Wait, this looks familiar, too...

"You see right here, the article says that the store owners, the O'Brien family, are missing, and there is even a reward in place for their whereabouts, but the very next day in this newspaper article..."

Mr. Gilbert grabs the next newspaper he had set aside and flips the page to reveal the article titled, *Irish Family Moves Out of State, Ashford's to Take Over Store.*

"All of a sudden, the family is not missing anymore, now they've *moved away*. And who takes over the store? The Ashfords. Does that sound right to you, Sarah? A free woman charged with her lover's murder without a dead body? A missing Irish family that's now 'moved away?' And all of this within a single day?! Smells fishier than my Mama's Sunday night tuna casserole, and she used *a lot* of tuna!" Mr. Gilbert's brows furrow, and his lips quiver from anger.

I gently grab the first article to take a closer look at the sketch of the O'Briens. Suddenly, vivid images flood my mind—the couple hanging from rusted spikes on the country store's pillars, their lifeless bodies swaying in the wind. The memory is so intense that a jolt of electricity shoots down my arm—the same arm that the woman with the *O'Brien* nametag had grabbed. I gasp and drop the newspaper.

Mr. Gilbert notices, "Is everything all right, Sarah? You look like you've seen a ghost."

Should I tell him? I pause for a moment, questioning if I can trust him. I look into Mr. Gilbert's kind, concerned eyes and a weight falls off my shoulders.

I sigh, "Can I tell you something in confidence, Mr. Gilbert?"

"Of course, this library is a safe place, my dear. What's troubling you?" He sits us both down and I tell him everything that has been happening to me. How I'm the only one seeing these ghosts and how now I believe they're the same people from his newspaper articles.

After I finish, Mr. Gilbert leans back into his chair, grabs a cigar and quietly lights it. Puffs of smoke slowly float to the ceiling.

"You know, Sarah, I don't know why you're seeing what you are, but there must be a very good reason for it. Maybe they're trying to tell you something." He takes another puff from the cigar before continuing. "Tell you what, I'll do some digging for you, see if there's something going on beneath the surface at Burrow Estate. But for now, try your best to avoid the Ashfords. It's evident that whatever's going on, they will do anything to keep it a secret." I nod and look over at the clock. It's 12:32 p.m.

"Oh no, I'm late! Emelia must be wondering where I am." I frantically start to get myself out of the chair and open the office door to leave.

"Oh, Sarah, before you go, will you write your number down on this sticky note? That way I can call you when I find something."

"Oh, right. Yes, that would be helpful." I quickly go to the desk and sloppily write down my number. I hope he can read my handwriting. I hurry to the door, "Thank you, Mr. Gilbert!"

"Anytime, dear! Oh, and Sarah?"

"Yes?" I turn my head to look back. Mr. Gilbert holds up a small stack of papers. "Don't forget your licensing paperwork."

"Oh, that's right!" I rush back over and grab the paperwork, then turn back to run out the door. "Thank you, Mr. Gilbert!"

"Of course! Be safe and keep your head down!"

"I will, you do the same," I reply as I leave the office and walk out the front door.

Chapter Nineteen
Picnic

Running up the steps, I swing open the door. "Emmie, I'm so sorry I'm late!" I yell as I enter the foyer and look into the living room. Many of the moving boxes have been opened, with a few items scattered across the dark hardwood floors. Pots and pans clang against each other in the kitchen. I look over and I see Emelia's head pop out from over the counter.

"Oh, hi, Mom! Close your eyes. I got a surprise for you."

"Oh, uh, okay." I hesitantly close my eyes and brace for whatever concoction awaits me. The squeaks from Emelia's wheelchair grow louder as she approaches.

"Okay, open them!" I open my eyes. Emelia is in front of me, a woven basket, her ground lawn chair, and a sloppily folded blanket on her lap. "I made us a picnic! I was hoping we could have it on the front lawn, and I can tell you about my book while we eat." I sigh in relief and smile.

"That is so thoughtful, sweetheart! Thank you for the wonderful surprise! Yes, let's go outside. I can't wait to eat some delicious…" Then it dawns on me. We don't have much in the house. What did she make? "Well, whatever you made, I can't wait to eat it. Let's go." I hold the door open for Emelia to roll out, but she stops.

"Can Oliver come outside, too?"

"Hmm. I'm not sure that is the best idea, hon."

"He can't run away. Plus, I made him lunch, too!" Emelia pulls a can of tuna out of the woven basket. "Oh, please, Mom? I will keep an eye on him. Pretty pleeeeeeaaaseee?" Emelia begs, widening her eyes while batting her eyelashes in an attempt to guilt me. It's working.

Well, I mean he can't run with that limp. I guess it couldn't hurt.

"Oh, okay, fine. Oliver can join the picnic. But you must keep an eye on him and make sure he doesn't go into the street."

"Yes, yes I will! Can you get him? I think he's under the bed again."

Great just what I want to do in a potentially haunted manor—look under a bed.

"I'll go get him. You continue down the side ramp and find the spot you want your picnic to be."

"Okay, Mom!" Emelia heads down the ramp as I go look in her room for Oliver.

I look around the room, but so far, no sign of Oliver anywhere. My heart skips a beat as I look straight at the bed. My imagination runs wild of the possible boogeymen that are awaiting me. God, I wish that mover had found those wheels, then I could've avoided this altogether!

Okay, Sarah, you got this. It's not real, remember? It's not real... I encourage myself, getting on all fours as I start to low crawl under the bed, but Oliver isn't there. A long, drawn-out creak emerges from my right. *What was that?!* I slowly turn my head toward the source of the sound—the armoire door is cracked open.

It was closed before I went under the bed.

I pause.

Unsure what to do.

Well, lying under the bed with my legs sticking out is probably the worst hiding spot imaginable. If something's out there, it's already seen me. I either commit and crawl all the way under—or get up and face it.

I glance at my exposed legs. It's too late to hide.

I guess I'm going out.

I take a big breath in and out, before I scramble out from under the bed and onto my feet in a fighting pose—but nothing's there. Just the slightly cracked armoire door. I look around for something to use as a weapon, and I see Emelia's book on her nightstand. I grab it and hold it over my shoulder, primed to swing as I kick open the armoire door.

"Meow." There in the middle of the armoire floor is Oliver, meowing up at me with the most pitiful look on his face. I lower the book with a deep exhale, then chuckle.

"You about scared me half to death, Oliver!" I toss the book on Emelia's bed, then squat down to pick Oliver up. I look at the armoire door, "How did you get in here, little buddy?"

"Mom, I found a spot!" Emelia yells from outside.

"Coming!" I head through the front doors to find Emelia in the middle of the front lawn.

"Oh good, you found Oliver! Isn't this spot perfect? It felt the warmest."

"Yes, it feels great, hon, now let's get this picnic started. I'm starving!" Emelia laughs with a huge grin as I trade her the picnic supplies for Oliver. I lay out the quilted, blue-and-white plaid blanket as flat as I can on the prickly grass before unfolding and setting out her lawn chair. I motion for Emelia to get closer, "All right, I'm going to need you to hold tight again, okay?"

"Okay."

I put Oliver on the blanket before putting my good arm around Emelia's waist.

"Three, two, one. Go!" I lift her one-handed, squatting her down on the blanket. After gently putting her down, I scoot over the lawn chair and help her sit up in it. Slightly out of breath, I plop down next to her, and put Oliver in her lap. I lean back my head, allowing the weight of my hair to fall back as I look up at the clear sky. There is no wind, just the sun's warm rays kissing my face and the melodies of birds singing off in the distance. For a brief moment, there is peace.

"Mom! Mom! Mom!"

And the peace is gone.

"Yes, Emmie?"

"Look at Oliver. Isn't he the cutest?!" Oliver is now out of Emelia's lap and playing with the pink ribbon tied to the basket's handle. I snicker. He really is quite adorable. I reach to the basket and slowly drag it toward us, enticing Oliver to chase the ribbon, his little booty wiggling before each adorable pounce.

Opening the basket, I see a can of tuna, a can opener, and two sandwiches wrapped in paper towels stacked on a plastic container. I grab the can of tuna and use the can opener to remove the lid before placing it in front of Oliver, who takes a big whiff starts to devour the contents.

"Look at that face!" Emelia giggles, as Oliver lifts his face out of the can, his whiskers weighed down with tuna chunks, and juice dripping off his fuzzy chin. He looks right at us, almost to say "what?!" We both laugh at the sight.

"Hey Emmie, would you like your sandwich now?"

"Yes, please!"

I reach into the basket and pull out the sandwiches and the slightly heavy plastic container.

"Hey, hon, what's in the container?"

"Oh, I made us ramen!"

"How wonderful!" I pass Emmie a sandwich and open the lid. An uncooked ramen square speckled with ramen seasoning floats in the center of cold water.

"I couldn't reach the microwave…" Emelia says softly. I try my best not to laugh. I am so exhausted that at this point, I might just eat it just for the crunchy sensation. I go to take a bite of the sandwich, and my mouth is filled with a thick layer of peanut butter that smacks the roof of my mouth.

"We didn't have any jelly…" Emelia's says softly as a tear falls off her cheek and onto the blanket. I grab her hand firmly and smile.

"Oh, sweetheart, this is all perfect! Thank you so much for the picnic. I love every bit of it, *especially* the sandwiches." Emelia sniffles.

"Really?"

"Yes! And Oliver clearly loves his lunch as well! Now, tell me all about the cool animals in your book."

Emelia's eyes, no longer full of tears, are bright and full of energy—energy I wish I could steal just a little bit of right about now.

"Okay! You're gonna love this. So, did you know tree frogs blend in with trees? Some look like leaves, others match bark!"

Her joy is contagious. But just as I raise my sandwich to take a bite—

DRIP.

A wet splash hits my forearm.

I look down. A thick black droplet slide down my skin like molasses. I blink, hoping it goes away.

You're just tired, Sarah.

I raise the sandwich again—

SPLAT!

A hunk of something the size of a baby's fist, heavy and wet, slams into my sandwich, sending splatters onto my cheeks and lips. My burning eyes cautiously look down. A veined, ragged chunk of rotten flesh is sinking into my sandwich like a crater as the bread changes from tan to a dark red from the juices that ooze out of the pulsating veins. The stench of sour, metallic blood chokes me. My throat tightens as I resist the urge to vomit. Then suddenly—

There is giggling.

Children's seemingly innocent laughter.

168

I turn.

About twenty feet away, a group of young children are playing long jump rope.

But not with rope—

With their own organs.

Twin girls, no older than six, clutch their own spilling intestines, the two cords grotesquely braided together into a single rope. swinging it end over end like some unholy carnival game. Vile, rotten intestines squish between their fingers as the innards still pulsate and twitch, not realizing it's already dead. Their white, ruffled dresses are shredded down the center, revealing gaping abdominal cavities where their slimy, glistening guts slip out in globs. The sisters giggle, exposing their blackened teeth as the devil's rope swings.

Round and round. Stretching and tightening as it whips the grass with each swing. Each slap shooting out undigested stomach juices and chunks of rotten flesh in all directions through the tears in the tubular tissue— painting a rotten canvas of decay.

The girls don't notice. Don't care. They just keep swinging their intestinal rope, laughing in euphoric innocence—lost in the rhythm of their revolting game.

In the center, a boy, maybe nine, with freckles and thick red curls. He's dressed in shredded bellbottoms and a polka-dot shirt which are stained with dried blood. He leaps over the swinging braided guts, laughing as yellow-green digestive juices mist across his face. His white shoes splash in a puddle of bile, sending up the reek of fermenting meat and stomach acid so thick it stings my throat.

The grotesque game continues—slinging sour bodily juices and pulpy organ fragments across the picnic.

Onto the blanket.

Onto the food.

Onto me.

Onto Emelia.

SPLAT.

Blackened intestinal fluid squirts across the quilt, soaking into the cloth and spreading like ink on paper.

SPLAT.

Rubbery, fat tissue crashes into the open ramen container, sending blood-tinged broth onto Emelia's lap. She's still smiling. Still talking about animals, oblivious to the horrors around her.

The twins giggle louder, swinging their intestinal jump rope with cheerful delight. Each whip of their braided innards hitting the grass sprays out chunks of rotten tissue, jelly-thick half-digested mush, and vile juices—all squirting through the air like hell's sprinkler system, spewing devils' stew.

SPLAT.

A gob of meat slides down my arm, still clinging to a string of slick intestinal lining, reeking of fermented iron.

SPLAT.

SPLAT.

My head swims. My stomach coils in on itself, threatening to purge what little I've eaten. I try to stay focused on Emelia's voice, but it's being drowned out by the sound of my own heartbeat pounding in my skull.

The air thickens. The bile clings to my skin, my hair, my food. The entire world seems to be spinning.

I'm unraveling.

No sleep.

Too many ghosts.

Too many whispers in the walls.

Too many children stomping on their own spoiled organs.

SPLAT.

SPLAT.

SPLAT!

The devil's rope keeps swinging—spilling everything a body's meant to keep inside.

I'm going to snap.

"This one spider pretends to be an ant so it can eat all the—"

"EMELIA, SHUT UP!!!" The scream tears from my throat like I'm being skinned alive. My heart instantly drops to my twisted gut.

Emelia's mouth stops moving. Her eyes widen. Then the tears come. I reach for her.

"Emmie, I'm sorry! I didn't mean that. Please, sweetheart…"

She pulls away.

I am disappointed in myself. How could I lose control like that? My daughter didn't deserve this. Suddenly, I sense something is wrong.

The children are gone.

So is Oliver.

"Hey Emmie, where is Oliver?" Just as I say the words, I look out toward the street.

And there he is, right on the edge of the sidewalk, limping onto the road.

"Oliver! Stop!" I leap to my feet and run to him—but I'm too late.

BAM.

Just as Oliver gets onto the road, he is hit by Sheriff Ashford's patrol car, which then fully runs over him with both front and back tires like he is nothing more than a small speed bump.

"OLIVER!!!" Emelia screams as she attempts to crawl toward the road, dragging her body across the dried, prickly grass. I run to Oliver's body. His stomach is split open with his guts squished into the cracked pavement. His eyeballs push against his closed lids as his broken jaw holds his mouth gaping open. I fall to my knees next to Oliver's corpse. My eyes burn, both from tears of rage and sadness. Sheriff Ashford steps out of his car and stands next to me. I don't look up at him.

"I had thought I ran over a squirrel or something. Guess I was wrong." I don't respond.

"Ah, poor little bugger. I reckon he wasn't going to make it long anyway based on my wife's description. Better now than when your daughter got any more attached—"

"Get out of here."

"Excuse me?"

"I said," I stand up and get in his face while pointing at his car. "GET THE FUCK OUT OF HERE!"

Sheriff Ashford's jaw drops. I don't think he was expecting a *proper woman* like me to cuss at him in that manner.

He looks over at Emelia, lying on the grass, hysterically crying, her arms red from being grazed repeatedly against the lawn.

"Fine. I'll leave you to it. Good day." He tips his hat and gets back into his vehicle.

I stand there until the vehicle disappears around the corner. I go and get down on the ground next to Emelia. I pull her upper body onto my lap and hold her, stroking her hair as her tears soak into my jeans. We both sit there for a while, mourning the loss of our dear Oliver.

Chapter Twenty
Chandelier

I open my eyes slowly, disoriented. The flickering light from the TV casts pale shadows across the living room, stretching long and thin over the worn floorboards and up the walls like restless spirits. I glance down at Emelia. She's curled up on my lap, her hands tucked beneath her cheek, her breathing soft and even. Her face is faintly streaked with dried tears. She looks almost angelic in the dim light. For a moment, I just watch her. It hurts to see her like this—resting only because exhaustion has finally overtaken her.

The evening had been long.

Too long.

Too cruel.

After Oliver died, we collected what we could of him from the street and wrapped him gently in a towel. I found a shoebox and together we buried him in the backyard. Emelia sang *You Are My Sunshine* through shaky sobs while I dug the hole and placed him in the earth. Her voice cracked on the final verse, but she sang every word. We both stayed there for a while, crying over the loss of our dear Oliver.

When we came back inside, the house felt too quiet, almost wrong without Oliver's sweet, soft meows. Neither of us had the heart to eat dinner. We didn't wash up or even change into pajamas. We just collapsed onto the couch, still smeared with dirt and grief, and turned on National Geographic—anything to fill the silence in our broken hearts.

We must have been asleep for quite some time, as the only thing remaining on the TV is buzzing black-and-white speckles, sending a static buzz throughout the estate.

I look over at the clock, and it is a little past 3 a.m.

I slowly stretch out my arms and smack my dry lips. I must've fallen asleep with my mouth open, because all I can think about right now is how dry my throat is and how desperately I need a glass of water.

While I am at it, I might as well take my medication.

I finish my stretch and gently slide my arms under Emelia's upper body, lifting her up just enough to slide out from under her. I set her down carefully, trying not to wake her, and start walking toward the kitchen counter where my medication is next to my purse. I twist open the lid when—

I hear a baby cooing from behind the counter in the kitchen.

Through motherly instinct, I walk around the corner with my open pill bottle when—I gasp. The blood drains from my face as every muscle in my body stiffens at the sight before me.

There, on the floor, are four children, between the ages of four and six, surrounding one of my kitchen pots.

Inside the pot—

A baby. Pale. Bloated.

Sitting there, cooing and softly babbling in what looks to be a pot filled with its own blood, which falls from the seeping, blackened gash on its cheek. It reaches into the rotten soup and plays with the maggot swimming in it—sticking one into its toothless mouth and sucking on it like a demented lollipop.

The children all look to be from different time periods. One of the little girls wears a blue dress with puffed sleeves and an apron, stained from where she's wiped her blood-coated hands. Worms crawl between the strands of her pulled-back brown hair, leaving a slimy trail across her dingy blue bow.

The other girl is dressed in red corduroy overalls, a long-sleeved daisy-print shirt underneath. Her messy red hair is pulled into pigtails with rainbow beaded hairbands. Her freckled face is speckled with blood as she dips her hand fully into my kitchen pot, soaking the ends of her sleeves in rotten blood.

The boys appear to be brothers, perhaps only a year or two apart. They both wear shaggy, brown wool knickers and black tweed flat caps. The only difference between their outfits is the color of their shirts under their cotton vests.

They begin to fight over the pot. Each boy gripping a handle, yanking it back and forth. Blood clots, death, and decay slosh out with every pull. The baby giggles as maggots splash onto its head, sliding off and flinging everywhere with each violent tug.

Until—

The younger brother lets go. The pot jerks backward, coating the older boy like an apple candied in chunky blood. The older brother crinkles his nose and furrows his brow in anger before lunging at his younger brother, sending the already tipped-over pot—baby and all—spinning in wild circles across the floor.

The girls giggle and scramble over, grabbing the bloated baby. They sit it upright in the middle of the soupy, bloody mess. The baby, still laughing, doesn't seem to notice as it continues to grab fistfuls of rot and maggots, squishing them between its chubby fingers before putting them into its mouth, where its fleshy gums smack the mushy blend as it chews with its mouth open.

The girls begin to draw innocent, child-like pictures in the pool of chunky blood. Their fingers swirl through the rot, squishing maggots as they paint flowers, butterflies, and suns into the blackish-red muck.

I instinctively cup my hands over my nose and mouth as I fight the urge to puke. The rotten concoction fills the kitchen with a sour, metallic, pungent aroma. As my hands fly to my face, I drop the bottle of pills, sending the medication scattering into the bloody soup.

Shit. That bottle is all *of my medication.*

I stare at the pills scattered across the floor, debating if I can stomach picking them up.

Then—

CREAK.

My head snaps toward the living room. But I don't see anything. Just Emelia, still peacefully sleeping on the couch. But something feels off.

I need to go check on her. Make sure she's okay...A chill crawls down my spine as I slowly step into the living room, cautiously walking toward Emelia.

The TV flickers, casting stuttering light across the walls. Buzzing static mixes with the children's laughter behind me, filling the manor's dimly lit room with an overwhelming sense of wrongness. My eyes scan the room, darting from shadow to shadow With each step I take, my body grows heavier, as if bracing for something to leap out at me.

The closer I get to Emelia, the stronger the dread creeps in—thick, suffocating. Like the estate itself doesn't want me here.

I reach Emelia, the flickering light illuminating the couch and her motionless body. I kneel next to her and lean my head in to listen.

She's breathing.

I let out a heavy sigh of relief as I start to relax. Placing my good elbow on the seat of the couch, I rest my head in my palm and lightly chuckle. "I'm losing it. I really do need some sleep—"

Suddenly, a large shadow creeps over us, leaving us bathed in darkness. Something is blocking the TV screen, and...and the giggling has stopped.

My veins run cold. My heart pounds in my ears, and my body tenses as I slowly turn my head to look at the TV.

The children are standing in front of the screen, the light silhouetting their frail bodies. Each leaves their hands hanging at their sides, except for the girl in the blue dress, who holds the bloated baby on her hip. The baby's wet skin gleams in the light, highlighting the maggots crawling across it.

The children's heads are slightly tilted downward, their hair dangling loose, covering their faces in shadow. Each flicker of light from the TV revealing glimmers of light in their large eyes and wide, stretched smiles that bear their jagged teeth.

They stare at me. Motionless. Their sick, sinister smiles growing wider—like a row of demented jack-o'-lanterns.

In unison, all four children begin to raise one hand to their mouths. Their fists close, leaving only the pointer finger extended as they press it to their lips.

"*Shhh.*"

Then, slowly, in unison, they point up. I strain my eyes, trying to look up without moving, but my chin naturally tilts upward to see what's above me—I wish I hadn't.

Clinging to the vaulted ceiling is a lanky teenage boy. His bony limbs are twisted and bent unnaturally, making him look like an insect as he clutches the wooden beams. His body faces the ceiling. His shirtless, pale back is marked with a crude pentagram tattoo, and a chain dangles from the belt loop of his baggy black cargo pants. His long, jagged toenails dig into the wood. He wears black fingerless gloves, which draws attention to the gleaming silver rings he wears on each finger— one with a lamb's head, the others adorned with spikes. Strands of stringy black hair hang straight down from his head, as he sways above me.

My heart drops to my gut. My teeth chatter and my body trembles. I hold my breath. I try not to make a sound. Try not to move. My eyes are locked on the boy hanging from the ceiling—

Emelia coughs.

CRUNCH.

The teenage boy's neck snaps back, his vertebrates grinding against each other as his neck breaks, twisting like an owl. His pale, sunken face twists into a snarl, his lips curling to show his sharpened teeth. His eyes black as night, void of any humanity.

He sees me.

He sees *us*.

His eyes locked on mine, he scurries across the ceiling like a spider, his limbs jerking in an unholy fashion and his long nails tapping as they claw against the wood.

A scream catches in my throat. I throw myself over Emelia, shielding her with my body as my eyes try to follow him. But he moves too fast—his figure a blur above us. Then—

Right above the candle chandelier—he slips.

BAM!

I let out a terrified shriek. The scream no longer lodged in my throat as his body crashes into the chandelier.

The cast iron frame groans as it swings. The candles, once cream, are now coated in black, chunky blood as the boy's impaled body slips against the curved metal candle holders and slides down. His broken limbs bend in every direction, twitching like a squished bug in its last seconds of life.

One of the chandelier's arms impales the boy through the mouth, his wide eyes staring at us from above as black globs splatter to the ground from his pulsating throat.

Onto the couch.

Onto *us.*

The clotted blood hits my cheek and slides down, no doubt forming a grotesque black tear stain on my skin.

The children laugh at me like it's a show—their shrill giggles burrow into my skull and echo through my mind.

I've lost it. I've gone insane. Fear consumes every inch of me—mind, body, breath. I scream uncontrollably.

Emelia's eyes flash open. She jerks upright, suddenly waking to the sound of me screaming. She looks at me and grabs my arm, shaking me urgently. Her vicelike grip breaks through to me and I stop screaming.

Emmie yells, panic in her voice, "Mom, what's wrong?!"

Just then, the front doors fly open. I jerk my head and see Sheriff Ashford storming into the house, gun in hand.

The room falls still as he glances around, leveling his gun every which way, looking for threats. He speaks while continuing to sweep the estate.

"Are you okay? What happened?"

I glance at the TV. The children are gone. I look up—the teenage boy is gone. I look down—the splattered blood is gone. A static ring ricochets into my ear canal.

Emelia looks at me with concern, "Mom... are you okay?"

Without saying a word, I stand up and start walking toward the kitchen. I look around the corner where I saw the children playing with a pot of baby stew.

Now—nothing.

No children.

No pot.

No baby.

Just my medication scattered across the tile floor. I stare blankly at the tiles as I hear Sheriff Ashford walk up behind me.

"All clear," he states. I hear the click of his pistol's safety and the sound of him holstering it. I feel his eyes watching me.

"Mrs. Gallo, would you like to tell me what happened? Did you have a nightmare or something?" He says as he walks around to face me, and as he does, he spots the medication spilled all over the kitchen floor.

"Have you been taking your medication? Your husband mentioned to me you take something for a head injury or some such?"

I watch as he squats down to the ground, acid climbing up my throat as images of my pills floating in the soupy mess flash into my mind.

Sheriff Ashford huffs as he reaches out and picks up a small, brown-looking turd from my floor.

"Seems you've got yourself rats, Mrs. Gallo. I wouldn't take any of the medication that hit the floor, if I were you."

Using his other hand, he picks up the pill bottle and gives it a shake, the sound of one lonely pill bounces off the plastic. "Luckily, looks like you've got one left," he says as he hands me the container.

Without a word, I take it.

He leans in, staring at my face, and waves his hand in front of it. "Hello? Earth to Sarah. You with me?"

I look at him. I'm exhausted. I'm stressed. But in the middle of my mind splintering, something occurs to me.

"How did you know I was screaming?"

The question catches him off guard. He stammers."Wh—what?"

I clear my throat, forcing the acid back down into my empty gut.

"You busted through the front door only moments after I started screaming." I narrow my eyes as my gaze meets his. "How did you get here so fast? No one called 911."

Sheriff Ashford shifts uneasily, pressing down on the cowboy hat already on his head. He clears his throat before replying.

"I was... I was just on patrol and happened to be in the vicinity when I noticed your light—"

"None of the lights were on."

"Right. I meant the TV light was on, and shortly after, I heard screaming." He quickly turns and walks toward the front door. "But anyways, I better be leaving now that the home is secured."

He tips his hat to me as he opens the front door. "Have a good morning." And with that, he leaves, shutting the door behind him.

My mind slowly starts to piece itself back together as I begin to relax. I immediately walk over to Emmie, who's still on the couch, concern washed across her face. I kneel down next to her and grab her hand.

"I'm so sorry, Emmie. I didn't mean to scare you. I just had a nightmare, is all."

Emelia's expression doesn't change. She leans her head against the couch cushions.

"Mom, you can be honest with me. What's going on?"

My daughter, always smarter than the average nine-year-old. Though I'm exhausted, I need to think of something to say—fast.

"I'm just sad about Oliver. I miss him." It's not a lie. I *am* sad about Oliver, and I *do* miss his fluffy little orange face. But it's not the whole truth.

I'm not about to tell her what's really going on. She'll think I'm crazy. And then it will get back to Kyle somehow and I don't want that to happen.

Emelia gives a small, sorrowful smile and holds open her arms, waiting for a hug. Tears stream down both our faces as we embrace. After a while, I glance up at the clock. It's almost 5 a.m. God, time really flies when you're going insane.

"Hey, sweetheart, it's almost five, and I have a doctor's appointment in about four hours. Let's get you back to sleep before I have to wake you up again. Do you want to stay on the couch or go to bed?"

"Couch. I'm already comfortable," Emelia yawns, stretching and snuggling deeper into the cushions. I chuckle softly.

185

"Okay, hon. I'm going to step outside for some fresh air. I'll wake you in a few hours before I leave. I love you."

"Love you too, Mom. Night!"

"Night."

I walk over to the counter to grab my purse and see the lid from the pill bottle still lying there. I pick it up, seal the bottle, and drop it into my purse. I grab my bag and step outside for a much-needed smoke.

Chapter Twenty-One
Gold's Primary and Pharmacy

Walking into the doctor's office, the aroma of disinfectants is so overwhelming, I have to fight the urge to cover my nose.

The waiting room is small, furnished with only a few retro chairs that look like they were pulled straight out of a 1970s porn film. The off-white walls have a handful of cheesy medical advertisements, and straight ahead is a sliding glass window with a red 'check in' sign above, and a wooden door to the right. I walk up to the window, and see an older woman sitting at a computer desk filled with various bobblehead nick-knacks and pictures of a small, puffy white poodle with a rhinestone pink collar and bow. The woman's straight brown hair flips off her paisley pink blouse, which is decorated with rhinestones and matched perfectly with her extra-large pink cat-eye reading glasses. Her hair almost covers her nametag that reads, 'Karen'.

Without looking up, the woman sighs, "How can I help you?" She says with a tinge of annoyance in her voice. I clench my fist, my blood boiling at her attitude.

Breathe, Sarah, breathe. She isn't worth it. I take a deep breath in and release my fist. "Um, yes, good morning, Karen. I have an appointment this morning to see Dr. Gold?"

"Name?"

"Sarah Gallo."

The woman starts to type on her keyboard, her pink acrylic nails tapping obnoxiously against the plastic keys. She instinctively grabs a clipboard with a small stack of papers and hands it to me through the window. She has yet to look up at me.

"Have a seat and fill this out. The doctor will take it when you are called."

"Thank you."

I go to the nearest chair and slump down, staring at the forms in front of me. The letters blur together on the page as I guess how to fill it out.

I give up, my eyes are way too tired for this.

I lean my head against the backrest. I usually would never sit like this in public, as it is very unladylike, but between my messy hair, runny makeup, and the lack of sleep, I don't give a shit how I sit. The door next to the check-in window creaks open. Standing there is a tall, muscular, bald black man with a perfectly trimmed goatee and hazel eyes a woman could drown in—and I am. I quickly sit up in my chair and cross my legs as if I'd been sitting like this the whole time.

"Mrs. Gallo?"

"Yes, I'm Sarah," I say sweetly, and not like I haven't slept in days.

"I'm Dr. Gold, follow me, we'll go to the back room."

"Yes…Doctor." I follow him back twirling one of my messy blonde curls. I catch eyes with Karen, who is shaking her head at me. I stick out my tongue at her and follow Dr. Gold to the back office.

The office is spacious, a desk on one side and a medical bed on the other. In between is a sink with several storage cabinets and a trash can next to a rolling stool. Dr. Gold gestures me to sit on the medical bed as he washes his hands.

"Now, how can I be of assistance today, Mrs. Gallo?"

Oh, there are many things I can think of…. Oh god, Sarah, get your head on straight!

"I tripped and fell over my daughter's piano bench. During the fall, I hit my elbow on the piano. I think it's sprained, it hurts when I try to bend it,"

Dr. Gold dries his hands then motions for the forms. I hand over the clipboard and Dr. Gold looks over what little is there and chuckles.

"Not much here."

"Oh yeah, Sorry. I'm very tired." I blush out of embarrassment. Dr. Gold smiles and sets the clipboard down on the counter.

"It's quite all right, let's take a look at that elbow. " Dr. Gold sits on the stool and rolls over to me. As he gets closer, I can smell his cologne, a fruity aroma with a hint of hardwood. Maybe it's my insomnia, but he may be the best-smelling, best-looking man I have ever met. He gently takes my elbow and slowly tries to bend it. I wince as pain runs down my arm.

"Does that hurt?"

"Yes, it feels like a sharp pain." While he is distracted with my elbow, I try to wipe away my runny mascara with my other hand but quickly pull it back when he looks up at me.

"Well, I would say your deduction is correct, you most likely have a mild sprain. Our x-ray machine is down right now, so I can't verify it, but I can give you a brace and some medication while it heals on its own."

He rolls over to his computer, his white coat doing little to hide the outline of his biceps flexing as he types on his keyboard. "Is there anything else I can help you with today?"

"Well, yes, actually." I reach into my purse, pull out the pill bottle, and hand it to Dr. Gold. "Can I possibly get a refill of my medication? It's for a TBI from the car accident I had last year. I only have one left." Dr. Gold looks at the label, opens the bottle and takes out the pill, holding between his thumb and index finger as he examines it closely.

"I have no problem giving you a refill, but this isn't the medication listed on the container."

WHAT?!

"Based on your expression, you must not have known. This does look familiar, though. One moment." Dr. Gold puts the pill back in the bottle, then goes to the neatly stacked pile of papers on the desk and begins flipping through them. He seems to find what he was looking for, as he pulls one page from the stack, holds it next to the pill, then smirks.

"I knew I recognized this pill! It's called Nurotrexilm. A pharmacy rep was in here trying to pitch this drug for pain treatment. I declined it because the fine print mentioned it caused vivid hallucinations and insomnia in most of the trial patients. I honestly hate how they have the BioTech corporation right outside of town. Why not put their home office in a city with more doctors, instead of making their sales reps drive all the way out here? Cheap bastards." Dr. Gold continues to rant about how corrupt the BioTech corporation is, as I start to drift off into my own thoughts.

Did Kyle know he was giving me this medication? Of course he did, how else would Nurotrexilm accidentally get switched for my original medication? But why would he do that? Does he want me to go insane? I know he's an asshole, but even this is pretty far for him...

Dr. Gold leans in, "Mrs. Gallo I must ask, have you been experiencing hallucinations and sleep loss?"

I look down at the floor, almost too embarrassed to reply. "Yes, I have. I haven't slept much at all since I started taking the medication a couple of days ago."

"Did you take any today?"

"No. I dropped all but one on the floor and wanted to save this last one in case you needed it to prescribe a refill." My mind flashes images of the pills swimming in the chunky black blood. I swallow hard trying to suppress the thoughts as I feel my mouth watering like I am getting ready to puke. Dr. Gold doesn't seem to notice as he continues.

"Well, that is reassuring at least. From what I recall, the medication leaves the system within 24 hours. Since you have only taken it for the past couple of days, most of it should be out of your system by now, but just in case, I'm going to prescribe you a sleep medication to use tonight. We'll also hook you up to an IV to replenish your fluids before you leave—you look dehydrated."

You mean I look like a hot mess.

"Okay, and what about my real prescription?" I say, gesturing at the pill bottle.

"Come back next week, we'll get that refilled in-house for you. I want to make sure the Nurotrexilm is fully out of your system before reintroducing your body to your original medication. We don't want any adverse side effects." Dr. Gold stands up and starts to walk out the door. "Just hold tight, one of the nurses will be in shortly to hook you up to the IV. The sleep medicine will be ready for you at the front when you check out and she will take your insurance information—verbally." Dr. Gold lightly jokes while looking at the barely filled out paperwork.

I laugh a little too much. "HA-HA Thank you, Doctor!" He smiles at me before gently closing the door. I shake my head at myself. Way to leave a lasting impression. As I sit in the now still and quiet room, my mind starts to wander.

So, does this mean everything really was in my own head? I was just hallucinating the whole time? I mean, that would explain why no one else saw anything and why it just all started to happen when we moved. But if none of this was real, why were my hallucinations the very same people from a 120-year-old newspaper? Or was the Nurotrexim playing tricks with my mind, and I only think *they look the same? This really would explain everything...*

I lay back onto the medical bed, and I feel my body start to relax. I close my eyes and smile. It's reassuring to know I'm not crazy, though that seems to be what Kyle was trying to make me believe.

But why?

Chapter Twenty-Two

Peace

Walking through the front doors, a familiar song fills the dark house.
"I said whoo whoo whoo whoo whoo!"

I look over and see Emelia sitting in the dimmed living room directly in front of the TV. She's cuddling her fluffy purple blanket, with only her head visible as the tears in her eyes reflect the dynamic animated colors of the cartoon playing on the screen.

"Why should I worry? Why should I care?"

Walking to Emelia, I finally recognize what she's watching: *Oliver & Company*—the animated movie with the orphaned orange kitten she named Oliver after. I sigh deeply as I look down at Emelia, who is sitting motionless, her eyes glued to the dancing cartoon dogs and the scrappy kitten chasing after them.

"Oh, sweetheart, why must you torture yourself like this?" Emelia's teary eyes begin to swell.

"I miss him, Mom." Emelia starts to cry. I turn off the TV and get on my knees to embrace my daughter as she cries out, "Why did he have to die, Mom?! He was such a sweet boy. He didn't do anything wrong. He was my friend. Why did God take him already?! I needed him, Mom! It's not fair! NONE OF THIS IS FAIR!!!" Emelia's screams echo throughout the manor.

I start to cry with her. She's right. None of this is fair. It takes a little bit before Emelia lifts her face from my shoulder, her cheeks damp from the tears soaking into her pores. Her puffy blue eyes look up at me. It is enough to make me cry all over again.

"I'm sorry, Emmie." Emelia wipes her face and looks away.

"It's okay, Mom. It's my fault—"

"No, it is not! I'm responsible for both of you." I gently lift her chin to look at me. "It's my fault. I'm sorry I failed you both. Will you forgive me?" Emelia's eyes water what little tears she has left, and she smiles.

"Yes, Mom. I love you."

"I love you too, my songbird."

A smile cracks from the corner of Emelia's mouth, "You know, after a storm there is—"

"Sun." I chuckle. My daughter is so strong and mature for her age, though at times I wish she weren't. I can't help but blame myself. If it wasn't for my running that red light, Emelia would've had a normal life. But because I did, she is forced to grow up faster than she should. I feel like a horrible mother for putting my daughter in the situation she's in now. I guess that's why I can't help but try to give her the world—because I already took away the one she had.

"Hey, Mom… when are you going to shower? You kinda smell." Emelia looks down at my feet, "And when did you start wearing tennis shoes?!"

I look down at my muddy white sneakers and my dirt-stained jeans. Now that I think about it, I haven't changed my clothes since yesterday. I lean over to try to sneak a sniff of my armpit—dear god, I reek! I guess going a couple of days without showering will do that. Then I realize something...Dr. Gold must have smelled how stinky I was. I feel my cheeks flush from the thought.

"I had to go on a little walk somewhere. Speaking of, how about I go shower and change, then we can go shopping and get ice cream? With this new brace the doctor gave me, I think it may be easier for me to get the wheelchair in the van."

"Ice cream? Shopping? Does that mean...go to the mall?!"

"Sure, we can go to the mall." Emelia's eyes widen and her hands start to shake out of pure excitement.

"YES!!!" She shrieks. Laughing, I get up and start to walk up the stairs.

"Okay, you go pick out what you want to wear. I'll be back down in a bit."

"Okay, Mom!" Emelia replies as she zooms her wheelchair across the living room to her bedroom, her purple blanket flying behind like a superhero's cape.

Now, at the top of the stairs, I slow my pace, glancing around the master suite, looking for any movement or sign of paranormal activity.

Nothing.

I walk into the room and toward the master bath, holding my breath, I poke my head inside and look at the

tub, the mirror, the lights, the floors, the sink—nothing.
No movement. No voices. No writing on the mirror.
Nothing.

I exhale in a rush. It feels weirdly normal. Well,
only weird because it hasn't felt like a normal bedroom
or bathroom since we arrived. But now, all I feel is the
hollow ambience of a half-unpacked home, with sorrow
and guilt being the only things fully settled in. Still
cautious, I strip down, leaving my clothes and muddy
shoes on the tile floor as I step into the shower.

Turning the knob, clear, hot, steamy water
splashes over my knotted hair and runs down my body,
filling the drain with cloudy runoff. My head grows
heavy as my hair soaks up the water, and dirt starts to
slide off me like hot butter on a pan. My calves and shins
sting as the water cleans my open scrapes, and the high-
pressure spray gently massages my back. My muscles
start to relax with the heat, the weight of expectations
washing off with the dirt. I gently scrub shampoo into
my hair, allowing the water to drag any leaves and debris
still tangled in my blonde curls. Then I massage my face
with soap, the leftover makeup and grime slithering off,
making my face feel light and airy. The knob squeaks as
I turn off the shower and step onto the blue memory
foam bathmat.

Now standing naked in front of the mirror, I
stare at my reflection, studying myself. I feel revived,
like I am born again, but as a different person. I don't
recognize parts of who I am. I'm not sure exactly what's
changed, but I feel that the woman I was before we
moved is gone.

"Mom, are you ready yet? I picked out my outfit!" Emelia yells from downstairs.

"Yes, hon, almost ready. Be down in a minute!" I yell back as I snap out of it and rush to get ready. I reapply my mascara, brush my hair and teeth, put on a white tank top and tan cargo pants, and then complete the look with my gold crucifix necklace and hoop earrings.

At least Kyle didn't give these to the whore...

"Ready yet, Mom?!"

"Yes, coming!" My brown, leather sandals slap against the steps as I rush down the spiral staircase. Down in her room, Emelia is next to her bed studying the outfit she'd laid out: a pink, ruffled skirt layered over boot-cut light blue jeans, a white tank top, and a big brown woven belt. Why wear both a skirt and jeans together? I have no idea. I don't think I will ever understand millennials and their fashion tastes. Emelia looks at me and sighs.

"Is that what you are wearing, Mom? That is so 1990!" She flicks her wrists as she rolls her eyes. I roll my eyes, too.

"Why yes, I am! And I will have you know this is still in style."

"Surrrrre."

"Do you still want me to take you to the mall?" Emelia straightens up in her wheelchair, but still tries to play it cool.

"Okay, I guess you can wear that. It doesn't look *terrible*."

I give a sarcastic curtsy, "Why thank you, your highness. Now let's get you dressed."

After changing out her diaper and catheter bag, I help Emelia put on her outfit and get her back into her wheelchair. As soon as I'm done, she immediately rolls out of the room and around the corner. I follow behind but keep my distance.

I look around the corner and into the bathroom, where Emelia is staring at herself in the bathroom mirror, grinning from ear to ear. I lean against the couch, silently watching my daughter as she fluffs out her hair, admiring her attire. A sense of joy and sadness consumes my heart.

I'm happy that she loves her outfit, yet saddened by the fact that she will never be a normal kid who gets dressed up on her own to meet up with friends at the mall. She will never be able to experience the joys of being a rebellious teenager who sneaks off with boys or goes to parties when she swore she was going to be studying at a friend's house. She'll never experience the awkwardness of stepping on her partner's feet while slow dancing at prom. She'll never grip the steering wheel of her first car, her heart pounding with anxiety as she merges onto the highway for the first time. She won't be able to walk at her graduation, neither high school nor any other.

And all of it—*all of it*—because I was stupid.

Because I crashed the car.

Emelia looks over at me with gentle eyes and a warm smile. I smile back, her kindness making me feel even worse.

Chapter Twenty-Three
Phone Call

I glance in my rearview mirror and see Emelia bobbing her head. She's twirling the cord of her headphones with one hand and tapping her new hot pink portable CD player with the other, completely lost in the music. While we were at the mall, we stopped at Barnes & Noble and picked up a new CD player with matching headphones for her, along with the latest Britney Spears album. With everything that's just happened, I felt a bit of spoiling was in order.

"Hey Emmie, did you have fun at the mall today?" I look in the rearview again, Emalia's still quietly singing along with the music bouncing in her eardrums, there's no chance she heard me.

"Oops, I did it again..."

I smirk while shaking my head and refocusing on the road. Emelia is at her own Britney Spears concert. The sales rep said they were good headphones—he wasn't kidding.

We arrive home, the smell of our leftover Mexican food is almost unbearable after the hour-long drive out of the city. I hadn't really noticed how strong the scent was until about thirty minutes in, when I started pressing a bit harder on the gas pedal. Still, it's better than having pizza for the fourth night in a row, though I doubt Emelia would complain.

I step out of the van and get the wheelchair out. The brace Dr. Gold gave me makes it a bit easier. I roll the wheelchair around to Emelia's side and open her door. She's still nodding her head to the music and has yet to notice I am standing next to her with the door open and her wheelchair ready to go. I tap her shoulder gently as she swings her head back and forth, her hair slapping my hand.

"Hit me baby one more time!" She belts as I grab her shoulder.

"Emmie!"

Startled, she yanks off her headphones and looks at me with utter annoyance.

"What?!"

"We're home." She looks around as if we had just time-traveled from the mall. I laugh at her shocked expression. "Come on, sweetheart, let's get you inside." Emelia reaches out her arms and I lift her into the wheelchair. I grab the leftover Mexican food and place it on her lap. "Hold onto this while we get in the house."

"Okay, Mom. Oh! Did you grab my Furby!?"

Oh. That's right.

We got a Furby.

While at the mall, Emelia saw the purple monstrosity in the window of a toy store and begged me for it, saying that all the kids had one at her old school and she felt left out. Of course, I am only hearing about this *after* we move to a new town, and she happens to see it in a store's window. Of course I gave in, and now we have one of those creepy, big-eyed hairballs in the trunk. I was kind of hoping she'd forgotten about it. The thing gives me the creeps. Even its voice wigs me out. I hang my head. I *do not* want that thing in the house. But what else am I going to do? I shut the van's door.

I could say we accidentally left it at the mall—

"Doo-ay!" The disturbing robotic voice cries out from the trunk. The vibration from me shutting the door must have triggered the purple monster.

Yep. Mistakes were made.

"Oh! I hear it, Mom! Can you grab it for me, please? I want to take it out of the box when we get inside.

Awesome.

"Okay, sweetheart." I say as I reluctantly walk to the trunk and open the hatch. There, staring at me through the plastic bag, is the Furby. I pick it up and point my finger at it. "Okay, no funny business."

"What did you say, Mom?"

"Oh, nothing, hon! I got it." I look back at the Furby, which is now blinking at me while cooing with its weird, beak-like mouth. I quickly walk back over to Emelia and put it on her lap next to the Mexican food. "Please, wait to open it until after we get into our pajamas."

"Okay..." Emelia mumbles through a pouty face.

Going up the ramp, I look at the doorknocker. The gaping woman's mouth with spider legs coming out of her mouth seems to be scrutinizing me. I quietly snicker. I can't believe I allowed it to bother me so much.

I mean, it's just a hunk of metal. I blame the drugs. Now that I think about it, what am I going to do with that last pill? Maybe I should hold onto it so I can confront Kyle about it when he gets home tomorrow.

I open the door, and Emelia immediately rolls to her room and shuts the door.

"Emmie, you still have the leftovers." I raise my voice just enough for her to hear me. One of her double doors slightly creaks open and I see her small hand poke out just long enough to drop the bag on the ground before shutting the door again.

I can't help but laugh. Maybe I spoiled her a little *too* much this go around?

I wait about an hour before putting one of the new DVDs we picked up today at the Blockbuster by the mall into the player. I open Emelia's French doors and find her listening to her CD player, holding the Furby...that she took out of the box. I walk up to her and tap her on the shoulder. She pulls her headphones off and looks up at me.

"Hey, hon, I put *Chicken Run* on the TV. Want to watch it with me?" Emelia's face lights up with excitement.

"Yes!" Emelia starts to roll out the room, but I stop her.

"Hold on, let's get you ready for bed first. Also, the Furby stays on your nightstand. I don't want it talking during the movie."

"Awwww, but I just got him!" She says as she reluctantly rolls to the side of her bed and places the toy on her nightstand. The Furby speaking as it is set down.

"Boo!"

"See, Emmie? It'd make noises throughout the whole movie. You'll have more time with it tomorrow."

Emelia rolls her eyes and lets out a heavy sigh. "Fine."

"Thank you. Now let's get ready, and then we can watch *Chicken Run*." I go into the armoire to pick out her outfit. As I dig through the boxes, I accidentally drop one of her fuzzy pink socks on the wooden floor of the armoire. I lean over to pick it up and notice it's now dirty, a layer of light brown dust clinging to one side

Huh? I lean back down and run my fingers along the armoire's floorboard. The floor is caked with dry soil that blends in perfectly with the hardwood. This was clean just last week. *How did it get so dirty* inside *an armoire?*

"Did you find pajamas for me yet, Mom?"

"Yep, looking right now, hon!" I quickly grab her pink-and-white pinstriped polyester pajama set and a pair of white fuzzy socks and close the armoire, leaving this mystery for later.

We quickly get ready for bed, then head out into the living room to watch the movie. We cuddle together on the couch, Emelia's head in my lap as we watch claymation chickens run around on the TV. It seems like an eternity since I last felt this at peace. After a near perfect afternoon and evening with my daughter, for a moment my life feels somewhat normal again. I look down at Emelia, whose eyes are glued to the screen and smile.

Suddenly, my thigh starts to vibrate.

BZZZ... BZZZ... BZZZ...

Who is calling me at this hour? I pull my flip phone out of my pocket. The caller ID reads Gilbert Hickcok. I answer it.

"Hello?"

"Oh good, you're up. Are you available?"

"Well, I'm sorta in the middle of—"

"Good! Something's been bothering me." Mr. Gilbert's raspy voice cracks. "You know how the journals found gunpowder and barrel pieces at all the entry points to the area below the Burrow Estate? Well maybe the reason John didn't want anyone to mine was because he knew something was down there. Gosh, I wish I could just talk to him directly!" Mr. Gilbert pauses for a brief moment, giving me the opportunity to speak.

"You're right, that is interesting, Mr. Gilbert, but I found out from the doctor that it was my medication that was causing me to hallucinate." I look down at Emelia, who appears to not have a heard a word I said, still glued to the TV. "I'm off the medication now, and I'm feeling much better. I'm truly sorry to have wasted your time. I hope you have a great night—"

"Wait, Sarah. I also found something."

"Whatever it is, I'm sure there's a reason for it."

"Just listen, Sarah! While I was digging through the estate's archives, I discovered something very troubling." Mr. Gilbert clears his throat before he explains. "Ever since John Burrow disappeared, the manor has had twelve owners, you being the thirteenth."

"Well, what's so weird about that?"

"Nothing."

"Forgive me, Mr. Gilbert, but I'm not following."

"It's not about how many owners, but how long they *lived* there before the manor went back on the market." I can hear the sound of pages turning as Mr. Gilbert continues, "You see, Sarah, almost every owner lived there less than a couple of weeks before moving out. The longest anyone's lived there is three months, and that was the first owners of the home after John Burrows' disappearance."

What?

"But why?"

"Well that's the kicker, I don't know! But there's something amiss with that manor, Sarah. There has to be a reason why no one's stayed there longer than three months. I wonder if the Ashfords know anything about it…" Mr. Gilbert coughs. I can hear him sipping what I assume is his coffee.

What could be going on with this manor that makes everyone leave? Were they seeing things like I am? No, it was the medication that made me see things. Come on, Sarah, snap out of it. Everything's okay again.

"That's certainly odd but everything is okay on my end now, Mr. Gilbert. I'll call you if anything else comes up. But for now, I am watching a movie with my daughter."

Mr. Gilbert sighs disappointedly, "Nevertheless, I'm still going to dig on my end. I need to know for myself that you and your daughter are safe. I'll call you when I find something. Have a good night, Sarah, and say goodnight to Emelia for me."

"Will do. Have a good night. Bye."

"Bye."

CLICK.

I put my phone back in my pocket and go back to watching the movie with my daughter, stroking her hair as I feel my body start to sink into the couch from pure exhaustion. Though my muscles are aching from being up for too long, my mind is now wide awake. Should I be worried about what Mr. Gilbert found, or is it all just a coincidence?

The movie finishes and I get Emelia into bed, careful not to nudge the Furby on the nightstand next to her. I tuck her into her pink and purple blankets, then sit on the edge of the bed and hold her hand. "I had a wonderful day with you, sweetheart."

"Me too! Thank you for the gifts, Mom. I love them all!" Emelia says as she lets out a big yawn.

"I'm glad, hon. Now let's go to sleep. I'm probably going to take some medicine tonight just to make sure I get a good amount of rest, but I'll be right on the couch if you need anything. I love you." I lean over and give her a kiss on the forehead, which Emelia immediately wipes away.

"Moooommm! I'm too old for that!"

I chuckle, "You're right, I'm sorry." I stand up and walk to the door. "I'm going to leave this open so I can hear you if you need anything. I love you, sweetheart. Sleep well."

"Love you too, Mom. Night!"

"Night."

I walk over to my purse on the counter, where I stashed the chewable sleep medication Dr. Gold prescribed for tonight. I open the sealed back and dump the tablet in my mouth, gnawing the chalky chunk that's nowhere near as chewable as advertised. Actual chalk would probably go down easier than whatever I just ate.

"Ew, that was gross." I whisper to myself while I walk over to the fridge and grab a bottle of Coke. I twist open the cap and take a swig, washing down the chalky taste in my mouth. The carbonation strangely balances out the powdery texture well. I put the bottle back in the fridge and drag myself to the couch.

The medicine tasted godawful, but it seems to be working fairly quickly. I fall back onto the couch, staring up at the candle chandelier, and laugh quietly. It's been a crazy couple of days, and I'm just grateful things are finally seeming to fall back into place. I feel my eyelids growing heavy, and I let them slowly shut. The subtle sounds of the manor fade into the distance, hushed and far away, the soft glow of its remaining lights paints rainbows behind my eyes—shifting, swirling, and slowly dissolving into black.

Chapter Twenty-Four
Sweet Dreams

A cool draft brushes my cheeks, carrying the scent of old books, melted beeswax, and something faintly floral. Lavender, I think? I slowly open my eyes and squint as I try to adjust to the soft, warm glow overhead. The once dusty, neglected chandelier now shines, its polished fixture flickering candlelight. Its flames dance in the cool draft, their glow reflecting across the high ceilings. I try to stretch out my arms, but I feel them weighed down.

Huh?

I look down at my arms—I'm no longer in the cargo pants and tank top I fell asleep in. Instead, I am dressed in a deep purple Victorian gown. The long silk sleeves fit perfectly, the black lace trim lightly tickling my palms. My breath catches in my chest as the tight, ribbed bodice cinches my waist, the heavy skirt fans out around me, its layers of fabric rustling softly with each movement. Silk and lace embrace my neck, brushing against my chin. I struggle to sit up and grab the headrest of the couch, but it's not my couch anymore. In its place is a curved chaise carved from dark walnut and upholstered in scarlet velvet. I look around, the entire living room has been redecorated with pristine antiques, as if plucked straight from the 1800s. Cream-colored wallpaper covers the walls, tulip motifs drifting in gentle arcs across the surface, as if caught mid-fall and frozen in time.

Suddenly, playful piano music and cheerful laughter fills the manor's halls. I turn toward the source of the melodies. Through the French doors of the great room, shadows dance along the candlelit walls. I stand and walk closer, my footsteps muffled by a plush, red rug swirled with gold floral designs. Peeking around the corner, I see a white man and an African American woman. The woman feels familiar as she sits at a cottage piano pressed against the wall. Her royal blue silk skirt drapes over the bench, and the lace of her sleeves lightly grazes the edge of the piano as her delicate hands playfully stroke the keys. Her hair is braided into a perfect bun, accenting her slender jawline. Her amber eyes glow in the candlelight as she smiles up at the man leaning over the piano, who is laughing and smiling through his scruffy brown handlebar mustache. The love between the two is unmistakable. The way they gaze into each other's eyes is so raw, so passionate, so intimate, I almost feel intrusive watching from the doorway.

The man looks directly at me, our eyes locking. I quickly swing around and hide behind the door, sliding down to sit on the floor. I rest my elbows on my knees and hide my face in my crossed arms. My heart races. I close my eyes as panic tightens in my chest, making it difficult to breathe through the restraining bodice.

How did women deal with these stupid things back in the day? I feel like I am going to pass out!

My eyes open and I see low heels of black leather at the edge of my skirt. I look up and see the woman standing over me, smiling gently. I finally recognize who she is—Mary Beth Freeman.

She reaches out her hand to me and, still in complete disbelief, I slowly take it. Keeping her grip on my hand, she guides me into the great room, where the man stands next to the piano, waiting. Tall and slender, he wears an off-white long-sleeve shirt and brown pants held up by black suspenders. His pushed-up sleeves reveal scars and bruises on his forearms and hands from years of hard labor. His brown hair is slicked back, a few strands falling over his gentle blue eyes. His calm presence puts me at ease, makes me feel like I can trust him.

If this is Mary Beth, then that must mean...

This is John Burrow.

Mary Beth walks to the piano, sits, and starts to play a waltz. John bows slightly and holds out his hand, as if asking me to dance.

Without thinking, I grab his hand and we begin to move across the floor.

The melodies echo and bounce off the cathedral ceiling, and time holds still as we dance like we have been for years. The stained-glass skylight paints our shadows in purples and reds across the cream-colored walls like dark puppets, copying our every twirl, swing, and timely step we make. My mind and soul become one with the piano, flowing with the rhythmic key strokes and the instability of the emotions behind every note.

Our heavy steps create a beat of their own against the hardwood floors, but I feel light as air, dancing on clouds in John's arms. The open bay windows blow in a cool, moist breeze from the clear, moonlit sky, adding crispness to the air I breathe with each swing and twirl. I never knew air could taste this good. I never knew I could feel *this* good. I am dancing on cloud nine, yearning for this ecstasy to never end. But then—a faint cry is carried in with the breeze. A voice so distant, it feels almost imaginary.

"Mom, wake up!!!"

The voice sounds familiar. I know that voice, but from where? My euphoric high fades as I continue to hear the cries for help growing louder.

"Get away from me! Mom! Help!"

Emelia? I'm now alert, frantically scanning the room for the source of the screams as John and I continue to waltz.

"Mom, help!!!"

"Emmie?" I can't figure out where the screams are coming from. Emelia sounds so far away, yet so close. Where is she?

"Mom, help me!!!"

"Emmie, where are you?!"

"MOM, HELP ME!!!!"

"EMMIE!" Just as I scream out, John abruptly stops the dance. His laughter turned to silence, his lips tensed. Tilting his head down at me, his once-warm eyes turn cold as they stare directly into mine before giving me a command.

"Kill it."

214

"What? Kill what!?" The candles start to gradually extinguish, the room darkening with each passing moment. I push off John and aggressively walk around the room, which is spinning faster and faster with each step. Emelia's screams are now everywhere but nowhere at the same time, as if she is screaming from within my mind, each breathy cry trying to escape through my eardrums.

"MOM, PLEASE!!! HELP MEEEE!!!!"

"Emmie, where are you!?" The room, now spinning at full speed, continues to get darker. John's command to kill it echoes through the tornado that inhabits my mind until the room falls into complete darkness, nothing but the color black fills my strained eyes.

"MOM, PLEEAASEE!!!"

"EMMIE!!!"

Suddenly, I wake up, jolting up like Frankenstein gasping for air. I look around, and I'm back in my living room, on my couch, wearing my clothes. My thoughts quickly turn to the great room, where blaring beeps from Emelia's medical bed alarm pulsate throughout the manor.

Oh no... Emmie!

I jump off the couch and run to the French doors, swinging them fully open—

Emelia is gone.

Chapter Twenty-Five

Epiphany

There is a knock on the door. It takes every bit of willpower to respond through my cracked voice. "Come in!"

The front door slowly creaks open. Sheriff Ashford steps into the foyer, removing his hat as he walks toward the living room where I sit on the couch staring blankly into the distance, Emelia's purple fuzzy blanket cradled in my arms.

"Morning, Mrs. Gallo. I got a call that something happened to your daughter?"

"Yes." I softly reply without looking up. I can feel Sheriff Ashford staring at me.

There is silence between us for a brief moment, before he asks with annoyed arrogance, "Well, tell me what happened?"

I clear my throat while attempting to wipe away the smeared mascara running down my cheeks,

"Last night we did our usual bedtime routine. Everything was fine. I took a sleeping pill and fell asleep on the couch, then woke up to the sound of the alarm on Emelia's medical bed. When I went to check, she was gone. I looked everywhere. I checked the windows and front door, both locked. After searching the rest of the manor, I called 911. And now you're here."

"Uh-huh."

Sheriff Ashford walks into the great room. I get up and follow him in. He looks around the room casually, not saying a word, not taking notes, just standing there like a jackass. I can't hold my tongue any longer.

"Well? Aren't you going to look around? Take some notes? Something?"

Sheriff Ashford crosses his arms and shifts his weight onto one leg. "Are you trying to tell me how to do my job?"

"No, but my daughter is missing and you haven't even asked for her description. I've watched enough *Law & Order* to know you're supposed to get a picture of what the person looks like, or at least get a—"

"This isn't some kind of TV show, *sweetheart*— we're living in reality. You got me?" Sheriff Ashford scowls.

Breathe, Sarah. I need to tread lightly. He is the sheriff in this town, and if I want to find Emelia, I need his help. I pause and take a big breath in before speaking.

"Okay. I'll find a recent picture of her, print out missing person flyers, and go into town, and—"

"No, you won't."

"And why the fuck not?!"

"It hasn't even been more than a couple of hours. You'll need to wait at least 24 before I let you staple tacky missing person signs all over my town."

Sheriff Ashford looks off into the distance, avoiding eye contact. It's exactly what my daughter does when she lies. Ashford continues with a shrug. "Plus, she's a girl; she might've run off with a boy or something. Just wait 'til tomorrow—"

"Oh yeah, she just walked right out the front door with the neighbor boy—she's paraplegic you asshole!!!" How is this happening right now?! My daughter is missing and he's acting like it's no big deal! He just stands there, annoyed that I interrupted his morning coffee with my *problem*. Sheriff Ashford raises an eyebrow and jabs a finger in my face.

"Now you watch that pretty little mouth of yours, or I'll arrest you for disorderly conduct."

His condescending voice makes my stomach twist and my fists clinch. I take a few deep breaths, resisting the urge to punch his wrinkly Adam's apple. *I'm no good to Emelia if I'm in jail.*

"I apologize, I'm just a bit stressed." Sheriff Ashford lowers his finger and straightens himself up, his demeanor calm once again.

"Is she with your husband? Did you even call your him before clogging up my emergency line?"

"I did, he didn't pick up. Please, Sheriff, someone or something has taken her."

"And how do you know that?"

My mind instantly flashes back like a movie reel—the waltz, Emelia's distant cries for help, and a downward spiral into darkness before waking up to the living nightmare I'm standing in now. I clear my throat.

"Uh, it's just a feeling."

219

"A... *feeling?*"

"Yep." I gulp.

Sheriff Ashford is clearly annoyed—until a slow, sinister grin spreads across his chapped lips like he's just had an epiphany.

"What medications are you on again?"

"Why are you asking? Why does it even matter?"

"Well, you've been pretty manic lately, Mrs. Gallo. Some might even say delusional. What's to say you didn't do in your own daughter? I mean, no one would blame you—taking care of a cripple must be unbearable."

My jaw drops. The nerve of this man, accusing me of killing my own child. I can't take it anymore.

"Get out of my house!" I command while pointing toward the front door. Sheriff Ashford chuckles and holds his hands up sarcastically.

"All right, I'm leaving." Shaking his head, he walks to the still-open door. Standing in the threshold, he puts on his cowboy hat, then tips it toward me. "Do yourself a favor and don't leave town," he says as he closes the front door. Moments later, the purr of an engine revs outside then fades off into the distance.

My body begins to shake violently, and my labored breathing quickens, keeping pace with the rapid thudding of my heartbeat. I'm completely in shock.

How is this happening? Why is this happening? Am I going to jail? No, I need to get a hold of myself. I don't have time for this. I need to find Emelia, but how?

I squeeze my eyes shut, my lips quivering as I fight to control my breathing. Several minutes pass before I can relax enough to focus, my heartbeat still slightly elevated. I begin pacing the room, thinking aloud.

"Okay, I need to find Emelia, but I have no support from law enforcement, and I can't hang missing person flyers without dickface tearing them down... so think, Sarah, how do you find your daughter?"

My sandals slap against the hardwood floors, creating a makeshift metronome that keeps my thoughts in rhythm.

"Right before all this happened, I dreamed Emelia was screaming for help, saying 'get away from me', like something was after her. And then John Burrow said to 'kill it'... could *it* be the same thing that took Emelia?" I shake my head, "No. Stop it, Sarah. None of it is real. You were just hallucinating off the pills."

I pause.

"Or was I?"

I glance through the French doors at the kitchen counter, where the very last pill sits in its yellow container.

"What if these pills actually open up a part of the brain that allows the user to see past the veil? What if that's why people kept reporting hallucinations and insomnia? They weren't hallucinating, they were seeing ghosts and couldn't sleep because of them."

My voice slowly rises as I cautiously walk toward the counter, "If that's the case... then the little boy in the back seat, the man standing in my doorway, the knocker going crazy, the spider tearing through my stomach, the writing on the mirror, the couple spiked on

221

the pillars, the children playing jump rope with their organs, the child being filleted and spilling his guts all over me, Mary Beth, John—everything was real!"

I pick up the container on the counter and stare at the pill inside. *Am I out of my mind?* No... This is the clearest my mind has been since we moved here. And I know exactly what I need to do to find my daughter— finish what I started.

My hands shake as I twist the lid and dump the pill into my palm. It feels heavier than it should. My face starts to tingle from the anticipation of the unknown, while knowing just enough to be terrified. I look up at nothing in particular and yell. "All right, no more games. Tell me where my daughter is!"

I look down at the pill and let out a labored sigh. "Here goes nothing." I slap my palm against my open mouth, chewing the pill in hopes the effects will take hold of my mind quicker—it does.

Suddenly, the floor vibrates beneath my feet like a stampede is approaching. One by one, lightbulbs explode with deafening cracks, their echoes ricocheting throughout the manor until only the natural light from the overcast morning remains.

A horde of rats erupts through every kitchen cabinet like an endless waterfall. Their slick bodies slapping against my ankles as they swarm toward the front door, each one vanishing the moment they hit the wooden door.

I look up, the floral pattern on the walls morphs before my eyes, its once placid cream color transforming into pink, then red, as blood excretes from the cracks in the wallpaper. The air fills with cries of screaming children, the sound is so piercing. I flinch, clasping my hands over my ears. I slowly spin in circles, the room overwhelming me. But then, the earsplitting wails fade into familiar whispers, followed by the sound of a dull scratching.

As I turn, my eyes land on the dining room where letters are carving themselves on the wall, one after another, slowly, as if by the blade of an unseen, jagged knife.

No...

Not just the dining room wall.

On *every* wall.

All around me, letters are etching themselves into the walls, over and over, filling every surface with gibberish—nonsense repeating incantations.

SUETATI SUETATI SUETATI SUETATI SUETATI SUETATI SUETATI SUETATI SUETATI SUETATI

SUETATI SUETATI SUETATI SUETATI SUETATI SUETATI SUETATI SUETATI SUETATI SUETATI

SUETATI SUETATI SUETATI SUETATI SUETATI SUETATI SUETATI SUETATI SUETATI SUETATI

"What does this mean?" I scream, the gears in my mind working overtime when I feel my pocket vibrate.

BZZZ... BZZZ... BZZZ.

Without taking my eyes off the wall, I flip open my phone, "Hello?"

"Sarah, thank goodness you answered! It's Mr. Gilbert. Now listen, I don't have much time. Sheriff

Ashford will be back any minute." Mr. Gilbert whispers. The sound of rustling paper echoes in my ear.

"Yes, I'm here," I reply, only halfway listening as I try to decode the message covering the walls.

"Okay good, you need to hear this. I was heading into Sheriff Ashford's office to ask for information on the Burrow Estate, but he ran to his car before I even made it to the front door! He didn't lock it, so I let myself in and started rummaging through his files. Oh Sarah, it's horrible!"

Mr. Gilbert's voice quivers as he struggles to continue, "Missing children—all the way back to the 1800s. Each and every one of them vanishing within weeks of their families moving into the Burrow Estate. And the worst part? Each missing person's report was taken by someone in the Ashford family. None of these cases made it past the front desk, none were reported to other law enforcement agencies, they were all buried at the bottom of this filthy filing cabinet. All unsolved. Each family left waiting for answers they'd never get. How could they do this?! How can someone just allow a child to stay lost, desperate for help that will never come? It is pure evil, I—"

"My daughter's missing." The silence on the other line is almost deafening.

"Sarah, you need to find her. Something evil lurks in that manor."

I suddenly have an epiphany—when the shadows were whispering in my room, I also thought it was gibberish, but what if it wasn't?

What if... I shove my legs through the horde of rats still rushing past my feet and lunge for my purse on the counter, grabbing Mr. Gilbert's business card and a pen. I lean over the counter and copy an etching before it repeats:

S U E T A T I

"Okay, but what if, because the veil between the living and the dead acts like a mirror, everything is reversed? That's what happens in horror movies, right? So that would mean…"

"Sarah, what are you talking about? Is everything okay?" I start writing the letters in reverse order, saying each one aloud.

"I-T-A-T-E-U-S—" My heart sinks into my gut. Painful, overwhelming fear crashes over me as if every crevice in my body has been filled with shattered glass.

No. It can't be…

IT ATE US.

This is what they have been trying to tell me ever since we moved here. They weren't trying to hurt me, they were trying to *warn* me.

To *scare* me.

They were trying to *save all of us*.

I let go of my pen. The moment it clatters against the wood of the counter, the whispers vanish, leaving the manor eerily silent. Whatever ate these kids has my daughter. But how am I going to find her? Will I be too late? The thought of hope feels nothing more than a fairytale, then Mr. Gilbert's raspy voice reverberates in my ear.

"Sarah, right before I called you, I called the police one county over, but you can't wait. You need to find your daughter. Oh, if only we could talk to the family of one of those missing children, but most aren't

225

even alive anymore to help." The instant he utters the sentence, something clicks—

My god, how did I miss it?! It's been right in my face the entire time! Shock surges through my veins and out my fingertips, revitalizing me. There is hope after all. "Oh my god, Mr. Gilbert, that's it!"

"*What's it? I don't understand.*"

"I need to talk to someone who's dead!"

Just then, the sound of a door chime and a familiar voice, "What are you doing in my office, you old coot? And who are you talking to?!"

"I got to go, good luck—"

CLICK.

"I know exactly who I need to talk to. Thank you, Mr. Gilbert," I reply to the dead line before snapping my phone shut and shoving it in my pocket.

I snatch my keys off the counter and run through the rats, before bursting out the front door toward the van. The swarm follows me out to the front patio, vanishing when they reach the brittle grass. I make it to the van, swinging the door open, sliding inside, then slamming it behind me. I twist the key in the ignition, the engine sputters, then roars to life—a deep, rumbling purr echoes through the minivan like it's been waiting for this day since it rolled off the line.

"Hold on until I can find you, Emmie. Momma's coming."

Chapter Twenty-Six
The Tree

"Where are you?" I mumble under my breath. I've been driving around town for about an hour now, scanning the brick sidewalks and antique iron benches, searching for Mary Beth. If anyone knows what happened in this town, if anyone knows where my daughter is, it's her. But where could she be? I've searched for miles with no sign of her.

Frustrated, I spot a parking space and pull in, throwing the van in park.

"You've popped up before without me wanting it, but now that I need you, you've disappeared?!" Irritated, I rest my head against the steering wheel. Time has been flying by, and it's not on my side. I need to find Emelia before *whatever it is* eats her. Sharp tapping on my driver's side window interrupts my thoughts.

TAP TAP TAP TAP.

And just when it can't get worse, I hear an all-too familiar woman's voice right outside my door.

"Hello? Are you all right in there?"

TAP TAP TAP TAP.

"Are you sick?" Amy. Her voice makes me want to lobotomize my ear canals. I seriously hate this bitch.

"Yes, I'm fine, Amy. Please go away."

"Well, if you're sick, I don't mind helping out a bit. I'm sure I'm more than capable of taking care of Kyle and Emelia—"

Something in me snaps. Rage that makes my blood boil from under my skin. For too long, I've turned the other cheek, stayed silent, tried to set a good example for my daughter. Well, I'm done. Done being used. Done being stepped on. Enough is enough—and it ends here.

"What did you just say?!" I snap back, flinging the door open so hard it slams into her. I step out and get in her face. I'm close, I can count the pores on the tip of her pointy little nose. I look into her eyes with daggers. Amy stammers, eyes full of fear as sweat starts to bead on her forehead. She's trying to find words. I don't let her.

"You think I don't know what you've been doing with my husband? You aren't as subtle as you think. The first time I met you, you looked—and smelled—of trash. Then a couple of days later, there you are. All dolled up in Calvin Klein, wearing *my dead mother's pearls*?!"

Amy instinctively grabs the heirlooms still hanging from her ears.

"I—I'm sorry—" she stutters.

"And now you have the nerve to suggest you can do what I do? That you can replace me?!" I laugh coldly. "Just because you threw on a decent outfit with *my money* and slapped on some lipstick? Please. Putting lipstick on a pig doesn't turn it into a show pony, *hon* ...

228

you'll always be trash." I lean in even closer to Amy, who is still frozen and trembling in her wedges, my lips brushing her ear as I whisper venom. "And let me let you in on a secret," I pause for dramatic effect, "...you still fucking reek."

I step toward my van before I continue, "Oh, and if you *ever* get anywhere near my Emelia, I will kill you. She is my daughter, and I will be damned if the likes of you or anyone gets near my—" I stop.

A realization hits me like a wrecking ball. I know where Mary Beth is.

"I've got to go." I get back into my van and slam the door shut. Amy tilts her head in confusion.

"Do you want your mother's earrings back?" She shouts through the closed window.

"Nah," I say, revving my engine. "My mother taught me not to play in the dumpster."

I drive off, catching a glimpse of Amy in my rearview mirror—jaw dropped and stunned. I smile so hard, my cheeks hurt.

Damn, that felt good. But I need to focus on finding Mary Beth, and now I know where she is. She's where any mother would be—with her child.

The couple-minute drive to the edge of town feels like hours. My anxiety climbs with each passing second. I just hope I'm right—that Mary Beth is at her daughter's grave on the hill. If I'm wrong, I've just wasted precious time that I don't have. There it is!

The tree line in sight, I slam the gas pedal, pushing my already fast speed to the van's limit. The tires squeal as they grind against the gravel, the van fishtailing into a sharp turn, all four wheels drifting as it jerks to a stop, the side door missing a tree by mere inches before I throw it in park.

I yank the key from the ignition and leap out. I run down the trail, my exposed feet being abused by the sharp grass blades through my sandals, sending waves of stings up my legs. I hardly notice or care. All that matters is reaching the hill.

Finding Mary Beth.

Saving my daughter.

There, the end of the trail is in sight. *Come on. Faster. Faster.* A renewed sense of energy bursts through me as I push my body beyond its limits. My legs pump harder against the rough terrain, my inner thighs burning where the thick cargo pants chafe them raw.

I'm almost there...

I break through the tree line and into a field of wildflowers. A calm breeze stirs the air, feathering faint scents of pollen and wet grass beneath my nose. Straight ahead, the hill stands tall, wrapped in even more wildflowers—it's breathtaking. I just wish I had taken the time to truly appreciate it before now.

Looking up at the long climb ahead, I feel my legs throb and pulse with exhaustion.

Why does it have to be so tall? Please be up there. I need you to be up there...

I start to climb hill, my heart pounding in cadence with each heavy, labored step, my nerves frayed, and my feet screaming from the punishment I'm putting them through. As I near the top of the hill, I see tree limbs swaying, their leaves rustling in the wind.

Huh, I don't remember a tree... only a stump.

Reaching the top, I find where a large, weathered stump once stood, is now a full-grown oak tree, its vibrant green leaves dancing in the breeze. Dark bark swirls in gorgeous patterns up the trunk, and its branches stretch so wide, they make the hilltop look small in comparison. I look around, and Mary Beth is nowhere to be found.

"But, I thought..."

My eyes fill with tears as if gravity itself is pressing down on me. What did I miss? I was so sure she'd be here—but I was wrong. And now, I may never find my baby girl.

Feeling defeated, I sink down beneath the tree, leaning my tired back and pounding head against the hard, bumpy bark.

"Emmie, please forgive me."

I close my eyes and feel a gust of wind carry tears across my face. My heart feels like it's being ripped from the inside out. Oh god, it aches!

I clutch my chest, trying to keep my heart from exploding out of my ribcage. The overwhelming sense of sorrow consuming my soul is almost unbearable, though a part of me feels I deserve it.

Suddenly, I feel something tap the top of my forehead. I open my eyes and see small, burnt children's feet, swaying in the breeze.

I slowly, hesitantly, look up and see the charred body of a child hanging above me.

"AHHHH!!!"

Screaming, I scramble out from under the tree and collapse onto my back, staring up in horror. Hanging by thick, frayed ropes looped around their necks, a woman and a little girl dangle from the oak's massive branches. Both burned beyond recognition. Their skin is blackened, with a few curled patches of exposed, pink, rotten flesh. Steam rises from the woman's shriveled chest as thick bodily fluids seeps down the length of her body, sizzling like a hot steak in a pan.

Rotten, chunky milk oozes out of the woman's blackened and cracked nipples, the terrible, sour odor carried with the stench of burning flesh in the breeze, burns my eyes.

The tips of their fingers are gone, melted down to the bone, and only scattered patches of hair are left on their charred scalps, the few strands poking out like stubborn weeds. The skin on their lips and eyelids is gone, and what's left of their eyeballs drips down their slack jaws, highlighting their yellowed, split teeth— proof they were screaming when they were burnt alive.

My body lurches onto all fours, and I violently projectile vomit yellow, foamy stomach acid from my empty, knotted gut. I squeeze my eyes shut as tears stream down my face, dripping into the acidic puddle below.

The manor.

The ghosts.

My missing daughter.

And now the burned bodies of an unknown woman and child? It's all too much. I don't know how much more of this I can take.

From somewhere in front of me, I hear the sound of footsteps crunching through charred leaves. I open my eyes but keep them low, fixed on the ground.

Just outside the puddle of my vomit, two black leather pumps come into view.

I look up.

Mary Beth is staring down at me. Her expression unreadable, but undoubtedly serious. The moment feels like déjà vu.

I push myself up and wipe my face and mouth with the back of my hand.

"Mary Beth, what's going on? What happened?"

We stand there in silence, the only the sound the wildflowers grazing the tall grass, moving in patterns with the wind. She doesn't speak, she just stares into my eyes like she is peering into my soul—studying me, judging me, deciding whether I'm ready for the truth. A moment passes and her eyes soften. She holds out her hand, not casually, but with purpose, like she wants to show me something.

Without hesitation, I take it.

Instantly, my world flashes out of existence. Every color of the spectrum spins in my mind as time itself collapses, unravels, the present dissolving into the past.

A heartbeat later, I'm somewhere else—*someone* else. No longer in my own body and no longer in control.

I am seeing, feeling, hearing, tasting this new world through someone else.

I am living through Mary Beth.

Chapter Twenty-Seven
Mary Beth Freeman

I impatiently bounce my bare feet against the cool, hardwood floors while clenching my jaw, waiting to hear John come back up from the mines, but I'm worried. He's been down there too long. Suddenly, a sequence of muffled explosions from below rumbles the ground beneath my feet, then, just as quickly, everything becomes still again.

Oh no, he didn't do what I think he did—did he?!

The front doors burst open, and the night air blows a faint smoky scent into the manor. My friend and accoucheuse, Alexandria, is standing in the doorway, frantically gesturing for me to come to her.

"Mary Beth, you've got to leave *now*! The sheriff has a mob of townsfolk, they are marching over here to take you and John. Quickly, we've got to go!"

"But John hasn't come back up yet. I won't leave without him." Alexandria sighs, then quickly comes to sit next to me on the velvet chaise.

"Oh, honey, if he hasn't come back up by now, I don't think he is coming back." My strong front quickly shatters as if my exterior were made of glass, tears pour down my face. Deep down, I know what's happened, what John had to do to save us.

Alexandria grabs my arm urgently. "Mary Beth, John would not want his death to be in vain; he'd want you to live. Go. I'll hide his journal and the rope in the usual spot. You need to leave before the mob gets here."

"What about you? I can't leave you—"

"Nonsense! You are family, and I always take care of my own." She wipes away my tears. "You need to leave me."

"No—no, I can't!" The chants from the approaching mob ride in on the wind, reverberating through the manor like the first rumble of an incoming storm, growing louder with each breath.

"Mary Beth!" Alexandria begs over the rising noise. "They're almost here! There's no sense in both of us dying. *Go!*"

She leaps to her feet and hauls me up with her, dragging me toward the door. Before I can protest, she shoves me out. I stumble down the porch steps and onto the wild grass, my heart pounding. Torchlight flickers in the distance, grim and steady, getting closer. I turn back. Alexandria stands framed in the doorway, her silhouette lit by the faint candlelight behind her.

"I'll be fine, I promise." She says with a reassuring smile, even though we both know it's a lie. "Now go, I'll slow them down."

I try to hold onto this moment, my friend's beautiful face blurred by the tears pouring down my face. I know this is farewell.

Forever.

I choke on my words, knowing they will be my last to her, "I love you, my dear friend."

My vision clears just enough to see tears run down Alexandria's smiling face. Her lips quivering from her knowledge of what's to come. She steps back inside, slowly raising her hand to wave goodbye.

"I love you, too. Go. Live. For *us*."

Goodbye.

I wipe my face with the back of my hand. I lift up my black skirt and sprint to the nearest thicket, pushing through the bushes, trying desperately to get to the other side but my skirts become ensnared in the thorny branches. The mob's angry shouts gain clarity as they draw nearer.

"No dig."

"No gold."

"John lies with a dusky whore!"

My heart is racing faster than a steeplechase on hop. Panic surges through me as I yank and claw at my entangled gown. Sweat stings my eyes and drips onto my arms. The silk fabric of my skirts are tearing at the seams, but not fast enough.

"Come on!" I grunt through my teeth, ripping the silk.

The mob's hateful shouts grow louder, ricocheting through my ears. Fear has now taken over, I rip at my bodice, my sleeves, my collar. My trembling fingers are raw from the friction. I need to free myself before mob gets here.

The last button on my bodice pops, and I fall out of the gown, clad only in my linen chemise and petticoat. Gasping and shivering, I drop to my knees and crawl through the thorny underbrush, leaving the ruined and entangled dress behind.

Not even a breath later, the rioting mob arrives at the manor. I watch through the branches as the townsfolk raise their torches and pitchforks, one even throws a brick through one of the estate's windows. Shouts erupt from all corners of the crowd, popping off like musket shots.

"Traitor!"

"We want our gold!"

"Sinner!"

Alexandria calmly opens the door and then stands in silence, resilient, like a stone wall blocking the entrance. Hushed murmurs scatter across the gathered townsfolk. A moment of still tension—until one man yells.

"Look, another one of John's wenches!" He spits in Alexandria's direction. "Fucken' disgusting, the lot of ya!"

Like matches to a dry haystack, his deep-rooted hatred ignites a spark in the mob. They raise their torches and makeshift weapons, screaming and shouting with wild abandon.

Among the crowd, a young boy—no more than ten—chucks a brick toward Alexandria. It hits the front porch with a dull thud. His mother throws the next one. Her aim is sharper. The brick strikes Alexandria's foot. Alexandria cries out, grabbing her injured foot and hopping on the other for balance.

By now, the townsfolk have gained momentum. Bricks sail from the crowd at random intervals, flying toward Alexandria as she ducks and stumbles, trying in vain to take cover.

A thunderous voice cracks through the chaos, followed by horse hooves stomping the ground.

"SILENCE!"

The crowd freezes.

A white man clad in all black gallops in on a stallion, its smooth ebony hair reflecting the torchlight as it heaves from the abrupt pull on its reins. Jumping off, the man tosses the reins to the closest town member, who nervously holds them tight.

The man struts leisurely forward as the mob parts around him like the Red Sea, the spurs on his black boots rattling with each slow, deliberate step. He wears a long black overcoat, and a thick brown ponytail trails down his back to the middle of his shoulder blades.

My blood runs cold, and my heartbeat pounds in my ears at the realization of who stands before me. Even though his wide-brimmed cowboy hat hides his face, I know exactly who he is—Sheriff Wyatt Ashford.

Standing between the mob and Alexandria, Sheriff Ashford turns to the crowd. "Now I thought this was a Godly town. A town with order. Tell me, who threw the first brick at the accused?"

The crowd falls silent, save for a few coughs and the clearing of a throat. One of the townsfolk kicks the boy out of the mob. Trembling in his weathered shoes, the boy stutters.

"I—I did, sir." The boy sheepishly looks down, his long blonde bangs covering his blue eyes.

Sheriff Ashford walks toward him, the boy flinching at each spur-rattling step. Now in front of him,

Sheriff Ashford grabs the boy's chin, forcefully lifting it towards him. The boy squeezes his eyes shut, bracing himself.

"Look at me, boy."

The boy opens his eyes, not out of want, but out of fear of what will happen if he doesn't. Sheriff Ashford leans in and speaks down to the boy as if he were a toddler, slow and condescending.

"Now, what did Sunday School teach you about inflicting judgment on others?"

The boy gulps so hard, those nearby must have heard it. "Ummm. Not to judge others?"

"Correct, my boy! And who is the *only* one allowed to judge?"

"Uh—uh, God?"

"Right, again! Now," Sheriff Ashford gives a cold grin, "whose job is it to enforce law and order in this God-fearing town?"

"Yours."

"Wow, sonny, you're full of fire!" Sheriff Ashford lets go of his chin. The boy smiles nervously as Sheriff Ashford squats down to eye level.

"So if I—a God-fearing man—am in charge of enforcing law and order, who is the *only* person in this town allowed to inflict judgment onto others?"

The boy hesitates, then stutters, "Y—You?"

The sheriff's grin curls menacingly. In a rage of fury, he grabs the boy by his tattered brown shirt and stands, suspending the boy midair. Screaming and spraying spit all over the boy's face.

"THEN WHY DID YOU THROW THE FIRST BRICK?!"

The boy is shaking. He wets himself, dampness soaking his trousers, trickling down his socks, then dripping to the ground. The boy struggles to catch his breath as the hand around his throat squeezes into a fist. Sheriff Ashford holds the boy suspended in the air. His eyes are filled with fire as he savors the terror he's inflicting on the boy.

"That's enough, Sheriff, leave the boy alone!"

Oh no, Alexandria. Why did you say something...

Sheriff Ashford's grin curdles into a scowl. The spark of amusement dies in his eyes, leaving them cold and merciless. He slowly turns his face to her as he releases his grasp.

The child falls, hitting the ground and gasping for air, before scrambling back to his awaiting mother, who falls to her knees, embracing her trembling son as tears stream down her face. The townsfolk stand hypnotized. No one dares speak. No one moves. They just watch as Sheriff Ashford slowly turns to face Alexandria.

"Now, don't think I forgot about you." Sheriff Ashford says as he walks up the porch, the air growing thick with tension as each deliberate step emits sharp thumps that fill the night sky. Alexandria stands tall, holding onto the doorway to support herself.

Now on the porch, Sheriff Ashford picks up one of the thrown bricks and stares at it for a while, allowing the terror to settle in. Sweat trickles down Alexandria's face, as she tries to hide her fear. Smiling, Ashford bows dramatically.

"We are so sorry to disturb you on this beautiful night, ma'am." he says, his tone dripping with mockery, "But we are in search of two individuals. John and Mary Beth. By chance, would you know where they are?"

Alexandria swallows hard. "What do they stand accused of?"

Sheriff Ashford chuckles, turning toward the people with a boisterous voice. "Why, stealing from the good folk of this town! Hoarding gold that wasn't theirs. And most importantly—" he raises a hand and points at the sky, "breaking God's law."

He paces slowly, theatrically.

"God said, *'Cursed be Canaan; a servant of servants shall he be unto his brethren.'* And He also said not to marry a Canaanite."

Gasps and murmurs of agreement ripple through the crowd.

"Now, my fellow brothers and sisters," Sheriff Ashford calls out, madness filling his eyes. "Should we stand by and let our brother John be condemned to hell? Or," his grin twists cruelly, "should we find him, take back the gold he has stolen, and show him mercy so that he may meet his Father at the holy gates?"

The mob erupts in cheers, swept up in ignorant zeal. Sheriff Ashford raises both arms in fake piety.

"Can I get an AMEN?!"

"AMEN!"

Alexandria steps forward, her voice hoarse from breathing the torchlit air. "Have you all gone mad from greed?! Do you not remember what John and Mary Beth have done for you?! None of you would even be here if it weren't for them! Please, stop this madness!"

.

For a brief second, there is silence. Then—

"Boo!"

"Sinner!"

"Filthy Jezebel!"

Sheriff Ashford motions the crowd to settle down. The mob instinctively falls silent like a pack of trained hounds. Ashford turns back to Alexandria, his voice soft, yet frightening.

"Now, I humbly ask: where are they?"

Though her lips are sealed, her eyes are screaming. Ashford notices and steps uncomfortably close. He breathes down her neck as he stares into her. Alexandria avoids his gaze as her eyes start to water.

Spit sprays on her face as Ashford screams, "WHERE ARE THEY?!"

"I don't know!" She lies through her teeth, turning her head away from his piercing stare.

He grabs her by the cheek, forcing her to look at him. "You know, lying is a sin against God. But just as God is merciful... so can I be." With the jagged brick in his other hand, he grazes the brick's rough edges against her forehead, scraping her skin. "So I will ask one last time. Where. Are. They?"

Alexandria's eyes shimmer off the torchlight as a tear falls down onto Ashford's greasy finger. The eyes that once told of a tale of fear now tell one of bravery. Her voice shakes with determination.

"I. Don't. Know."

Ashford chuckles coldly, releasing her face. He turns halfway to the mob—but the sneer vanishes. In one fluid motion, he spins back around and slams the brick into Alexandria's head with a dull crack.

She collapses.

He follows her down like a wolf on a wounded deer and then continues to beat her.

Again.

And again.

The crowd remains frozen. The sound of Alexandra's crushing wet bones filling the air.

"NO!" I shriek before slapping a hand over my mouth, holding my breath, terrified I was heard. But it's too late.

Ashford pauses, his last swing still elevated above Alexandria's motionless body, blood dripping off of the brick onto what's left of her face. He rises slowly to his feet, blood smeared across his cheeks like war paint.

A sinister smile curls wide as he bounds off the porch, "There you are, little mouse."

Just as he is about to walk through the parted crowd, Alexandria lets out a quiet, pained moan. Ashford looks at the boy still standing next to his mother and tosses him the brick. The boy shakes as he fumbles to catch it in his hands.

"Boy." His voice is eerily calm. "Go finish what the Lord started."

The boy looks at his mother for guidance, but she turns her gaze away in shame. The boy stutters.

"I—Uh... I—don't..."

"Do as you're told, boy!"

The boy, slowly and with doubt, starts toward the steps of the porch.

Sheriff Ashford grabs his shoulder. "Remember, you are doing the Lord's work by sending that heathen back where she came from. Don't fail Him."

"Yes, Pa." The boy doesn't look up at his father, but walks straight toward the house. Ashford smiles at his son, then turns and walks towards the parted crowd.

Towards me.

My body shakes, pressing the scattered thorns and debris deeper into my stomach. I feel my petticoat dampen as soil and blood soaks through in a warm, filthy blend. My heartbeat pounds like a war drum as I clench my jaw, biting back a scream. Ashford's lazy footsteps grow louder.

Heavier.

Each step lands with the same sick rhythm as the brick breaking what's left of Alexandria's soul. The tension stretches out like a noose until finally, it's tight.

Black leather cowboy boots are now only inches away from me, the gold-colored metal spurs caked with dirt and tacky splatters of blood. Ashford picks up a branch and uses it to lift my tangled and ripped gown like it's laced with plague.

"Looks like the she-devil has shed her skin!"

Ashford calls back to the mob as he examines the dress.

I dare not move.

Dare not breathe.

One flinch, and I'm done for.

He leans towards the gown and gives an obnoxiously loud sniff. It sends shivers down my spine.

"But by the smell of it, she hasn't gone far!"

He slowly raises the stick—then, without warning, begins thrashing the bushes violently. Each strike sends chunks of stems, thorns, and leaves piling over my trembling body. I instinctively squeeze my eyes shut.

Oh, Lord... he's going to find me. I brace for the inevitable—until the galloping sound of an approaching horse interrupts the tension, followed by a voice.

"Sheriff, we searched the town. There's no sign of them anywhere."

The branch stops whipping. I crack one eye open. Another horse now stands next to the sheriff's, and a second pair of boots now stands behind Ashford, but these are worn, brown, and spur-less. I slowly raise my head up, my eyes straining from looking so high up from the ground. It's Deputy Dale.

Ashford's voice turns sharp. "Deputy, how many times do I have to tell you," he holds up the stick like it carries divine weight, "not to interrupt me when I'm busy!"

"I apologize, sir. I'm just following your orders to report back if I find anything."

"And did you?"

"Well… no, but that's why—"

"THEN NOTHING!"

He throws the stick down violently—it lands an inch from my nose.

"Did you search every establishment?"

"No, but we asked all the folk still in town. They all said they haven't seen anything."

Ashford pinches the bridge of his nose and exhales hard. "Of course they didn't! They're all sympathizers. Have you learned *nothing* about the power these devils wield?" He drops his hand and gestures toward the estate. "Just look what they did to poor John! Our town's leader, wrapped in the succubus's grasp. Condemned, for all eternity."

Ashford's eyes blaze as he turns back to the deputy. "Is that what you want loose in the world? Think of your daughter, Deputy. Would you want *her* to fall into the darkness?"

Deputy Dale lowers his gaze as if disappointed. "No, I wouldn't."

Ashford steps closer and gives the deputy's cheeks a few condescending pats.

"Good. Now, take some townsfolk and search the estate. That much gold shouldn't be hard to find."

His gaze drops back to the gown and a cold grin spreads across his blood-smeared face, "Then pay the town another visit—a personal one. Especially those sympathizers the O'Briens." He chuckles menacingly. "See what you can wring out of them."

"Yes, sir!"

They both walk toward the estate. Sheriff Ashford pauses and turns back toward the bushes and says calmly before continuing.

"I'm going to find you, my little mouse."

It feels like an ominous promise, almost like he knows I can hear him.

The sheriff and deputy pass through the crowd and ascend the porch, stepping over Alexandria's cold body without so much as a glance as they walk in. The boy still kneels by her, clutching the bloodied brick, his expression blank—his spirit hollowed out, like something sacred has been scraped out of his once youthful soul, leaving him dead inside.

The deputy yells out of a broken window, "Come search the manor for gold!"

The mob cheers and storms inside, leaving the mother still on her knees out in the field, tears streaming down her face as she blankly stares at her son.

"The O'Briens!" I whisper.

With everyone distracted, I quietly stand, my muddied bare feet crunching the leaves beneath me. I tiptoe slowly away from the estate, my heart racing. Expecting to be caught at any moment.

But I'm not.

Once I know I'm out of sight, I break into a sprint. Pain explodes through my legs with every step, raw feet screaming against the unforgiving terrain. The night air stings my torn skin and sweat-slicked body as I push forward through the pain, through the fear, through the unknown that lies ahead.

I stop abruptly when I reach the brick road at the edge of town. Something's wrong.

The diverse town is alive, not out of celebration, but panic.

Children's cries echo off the brick storefronts, their mothers trying to calm them in vain as their fathers frantically board up windows. Others are gathering their belongings, hoping to escape with their lives. Dust clouds the air as townsfolk scramble in all directions. The once peaceful town is now a battleground full of panic and dread of what's to come.

I run down the streets, pushing through the frightened crowd as I head to O'Brien Market on the far side of town, hoping to get to them in time before the sheriff and his henchmen do.

Through the cloud of dust, I see the store. Donald O'Brien is up on a ladder, hammering a plank across the storefront's window. My chest is heavy and I try to catch my breath as I manage to yell.

"Don! You and your family need to run!" I rush over as he climbs down off his ladder.

"What? What's going on, Mary Beth?"

"Your family is in grave danger. You all must run. Now. Before it's too late!"

Donald wipes off his hands on his work apron. "We can take care of our own. You're the one that should run; trust me, the sheriff isn't going to get a word out of us. You just need to run, Mary Beth."

I grab his hand and beg, "Please. They'll kill anyone who helps me. That includes *your family.*"

His wife, Laura, steps outside. Confused, she asks, "What is going on? Are you okay, Mary Beth?"

I turn to her, frantic. "You all need to leave! The sheriff is coming!"

Donald interjects. "We'll be fine, just go, Mary Beth—"

"Stop being a mule!" I'm furious. *Why can't they understand they're not safe here?!*

Donald and Laura exchange a look. A soft, familiar smile passes between them, then they turn back to me.

"You underestimate the stubbornness of the Irish," Donald says gently. "Now go, before—"

Suddenly, a horse's shrill cry stretches across the night sky. The dust starts to cloud, warning of an incoming stampede.

It's too late. They're already here.

Laura turns to me. "Quick, come with me!"

Before I can object, she grabs my hand and drags me through the open door and into the store. Near the opening of the front, a large, empty wine barrel stands, displaying a *Wine and Cheese* sign. Dust dances in the stale air as Laura lifts the lid.

"Quickly, hide in here!" She helps me climb into the barrel, my knees pressing against my chest as she puts the lid on top of me. The tab hole is my only source of air, light, of vision. I watch Laura run back out to the front of the store, leaving the doors open.

Donald and Laura embrace each other as they lean against one of their store's front pillars, waiting in anticipation.

They don't have to wait long.

Clouds of dust kick up as several horses gallop in, shaking the ground. The horses and their mad riders pace back and forth intimidatingly in front of the store. The horses huffing and snorting as they stomp into the earth. Then suddenly, they become still as a lone black stallion trots in front of them—it's Sheriff Ashford.

I watch in agony. The air in the claustrophobic barrel is muggy. Sweat drenches my whole body, my cream-colored undergarments sticking to me like honey on bread. It almost feels like I can hear my heartbeat echo off the barrel's wooden walls. I want to scream. I want to tell them to run while they can. But I hold my breath. I know any sound I make is a death sentence.

250

Sheriff Ashford hops off his horse and throws his reins to Deputy Dale, who looks away from the O'Briens. Ashford walks casually up to the couple with his arms up as his men gradually descend from their horses behind him.

"I mean no trouble. I am just in search of two wanted fugitives. You wouldn't have happened to see anyone passing through?" Ashford now stands within arm's reach.

Donald gently positions his wife to the side. "No, sir, we haven't seen anyone. But if you and your search party would like some pie..." Donald gives a glance to Laura, who then nods back nervously. "My wife just made a few of her famous apple pies...We can wrap them up for you to take with you."

Laura turns to head into the store—but Ashford grabs her arm. Donald's calm cracks. His hand clamps around Ashford's wrist, his voice tense as he commands through his clenched teeth.

"Don't you ever touch my wife."

Ashford releases her, raises both hands in feigned surrender.

"Okay, okay. Didn't mean anything by it." He chuckles coldly—but then his face hardens. In a single, brutal motion, he slams his fist into the side of Donald's face, cracking his jawbone.

"DONALD!!!" Laura screams, rushing over to her husband, trying to balance him as he stumbles back in a daze.

I grab my mouth, holding a scream in the back of my throat, tears streaming down my face as I watch the horror unfolding in front of me. *Run while you can! Please, save yourselves!*

Ashford snaps his fingers, and his henchmen swarm in like vultures, grabbing hold of their prey. They separate the couple and press each one up against one of the two storefront pillars, facing each other. Ashford takes out a handkerchief from his long coat and calmly wipes his bloody fist as he paces between the two pillars.

"Ya know, I've always hated the Irish. I just find them...oh, what's the word?" He pauses in front of Donald who is breathing heavy, his face flushed with rage. Ashford sneers. "Bullheaded."

He flicks Donald's head tauntingly. Ashford turns and walks slowly back to Laura, who's now sobbing uncontrollably—tears running down her lips, her face blotched and red. He stuffs the bloodied handkerchief into her mouth. Her muffled cries make my heart ache.

"Now, Don," Ashford says softly, almost sweetly, "I'll give you one more chance."

He reaches under his coat and pulls out a flintlock pistol, pressing its barrel against Laura's temple. Then he leans in, forehead to forehead—his voice dripping with feigned sympathy as he stares into Laura's frightened eyes.

"Tell me where they are..." He cocks back the hammer with his thumb.

CLICK.

Laura flinches and shrieks at the sharp sound. "Or God's just going to get one of His angels back early."

Donald trembles, his lips quivering as blood-tinged saliva slips down his chin. He tries to overpower his captors, but it's no use. His eyes lock on Laura, as they share a moment of both clarity and terror.

Ashford's grin spreads, his gaze glowing with madness. "I'M GOING TO DO IT!"

Laura's muffled cries grow frantic.

Ashford yanks the handkerchief from her mouth. "Something you wish to say, missy?!"

Laura screams—a raw, guttural wail of horror. Ashford mock-screams with her, laughing in her face, their spit mixing midair like something unholy. Then suddenly he stops. He smiles like a wolf in Sunday clothes—all teeth and no soul.

He's had an idea.

A cruel one.

Ashford holsters his pistol and steps back. Laura's screams taper off into exhausted sobs, her eyes remain locked on Donald's, unspoken terror passing between them.

Ashford steps off the porch, then turns to face the restrained couple.

"Well... if you won't talk, I guess I'll just have to open your mouths for ya." Without breaking his gaze from them, he tilts his head toward his deputy. "We still got those railroad spikes lyin' around?"

"Yes, I believe so, sir."

"Good. Fetch me two."

"Yes, sir."

Ashford pauses. His presence dark, evil.

"And, Deputy?"

"Yes, sir?"

"Bring hammers, too."

Chapter Twenty-Eight
Mary Beth Freeman—Part Two

I watch through the tab hole as the deputy comes running back from his *errand*. Panting, he extends two rusted railroad spikes and battered claw hammers to Sheriff Ashford.

Ashford doesn't touch them, doesn't even look at them. Instead, he lets out a sharp whistle and two of his men come running over like trained hounds being called by their master. They stand in front of Ashford, waiting for their next command.

"Each of you, take a spike," Ashford orders calmly. Too calmly. "Stand in front of one of the sympathizers."

"Yes, sir."

The henchmen snatch the spikes and eagerly skip up the storefront steps, stopping just inches from the captive couple. The O'Briens' eyes remain locked, desperately clinging onto each other's fortitude—until the men block their view, lifting up the spikes like fresh kill. Sinister grins wash across the henchmen's faces as they graze the rusted spike tips across their victims' cheeks. Teasing them of the pain to come. Laura trembles, chest heaving, her breath shallow and fast. She squeezes her eyes shut.

Donald cries out, voice cracking, "It's okay, Laura—I'll get us out of this—"

"Now, Don…" Ashford's calm drawl slices through the heavy air, "don't go makin' promises you can't keep."

He steps forward, slow and deliberate. Each footstep landing heavy on the porch, the wood creaking beneath his boots. His spurs jangling behind him like the hiss of a rattlesnake.

My stomach turns. I don't know what he's planning, but it can't be good.

Ashford approaches Laura and gently brushes her curly red bangs behind her ear, his gaze trailing over her with a sick, lustful gleam. Laura keeps her eyes clenched shut, too terrified to see the look on his face.

Ashford suddenly grips a fistful of her hair and yanks it back hard. Her head jerks up, slamming against the wooden pillar with a crack. Laura screams, tears spilling down her cheeks.

"Don, help me!"

Donald roars like a trapped animal, veins bulging from his neck as he strains against his captors. He lunges forward a step, but more men rush in, pinning him back against the pillar.

Ashford throws his head back, laughing wildly, relishing the chaotic terror he is inflicting. Then, just as quickly, his laughter stops. He leans in close to Laura, eyes burning with madness, and speaks lowly, as he delivers a final warning.

"Don... God will not ask for your cooperation again."

Say something, Donald. Please. Save yourselves...

I want to look away—but I can't. My eyes are locked on the horror unfolding before me, my breath frozen in my chest. Every second stretches, like thick, dripping molasses onto my frayed nerves.

Donald exhales through his nose, sharp and angry, like a bull being dragged to its knees. But still, he says nothing. His gaze meets Laura's again. They stare into each other's eyes as if to communicate between souls. Then there is a shift in the air. The defiance fades as the fight drains from both of their faces. A heavy sadness washes over them, drenched in a deep aching grief. There's no panic now. No struggle. Just a devastating, shared understanding.

They've made a choice.

A choice to stand by what's right—even if it costs them everything. And somehow, that quiet bravery, cuts deeper than any blade ever could.

Ashford sees the change in their eyes, and with a gleam of false disappointment, releases his grasp on Laura's hair and steps off the porch to stand beside the deputy still clutching the hammers.

"Well, if you won't open your mouth for God," he drawls, "I guess I'll have to do it for you."

Ashford glances at his men, who are shaking in delighted anticipation. He motions to one, and the man walks over to the deputy, grabbing the hammers from his hands before running back up and handing them to the men with the spikes.

Ashford grins as he removes his cowboy hat and presses it to his chest with put-on heartache. "It is with great sadness," he says insincerely, "that I must deem you both guilty of breaking God's law and withholding information needed to complete His work."

He snaps his fingers and raises his hands. "Boys, raise them up."

The thugs laugh as several lift the O'Briens against the pillars. The couple doesn't resist. Their bodies limp like ragdolls as their feet dangle several inches off the ground.

Ashford begins pacing, his voice rising with false righteous rhythm. "Now, just as Jesus was nailed to the cross for our sins… so shall you be nailed to the cross for yours. Your blood shall be His blood, and may it purify your souls." He lifts his gaze to the heavens. "Ensuring your access to the pearly gates of our Lord. That's the least a Godly man like me can do for you."

He looks back down. The deputy stands idly by in horror, but says nothing.

"Boys, it's time." Ashford's eyes burn with deep-seated hatred as he stands at the base of the steps with a commanding presence.

"On the count of three."

The cruel men shout with excitement. Raising what fists they have free from tormenting the couple.

"One!"

The men shove the spikes into the O'Briens' mouths. Terror returns to the whites of their eyes, crawling back in as the full horror of what's about to happen settles in.

How many more people have to be sacrificed like lambs to the slaughter...for me?

I can feel the guilt pooling in my chest. If they die—if this happens because of me—I don't know how I'll live with it. I don't know if I *should.*

"Two!"

The men holding the spikes raise their claw hammers. Panic floods back into the couple as they choke on the rusted metal pressing against their throats.

No. I can't let them die!!!

I shoot to my feet, knocking the lid of the barrel off. It crashes to the floor with a bang, spinning in wild circles until it slams into a shelf.

I run through the open doors.

"STOP!" I scream, throwing my arms up as I stand between the couple, my breath ragged as my heart pounds against my compressed lungs.

Ashford's gleaming grin stretches wide, like a Cheshire Cat drunk on cruelty.

"There you are, little mouse."

He snaps his fingers, and one of his men lunges forward. Rough hands grab my arms, yanking them behind my back as rope coils tightly around my wrists. My shoulder blades pinch together, burning from the strain. They shove me down to my knees. Ashford gently presses his cowboy hat back onto his head and slowly walks up the steps, savoring the moment before he finally stops inches away from me. Towering over me with a smug satisfaction like a predator who has caught its prey. "Well, hello there."

Ashford's eyes crawl over me, lingering on the patches of exposed skin showing through the tears in my petticoat and stained camisole.

"*Jezebel.*"

"I'm no Jezebel!" I spit back through my gritted teeth. "You have me—now let them go!"

"Hmmm…"Ashford tilts his head, looking upward as if deep in thought, though the glint in his eye makes it clear—he's already made up his mind.

"I don't think so. You see, little mouse," Ashford smiles with cruel amusement, "they have already broken the law and most importantly, they have gone against God by hiding one of the devil's witches." He crosses his arms across his chest. "It is only right that I wash their sins away before they meet our Heavenly Father."

His men nod and mumble in agreement. Ashford squats slightly, holding both of his knees as he leans in, inches away from my face. His eyes are cold with an unworldly darkness. His spirit long dead, a sinister evil in its place. His rancid breath fills my nostrils when he gives the command.

"Three."

The men hammer the spikes into the O'Briens' mouths. Wet crunches dully thud into the pillar as the spikes are hammered through their gaped teeth. Through their throats. Their spines. Cracking and crunching in an unbearable rhythm to the swinging hammers. Blood gushes out of their mouths in sick, choking bursts, the strikes just slow enough for the couple to gasp for breath between each surge of blood, yet fast enough to drown out their screams beneath the pounding.

"NOOO!!!" I desperately scream.

But they don't stop.

They just keep hammering.

Again.

And again.

The spikes hit something vital, causing their bodies to seize violently then go limp against the storefront pillars. It's unbearable to watch this unholy torture. I look away. Ashford laughs manically.

"Keep going, boys, until the spikes are driven into the poles. I want them to hang there, as decorations!"

The men cheer as they continue to pound the spikes. The cracking fading into mushy thuds as the spikes are pounded further into the wooden pillars.

Tears pour down my cheeks like rainfall. My face tingles. A weight of guilt and shame presses into my chest. I struggle to breathe.

Mucus runs down into my gaping mouth. I can taste the rust mixed with blood filling the torchlit air. Ashford continues to laugh as the O'Brien's bodies slowly transition from convulsion.

To twitching.

To finally—

Dead weight.

Ashford stops laughing as he walks over to Donald, now hanging by the spike nailed through his mouth. Ashford inspects the spike dripping in Donald's blood. Ashford nods, like he is impressed with his own handywork.

"Irish. Always so stubborn." He coldly chuckles as he kicks Donald's dangling foot.

Deputy Dale slowly walks up the steps toward Sheriff Ashford with hesitation.

"Sheriff..."

Without turning toward him, Ashford rolls his eyes with annoyance.

"Yes, what is it now, Dale?"

Dale stutters, fearful of his boss's reaction. "I'm not sure this will go over well." Ashford whips around in irritation toward Dale.

"What won't go over well? Haven't you forgotten who is in charge in this here town?"

Dale fumbles with his hands, avoiding Ashford's condescending glare. "You are, and you have every right to rid our town of devil folk...but—"

"But what?!"

"Uhmm..."

"Spit it out!!!"

Dale flinches, his voice cracking. "The O'Briens...They're Irish, Sheriff. That's a white family, and well known, too. You leave 'em hanging on their own storefront—that's murder plain as day. And if word gets out? It might reach Washington and with Quincy Adams sittin' in office—they might send men. Soldiers. The town might be taken or worse. We might get arrested for—"

Suddenly, a small voice echoes from inside the store behind me.

"Mommy? ...Daddy?... Where are you?"

Oh, no. Elizabeth.

I turn to look at the O'Briens' daughter, Elizabeth. She's no more than eight years old, she wears a white linen nightgown, her curly red hair resting gently against her shoulders, plaited into twin braids tied with blue ribbon. Barefoot, she yawns while rubbing her green eyes. I try to warn her.

"Elizabeth, ru—"

The thug holding me grabs my mouth and stuffs a dirt-stained rag in it. I can taste the sweat and grease in the rough fabric—trapping the warning in my throat as she steps further into the nightmare.

Elizabeth stops rubbing her eyes. The blood drains from her face as she stares at the horrific sight of her parents hanging against the pillars.

"Mommy?! Daddy?!"

Tears flood her eyes as she runs toward her mother's hanging body—but Ashford catches her.

He grabs her by the shoulders, kneeling to meet her at eye level. With a twisted softness, he wipes away her falling tears as she sobs uncontrollably.

"Shhhh. There, there. It's all right," he coos, his voice gentle—too gentle.

Elizabeth sniffles, still shaking. "Why are they up there?"

Ashford pats her head like a stray mutt. "Well, you see… your parents broke God's law. And we had to punish them so they could have a chance at going to heaven." He tilts his head. "You *do* want your parents to go to heaven, don't you?"

Elizabeth wails. "No! I want my Mommy and Daddy!!!"

"Well," Ashford says, snapping his fingers toward one of his men, "I guess it's a good thing you'll see them real soon. Take her."

The man grabs the screaming child, binding her arms and legs. She thrashes and shrieks, but it's no use. They gag her with a sweat-stained rag and throw her rope-bound body over one of the thugs' shoulders.

Ashford rises slowly, brushing the blood-soaked dirt from his trousers. He casually makes his way down the steps, as if it's any ordinary day. When he reaches Dale, he pauses, pulls out a pipe, and motions for him to light it.

Dale hesitates, then fumbles for a nearby torch. Shaking, he lights Ashford's pipe. Ashford takes a few slow puffs, then exhales, blowing smoke directly into Dale's face before it drifts into the torchlit air.

"Word can't get out. Right?"

Deputy Dale's eyes grow wide as he gulps. "Yes, sir."

Ashford grins and looks back at us, bound and gagged.

"I know the perfect spot," he says while emptying his pipe, and then with a single stomp rubs the ash into the sandy dirt. He stares at me with an evil gleam. He snaps his fingers. His men freeze as they await his command. "Let's go."

Elizabeth and I scream through our gagged mouths. Just as we are being taken, Laura's eyes fly open—like some deep motherly instinct has pulled her back from the grave. Her muffled scream pierces the night as she sees her daughter being carried away. Laura lifts her arm, blood trickling down the back of her neck as she uses all her strength to reach for Elizabeth. One mother's last attempt at saving her daughter's life. Her hand grabs one of Elizabeth's braids, but she loses her grip as the man pulls Elizabeth away, leaving only a blue ribbon in Laura's hand.

Ashford gives a slow clap like he is applauding a performance.

"Wow, what a performance! Brava, Laura!" He walks up to her. Laura struggles to keep her eyes open, struggling with all her might to stay in this realm. With an open palm, Ashford pushes her forehead back against the pillar, the spike grinding against her spine. The life in Laura's eyes fades, and with one last crack of her neck snapping against the pillar—she's gone.

Elizabeth's muffled wails shriek through the night as the last of her mother's blood drops down her body.

Ashford walks over to the child, still bound and slung over one of his men's shoulders. Now at eye level, he gently brushes back her loose braid and offers a monstrous promise disguised as comfort.

"Shhh, it's okay, sweetheart. You'll see her again. Real soon."

My eyes burn, raw and dry, as I struggle to summon another tear. *If only they had listened... if only they'd run when they had the chance...*

Ashford glances over at me with the same look of contempt.

"Oh, and don't you worry either, my little mouse. You'll be seeing your loved one very soon."

He turns to his deputy, "Dale, blindfold them." An evil grin spreads across his lips. "I want our next destination to be a surprise."

Chapter Twenty-Nine

Mary Beth Freeman—Part Three

My legs are numb, my shins rubbed raw and bleeding from being dragged across the ground. Wherever they're taking me, it must be wooded—the earth beneath me shifts from dusty bricks to tangled roots as my stomach scrapes against blades of grass and sharp twigs stab at my thighs. Dry pollen bursts into the air with every bump in the terrain, spritzing my face like face powder. I'd sneeze if it weren't for the mucus clogging my nose and running down my lips, coating them in a sticky, phlegm-slicked salve. In between the men cackling, I hear Elizabeth's soft cries blending with the crackling torches, guiding us toward our doom.

Then—we stop. The stillness allows me to notice the many voices whispering.

Spurs rattle as they strike the earth. They grow louder as they approach, then halt in front of me. Ashford's sickeningly cheerful voice whispers in my ear.

"We're here, my little mouse."

The blindfold is ripped from my face. My blurry vision slowly gains clarity as I glance at my environment. The air is thick with torch smoke that stretches across the growing mob. Men, women, children—it seems the whole town is here.

Surrounding us.

Further out, a grassy hill looms over the crowd, crowned by a large oak tree resting at its peak. A breeze gently rustles the leaves as torchlight paints the night sky with flickering streaks of orange and red smoke. The place feels familiar. But why?

Then it hits me. This is the hill where John and I buried our daughter only a few hours ago.

Still on the ground, I see Ashford squatting next to me, he waves his hands theatrically and whispers in my ear.

"Surprise!"

I look away from him, fighting back tears, my heart breaking all over again from the loss of my beautiful baby girl. To mock us here—at her freshly dug grave—is beyond cruel.

Ashford's eyes gleam at my pain, his evil spirit splashing through the lake of sorrow my heart now drowns in. But then, his demeanor flips like a coin. A smile stretches across his face. He looks at me like I'm his meal ticket. He leans in closer, his sour breath warming my bruised ear.

"I could let you go, if…" Ashford's grin curls wider, his eyes flashing with lust as he continues to whisper, "you tell me where John stashes the gold."

I snap my head toward him so fast I fear I might've broken my neck. I mumble furiously through the rag stuffed in my mouth. With a sigh, Ashford rolls his eyes and rips it out. I immediately turn my head to spit the foul taste of sweat and phlegm onto the ground.

Turning back to him, I fire back. "What about Elizabeth?"

"Well, unfortunately," Ashford shrugs arrogantly, "she's seen too much. And to preserve this Godly town... well, some sacrifices must be made." Ashford shifts in front of me, so we're eye to eye. He speaks like the devil offering a deal.

"So, how 'bout it? Your life... for the gold?"

Rage ignites in my chest like wildfire. I spit hard at him, my saliva splattering across his face and dripping down his cheek. Ashford wipes it away, his nose wrinkling in disgust as he glares at me.

Then, without so much as a blink, he grabs my braided bun and yanks me to my feet as he rises. Pain shoots through my scalp as the roots of my hair stretch and burn, sending shockwaves down my bound arms. I'm barely on the tips of my toes, suspended by his grip. His stance is solid, entitled—holding me by my hair like I'm nothing, my feet barely brushing the earth. His voice roars like an angry lion.

"You bitch!" Fuming with rage, Ashford tosses me to the ground like a used-up whore. He yells to his men. "Take them to the tree so they may stand trial!"

The gathered townsfolk cheer as we are dragged past them.

"Wretch!"

"Jezebel!"

"Dusky whore!"

As we reach the top of the hill, I see the tree— and it's already prepared.

Two nooses hang from the dark oak branches. The thick ropes are dusty and frayed, as if they'd once been used for something other than hanging an innocent woman and child. Two medium-sized logs stand just beneath the nooses, one slightly taller than the other. I glance over at Elizabeth—her eyes barely open from the pain of being slung over someone's shoulder like a butchered hog. My pain sinks deep into my core. How evil must someone be to plan the death of an innocent child?

We reach the summit, and the men throw us at the base of the logs. The townsfolk surround us, staring, judging. Some older women in bonnets shake their heads in disappointment, while mothers, knowing a trial is about to start, try to hush their excited children. The fathers stand tall, watching, waiting for their sheriff to make his case.

Sheriff Ashford slowly, yet confidently, walks up the hill. The crowd parts as he strides through them and straight to us. I rest my head against the log, breathing heavily through my grunts as I struggle to position myself. Elizabeth doesn't move, but instead lies curled on the ground, softly crying out for her mother.

Her cries rip through my heart as memories crash over me like a river swelling its banks after a storm. I see myself holding my sweet baby Ada in my arms, singing lullabies passed down from generations— soft songs my mother once sang to me, and her mother before her—as I gently rock her to sleep in the creaky chair John built with his calloused hands and tender heart.

*Oh, John, I wish you were here! I miss you
already. I miss you so deeply it aches. Why did you have
to be so brave in my darkest hour? We could've run
away together—left all of this behind. But, no. You
cared. You loved these people. You sacrificed yourself for
them. For me. And now you're gone. God, why must you
be such a good man? I hate you for it. I hate your
selfless, noble heart right now.*

I am drowning in this rage, this sorrow. Tears
form in the corner of my dry eyes. *Why, God?! Why
would You take my whole world from me in a single
day?! I loved my precious Ada. And You took her. And
now You've taken him, too.*

My chest aches. My body trembles. I can't
contain the anguish any longer. I let out a long, blood-
curdling scream—a sound torn from the deepest pit of
my soul. A scream drenched in grief. The scream of
someone whose heart has been shredded by a thousand
unseen blades. The scream of a mother who has lost
everything.

The mob falls silent as they watch me unravel.
Their smiles fading into something almost like shame.
Like recognition. It's as though for the first time, they
are truly seeing me for what I am.

Human.

Ashford notices the shift immediately. He steps
forward quickly, raising his hands high, his voice
booming with deceitful charm.

"Brothers and Sisters!" Ashford declares
charismatically. "The accused stand before you today,
drenched in a sin only God can forgive." Ashford pauses,

271

drawing out the suspense long enough for the townsfolk to lean in.

"Murder!"

A collective gasp ripples through those assembled. They murmur to each other in disbelief and whisper loudly amongst themselves. From somewhere in the back, a man yells out with a high-pitched squeak.

"Is it the little girl?"

Ashford slaps his forehead. He mockingly mimics back. *"Is it the little girl? No! It is not the little girl, you idiot!"* Ashford points at me. "It's Mary Beth!"

Gasps again—louder this time, like the townsfolk have never heard of me in their lives. I nearly laugh through the pain. Ashford's lies are so overdone, I'm amazed his tongue doesn't tie itself in a knot.

He paces before the crowd, his overcoat flapping like a magician's cape.

"Three-month-old Ada Marie—bless her innocent soul—dead before her time. And on that *very same day*, our good and noble leader John vanishes, without a trace. You think that's a coincidence?"

Without warning, he spins on his heel and charges back toward me. His hand grips around the back of my neck and he yanks me upright like a weightless ragdoll. My toes scrape against the dirt. I feel the heat of the mob on my skin as they enjoy the show of my torment.

"She was there," he shouts, "at both places! No one else. Only her. And there is one witness who saw it all." He lifts his free hand to the sky, eyes glinting with false rapture. "God. Almighty God. And He spoke to me—His faithful servant." He twists my neck, forcing me to face him, his voice venomous. "God told me the truth," he says with unholy grief. "Mary Beth was a jealous little whore who couldn't stomach the thought of raising a child not born of righteousness. So she smothered the babe. And after the funeral, when John discovered what she'd done, Mary Beth slit his throat and stole his gold."

Then he turns dramatically to the crowd again, as if overcome with secular sorrow, and places the back of his hand against his forehead as if he is going to faint.

"She butchered them both, my friends. Mother. Murderer. Temptress of Satan."

I yell out through the pain. "Liar!" But it's no use. The townsfolk have already exploded into shouts of angry protests and hate.

"Murderer!"

"Witch!"

"Hellspawn!"

Ashford stares into my eyes, savoring this moment. Without looking away, he gestures to the crowd by outstretching his hand. The mob quiets down, reluctantly obeying the silent command and waiting impatiently for him to speak. Ashford addresses to the masses.

"Now, now, let's not forget that it is only God who may condemn the unrighteous. So let us send her to Him, that He may judge her at the holy gates." He looks away with a false sense of sorrow, like he's putting down a wounded dog. "Put her on the block."

I scream as they yank me, my heels scraping against the dirt. "No! You greedy, lying bastard!" But my cries are swallowed by the roaring cheers of the mob.

Two of Ashford's men slam me on top of the log, then roughly fit the noose around my neck. My bound hands and feet make it nearly impossible to balance on the unsteady wood beneath me. I wobble, breath catching, then scream at the top of my lungs.

"What about the O'Briens?!!!"

This time, the crowd hears me. Their cheers falter into low murmurs, now curious of what I have to say. I continue, my eyes like daggers as I glare at Ashford.

"You murdered them in cold blood! And now you're about to murder an innocent child because she saw too much!" I'm shaking, furious, spit flying from my mouth as I shout. "You, Wyatt, are a devil in sheep's clothing!"

The townsfolk turn their gaze to Ashford, awaiting his response. Slowly, he removes his cowboy hat, as if in mourning.

"It's true," he says solemnly, "the O'Briens are no longer with us."

A wave of whispers ripples through the crowd.

Ashford chokes on his false sorrow, "The O'Briens had lost their way. They had fallen in with the devil. I *tried* to save them, but they would not heed God's commands. To cleanse their souls, I was *forced* to nail them to the beams—just as Jesus was nailed to the cross—so their sins could be washed away by blood. Christ's blood."

Some in the crowd nod. Others shift uncomfortably. Sharp little frays from the noose stab me under my chin as my jaw drops, I'm struck dumb at how the townsfolk are reacting. How can they believe this?

No—*they want* to believe. It spares them the guilt of what they're about to do.

Ashford strolls over to Elizabeth, who still lies curled on the ground. He kneels beside her and gently lifts her into his arms, cradling her like a grieving father.

"This child of God saw her parents pay for their sins," he says softly, stroking her hair with false tenderness. "And that, in itself, is no sin." He pauses— just long enough for the silence to settle.

"But sometimes...obedience to God requires sacrifice. You all remember your Bible. When the Lord asked Abraham to put the knife to his own son—did Abraham flinch? No. He raised that blade, because faith demands action, not comfort."

"And I say to you now—this is no different." Ashford slowly rises with the girl still in his arms, facing the crowd.

"The world won't care that her folks were sinners. They won't care that we were defending God's order. All they'll see is a graveyard...and a child left alive to speak it. And when word spreads, they'll come with questions. Then shackles. And when they come, they'll take everything—your homes, your names, your children. Everything we built will be burned to ash." He gazes down at the girl in his arms, as if he is grieving. "But if we do this—if we finish what the Lord has laid before us—then maybe, just maybe, He will spare this town. Like He spared Abraham. Letting this child live would be the sin. Turning our backs now would be disobedience."

He looks back up at the crowd, "So I ask you—not as your sheriff, but as a man of faith…who among you will help me carry out the Lord's will?"

The whispers swell into blasphemous cheers. I scream over them, my voice ragged with desperation.

"Please, don't do this! She's just a child!"

But it's no use. They've already chosen. Their comfort, their delusions, their way of life—it all outweighs the life of an innocent girl.

Ashford's face glows like a demented jack-o'-lantern in the torchlight, his jagged, stained teeth catching the firelight like broken glass.

Elizabeth regains awareness as she's placed on the log beside me, her eyes going wide with terror. She struggles to keep her balance, the noose yanking and tightening at her throat every time she falters.

She coughs hoarsely through her sobs, her small body trembling. She turns to me, her big green eyes pleading and desperate for comfort, for a miracle, for something *human* in this Godforsaken crowd.

"Mary Beth," she whispers just loud enough for me to hear, choking between sobs, "I'm scared."

The pain I feel for this child is worse than any wound inflicted on me. It hits my spirit like a bull charging headfirst into my chest, its horns harpooning through my heart. Right now, I wish it were only me up here. This child hasn't lived long enough to deserve this. I force a smile, trying to offer comfort where none exists, choking back the lump in my throat, I whisper loud enough for her to hear.

"I know, honey. I am, too."

Then, out of motherly instinct—or maybe desperation—I begin to sing. The same melody my mother once sang to me, but with words now meant only for Elizabeth.

Close your eyes, still your heart,
Drift where sorrow can't depart.
The warm sun kisses you, my dear,
No more pain, no more fear,

The mob's roar softens. The crowd turns toward me, their expressions easing with awe. Even Ashford's laughter fades as he notices the shift—the way my voice weaves through the flames and noise like a spirit in the wind.

Run through fields of wildflowers bright,
Bathed in gold and morning light.
Their colors dance, so soft, so true,
A world of peace waits there for you.

Their anger drains into silence. A few townsfolk lower their heads. Some wipe their eyes. Others openly weep. The fury Ashford once fueled is now dissolving into sorrow, and he sees it. His grip on the crowd—on his fantasy—is slipping with every note.

Run, my love, don't be afraid,
Where your parents' love was laid.
Their arms are open, skies are blue,
They wait in the flowers just—

Ashford snarls and snatches a torch from one of his men.

"Silence, you witch!" he screams, overtaken by madness.

With a violent swing, he hurls the torch toward us. It lands between the two logs with a dull thud—then *erupts*.

The brittle grass explodes into flames. Fire licks upward, ravenous, and smoke coils thick and fast into the air. It stings my eyes, scorches my throat, and fills my lungs with heat and ash. Breathing feels like swallowing a pincushion, each inhale slicing down my esophagus with a hundred tiny cuts.

I turn to Elizabeth. She's coughing violently, eyes red and watering, her small frame trembling as she chokes on the noose. She's feeling it, too.

The air thickens with smoke. It coils around our heads like a serpent. I'm losing oxygen. My vision blurs, and the world starts to spin. I sway on the log.

It wobbles.

The noose jerks tight as I fall forward, catching me mid-collapse. The rope grinds into my throat, the rope burn ripping at my skin as I gag. The rope digs deeper, stealing my air. The flames are higher now, devouring the grass and licking at the edges of the dry logs beneath us. The wood *crackles*— the flames gnawing at the logs. The fire is no longer a threat—it is upon us.

The townsfolk watch in silence as our feet catch on fire, burning my already abraded feet, the layers of my skin peeling away with each burst of flame. Thrusting my body back, I rebalance my bound feet on the log as I let out a blood-curdling scream—but only a breath before Elizabeth's choking, raspy shriek pierces my ear.

I look over. Elizabeth's frail body hangs over the edge of the log, suspended above the flames by her noose. The fire, just inches from her face, flickers against her cheek.

Her noose catches fire. The flames burn up onto her face. Her hair catches, the fire racing up her head like a snake, eating away at her scalp.

Then her forehead.

Then her eyes.

Her whole face is on fire—until the only thing left visible is her mouth, open but no scream can escape.

Choking.

Gasping.

Swallowed whole in the flames.

The mob looks on in horror at the sight in front of them. And Ashford—Ashford smiles sharply, laughing as he watches Elizabeth's face being eaten by unholy flames until finally, her raspy chokes stop. Her body, having hung to life as long as it could, finally succumbs to the flames' deadly grip.

I cry, both in painful agony and sorrow. Ashford stands there, enjoying Elizabeth's death like he was watching the derby. My anger boils under the fire's heat. With my last breath, I curse Ashford.

"You can't kill the truth, Ashford. It will rise, and your sons and their sons will wear your shame like chains!"

Ashford looks at me like he's seeing a ghost. My words striking fear into him. For a moment, his mask slips. Then, desperate to regain control, he sneers and grabs another torch. He storms up to me, eyes blazing in righteous fury.

"Die already, you witch!" he hisses through gritted teeth, and presses the torch into my stomach—like someone snuffing out a flame.

I scream.

Agony tears through me as the flames curl back the layers of my belly, still thin and tender from bringing Ada into the world. Ashford pushes the torch into me. Layer by layer, my skin burns away—until I can't feel it anymore. The fire smells different now. The air tastes metallic, like blood and iron and smoke.

I glance down.

My innards are spilling down my pelvis, my thighs, my shins, then slipping off my bone-exposed feet and steaming in the flames.

The world tilts. Spins. The air thins. My lungs collapse in on themselves, drowning in ash. My eyes flutter. The pain is too much. I struggle to stay conscious as the world around me fades into darkness. My mind desperately clings to any light that is left.

But it keeps getting darker.

And darker.

Like a dream, my life flashes before my eyes. Sipping my mother's famous potato stew in the kitchen, never realizing we were starving. My mother teaching me how to sew dresses for our ragdolls, pricking my finger for the first time and her gently giving it a kiss to make it better.

Running barefoot through fields of grass while she watches from a distance, a tear rolling down her cheek as she sees her child happy in such a cruel, unforgiving world. I never understood those tears—until now.

The first time I met John. His contagious laugh warming my cold heart, letting me love again. The two of us dancing through the manor's halls, swaying in each other's arms, forgetting the evil that waited just beyond the doors. Me twirling, falling into his gentle embrace. A love like no other.

My child's birth, the moment when I touched her for the very first time. Her soft eyes giving me a hope I thought had long since died. Her coos, gentle and loving—no fear, no pain—just her joy in being with her mother and father.

A tear slips down my blinded eyes as I smile one last time.

I'm coming, baby girl.

Chapter Thirty
Hidden Secrets

The world spins violently, every color of the spectrum swirling around me as I'm ripped back into the present. A single breath later, I'm no longer in Mary Beth's past—I'm back in my own body. I'm standing on the hill, Mary Beth's hand still in mine.

Seeing the world through her eyes was like being dragged through hell. The pain—raw, unrelenting. The agony tears through me like fire in my veins. My chest heaves as the torment consumes me. I feel it all. Her grief, her fear, her hopelessness.

Tears flood my eyes before I even realize I'm crying. I yank my hand from hers and collapse to the ground, sobbing uncontrollably. My body trembles beneath the weight of what she carries—what she still carries.

To lose a child, only to be mocked, hunted, and destroyed…It's more than cruelty. It's evil in its purest form.

And I feel every second of it.

I look up at Mary Beth, my vision blurred by tears. I choke on a sob. "I'm so sorry, Mary Beth…" I cry uncontrollably, the weight of her suffering crushing me.

She gazes down at me with a hollow compassion—like someone too used to pain to feel it anymore. I wipe my face, trying to steady my breathing. Her hand rests gently on my shoulder. There's kindness in the touch, but it only makes my heart ache more. I force a trembling smile and let out a weak laugh.

"Why am I the one crying? You're the one who suffered..."

Mary Beth gives a faint smile, then quietly releases my shoulder. She walks to the old stump at the edge of the hill and looks out across the golden fields below, the sun sinking behind the trees.

Then it hits me.

"Wait... why did you show me your past?" I whisper, still collapsed on the ground, trying to make sense of it all. I sit up, trying to catch my breath. Trying to focus.

How does her death connect to Emmie's disappearance?

Mary Beth.

Sheriff Ashford.

The O'Briens.

Elizabeth.

My mind flashes back to when Mr. Gilbert showed me those dusty old newspapers. At the time, I didn't think much of it. First, the article said O'Briens were missing, then the next day the article said they moved and the store was to be taken over by the Ashfords.

But the O'Briens were never missing. They didn't move. They were silenced. Murdered for their values. And almost immediately, the Ashfords took over their store... and eventually, the town.

Wyatt Ashford built his empire on stolen ground.

And if that truth had ever come out—if the government had known he murdered an Irish family in cold blood, if they knew he burned a free woman and a child alive—everything would've collapsed. The land. The wealth. All of it seized.

He would've been arrested—for the murder of an Irish family and their child, for arson, for the crimes buried beneath the soil he claimed as his own.

Even now, if it can be proven that the land was wrongfully taken, the family could be sued for restitution and damages. The store, heck, the town itself could be stripped away, returned to the descendants of those it was stolen from.

But then, why? Why not report the missing children? Why let them vanish without even a glimmer of hope that they will be reunited with their loved ones?

A chill crawls down my spine as my blood freezes at the horrifying realization. The answer hits me like the Titanic crashing into the iceberg.

Because even if one case was reported, with just a few phone calls, investigators would eventually figure out that this isn't the only missing child case to emerge from the Burrow Estate. And moreover, every family who has lived in the estate had a child go missing, and none of it reported. It would trigger a pattern case review, and they would undercover the truth.

I grip my cargo pants, squeezing them so hard my fingers turn white as I am filled with anger. Tears stream freely now, but they're hot with rage.

"Oh my god..." I whisper. "They buried it. They buried *everything*."

All the missing children. All the broken families. Every case file collecting dust...It was never just negligence.

It was protection. Preservation of evil.

The town chose silence, ripping out the pages in their journals to bury the evidence of their sins. They chose compliance. Not knowing they were letting something feed off the lives of innocent children. And because of their silence, the cycle continues.

The townsfolk just watch, numb to it all as their morals have long since rotted with their ancestors. Their souls hardened by years of silence and complicity. They know another child will vanish from Burrow Estate because it has happened to every family that has moved in. And still, they do nothing but whisper among themselves on the streets while new families frantically search for their missing children. Desperate parents place their trust in law enforcement, believing they'll bring their child home. But the cases are quietly pushed aside—left to collect dust at the bottom of a filing cabinet, forgotten. No one says a word. Because if they did, the truth would come out. And they could never sell the Burrow Estate. Who would buy a home tied to unsolved cases of missing children?

So the cycle repeats. Again and again.

Now, that missing child is my daughter. I leap to
my feet, screaming—rage, sorrow, agony pouring from
my lungs.

"Fucking cowards!"

I kick at the dirt, not caring that soil shoves
under my toenails and into the seams of my torn sandals.
My chest heaves, my body trembling, my eyes burning
with unholy fury. Fury at their silence. Fury at their rot.
Fury at myself.

I look up at the sky, emotions scattered in the
wind as I try to grasp even one to hold onto. Mary Beth's
torment still burns in my lungs, my rage spreading
wildfire through my veins, and hope for my daughter is
flickering, like a candle about to go out. I walk over to
the stump and haphazardly drop onto it, my elbows
digging into my knees as I grasp my scalp and cry.

My tears dripping from my eyes like a leaky
faucet, each falling to the earth. As they do, something
catches my eye. Looking down, my tears land on the
edge of Ada's grave. My mind pauses, a buzz rings in
my ear for a moment, my mind trying to recalibrate
itself. Until a realization, no, a question forms in my
mind.

How did Ada die?

I flash back to Mary Beth's memory. The fear in
her eyes as she was waiting for John to come back from
the mines. And Alexandria—she said she would hide his
journal. His rope. But…*How did John access the mine
from the estate?*

I lift my gaze to Mary Beth, who still stands
staring into the sinking sun.

"How did Ada die?" I ask quietly.

She doesn't move, doesn't flinch, but the air around her tightens.

I've struck a nerve.

I rise slowly to my feet, "Did something kill her?" I ask. "Is *that* what's taking these children?"

Mary Beth's face tightens with anger. No, with *guilt*. I step closer. "Is it in the mines?" I press. "Is that what John was doing? Was he trying to stop it?" Her eyes narrow, warning me to stop while I'm ahead.

"Mary Beth—" I reach for her shoulder. She jerks away from me and begins storming down the hill. "Wait!" I call out, the desperation cracking my voice. "My daughter is missing! I think it took her!"

Mary Beth halts. But she doesn't turn.

I approach slowly, cautious not to spook her.

"I'm sorry for what happened to your daughter," My voice trembling. "It's tragic. It's a pain that—*even after reliving your final day*—I still can't fully comprehend."

I'm standing just behind her now. She hasn't moved. Tears start to roll down my face. My voice choking on my words.

"But please, Mary Beth… don't make me live through that same pain."

There is silence. The wind is breathing through our hair as time stands unmoving. It's painful to break the stillness.

"Please," I plead, "help me save my daughter." Mary Beth's shoulders soften as she slowly turns toward me, her face bathed in the golden shimmer of the setting sun. Tears stream down her cheeks. Her lips do not move.

But her body does.

Without a word, Mary Beth lifts her left hand to the sky, her fingers curling around something unseen—gripping an invisible object—as the delicate lace of her sleeve falls back from her wrist and drapes over her shoulder. Her eyes lower toward her other hand, open and gently elevated, as if something is resting in her empty palm. She stares at it with solemn reverence, as though waiting for me to understand.

It's familiar.

Her pose hits me like déjà vu, like something I've seen in a dream but forgot until now. She's trying to tell me something.

But *what?*

I pace in front of her, heart racing, smacking my open palm against my forehead like I can force the answer loose.

"Think, Sarah… *think!* Where have you seen this before?"

And then—it hits me. My eyes widen, catching the warm orange rays of the setting sun. My jaw drops. I stop pacing. I turn to her, breath catching in my throat.

"The skylight in the great room…" I gasp, lifting my hands in stunned realization. "Is that it? Can I find her through the stained-glass skylight?!"

Mary Beth doesn't move. But she smiles.

It's all the answer I need.

I throw my arms around her posed form, hugging her tightly, the relief flooding my body in an overwhelming rush.

I look out to the horizon—the sun is nearly gone.

"Oh no," I murmur. "It's almost night. I don't have much time."

Stepping backwards, I turn and break into a sprint down the hill, legs flying beneath me like Hermes. Dirt kicking up behind my heels as the shadows grow long across the grass with the setting sun.

Halfway down, I skid to a stop and spin around.

Mary Beth is gone. Only the stump remains as the sun sets behind it.

I smile.

"Thank you, Mary Beth," I say softly to the empty hill.

I turn around and run through the path.

Toward the stained-glass skylight.

Toward my daughter.

Just hold on, Emmie. I'm coming.

Chapter Thirty-One
Stained-Glass Skylight

Swinging the front doors open, I rush into the great room. I come to an abrupt stop in the center, my heart racing, competing with time. Standing in the middle of the room, I look up at the stained-glass skylight, glowing in the moonlight.

The beautiful woman is dressed in reds and purples, her empire-waisted gown draping over her feet. The delicate adornments and jewels shimmer in the early moonlight, throwing glittering rubies and amethysts over the dark hardwood floors. The colors dance around me, the artwork a masterpiece of its time. I squint, studying every inch. There's a reason Mary Beth wanted me to look here. She was trying to show me something.

What are you hiding... I scan the glass feverishly. Memorizing every fold of the dress, every delicate border, every gem. Then my eyes stop at her open hand and the spider nestled in her palm. I instinctively hold my breath in my throat as my stomach twists in knots. It lies delicately on the woman's frail fingers, its long legs outlined by melted silver metal. It's oddly elegant, yet for some reason, it feels out of place.

And then Mr. Gilbert's voice echoes in my mind, as clear as if he's standing behind me:

"Peculiar. That's the only part of the glass not stained. Makes you wonder what John Burrow's intention was."

I whisper, " *Peculiar* ... you might be on to something, Mr. Gilbert."

I stare harder at the spider. The glass is clear. Not red. Not purple. Not stained at all. Just delicately shaped to give the spider's legs the illusion of crawling across her hand.

It gives me the creeps—of course, it had to be a spider. I hate spiders. I shake off my nerves and contemplate.

"Now…" I mutter to myself, "why did you make the spider clear, John?"

I take a slow step back.

Just then, a shard of crimson moonlight refracts through one of the red jewels in the skylight. A sharp beam stabs straight into my eyes.

"Ugh, that's *so* bright—" I wince. Then freeze. *Wait.*

I lower my gaze. The room around me glows in red and purple light, fractured and scattered across the floor like a kaleidoscope.

"Maybe it's not about where the color touches…." I mumble under my breath, scanning the floor. "Maybe it's where the color *isn't*. The truth, not in sunshine and rainbows, but in the spaces between."

My eyes dart across the floor, scanning the sea of glistening colors.

Then, I see it.

Within the hues of reds and purples, a small, yet perfect outline of a spider floating in the wave of shimmering colors on the floor. I gasp.

"There it is!" I rush over and drop to my knees. Knocking and pulling at the wooden floorboard. It won't budge. I slump backward, falling into a sitting position, the weight of disappointment sinking into my chest like a stone.

What did I miss?

I stare at the spider's shadow, blinking at it through blurred vision. Then—something shifts.

It moves.

Ever so slightly, crawling to the west.

Wait...

My mind races. "What if John only accessed the mines at a specific time at night? That would mean..."

I look up at the skylight, eyes tracing the angle of the moonlight, measuring what direction it would move. Using my finger, I follow the light down until I am pointing at Emelia's bed. It has to be one of the panels between here and the bed. I get on all fours and crawl slowly toward the bed, knocking each panel in my path.

THUD.

THUD.

THUD.

THUMP.

I freeze.

"Oh my god." I gasp. "I found it!"

Frantically, I dig my fingers into the edges of the panel, clawing at the seams. It begins to give way—but it's stuck, sealed tight from a century of being undisturbed. I shift into a squat, planting my feet like a sumo wrestler, and grip the panel with both hands.

"Come on..." I growl through clenched teeth, using every ounce of strength to pry it loose.

Then—

CRACK.

It snaps free.

The panel rips from its frame, and I go flying backward, landing flat on my ass with a dull thump.

Dust swirls up around me, but I'm already scrambling on my hands and knees forward, desperate to see what's inside.

Inching my face toward the opening in the floor, I brace for whatever is in there. Peering over the edge, dust still floats out from its captivity, bringing with it scent of old wood. The moonlight filters through the stained-glass skylight, shooting beams of rubies into the hole, revealing its contents.

Inside, tangled in cobwebs, rests a coiled rope— thick, weathered, and curled into a perfect bundle, and resting on top of it—a journal.

Its cover is burgundy leather, worn and curling at the edges, cracked from decades of handling and time. My heart pounds as I reach in carefully, brushing off centuries' worth of dust with my fingertips. I gently grab the journal, its yellowed pages tapping against my hands. I ease it open, eyes gliding down the first page, and jaw tightening as I read the heading.

This Journal Belongs to:
John Burrow.

A sharp gasp passes through my lips. My heartbeat pounds in my throat. I can't believe I actually found it. I start to flip through the pages, urgently skimming through the journal, searching for answers. Searching for a way to save my daughter.

Chapter Thirty-Two
John Burrow's Journal

April 22, 1823

By God, I just might have done it! Sixteen days of fruitless searching in this empty, unclaimed land, and finally, my pike and my foot broke through. When the townsfolk back in Charleston joked and whispered rumors of abandoned mines out west of the Appalachians, I felt God's voice, God's hand, telling me to go. Telling me if I were to seek out this land, he would guide me, and together we would build a free town in His image.

When the land underneath my pike gave way, and when I widened it and saw the great cavern below, I knew for certain He was with me.

April 23, 1823

I descended into God's earth today. I staked my rope at the surface, tied it about my waist, and then with a lantern in my hand and a prayer in my heart, I lowered myself into the pit.

Some thirty feet down, maybe more, my boots hit solid ground. There, stretching before me in the darkness was a tunnel clearly made from man. Timber reinforced walls and spent torches wedged into the dirt, all covered in cobwebs thick enough to drape a ghost parlor. I ventured into the tunnel's deep, descending darkness, trusting God's will over my panic as the walls seemed to close around me.

And then, the tunnel opened. A vast, great chamber, larger than any church and near twice as high, with a great stone pillar rising straight up through the center. Overturned mining carts, old gun powder barrels and rusted, forgotten tools lay scattered throughout; thick cobwebs covering nearly every surface.

It is certain—I have found the mines. Tomorrow, I return with my pike. The Lord led me here. If there's gold, He will guide my hand to it, and it shall be uncovered and used for His glory.

April 24, 1823

Oh, how the Lord tests me!

I went down into the mines, started about my work when I saw it—movement beyond the stones. I braced myself, certain it be snake or rat, but what came forth was like that of a folk tale.

A spider, but unlike any I've seen or heard tale of before. Huge, near the size of a rabbit, brown and slick with earth. At first glance, I thought it deformed, but then it moved, and I saw the beast not only has huge fangs upon its face, but along the top of its rear, in full length, lays another maw. As it turned, my lantern's light caught upon what it held underneath — gold!

Without thought, I reached forward, and the creature raised one of its front legs with a hiss. It did not flee, it did not attack, it just stood firm, each of its frightening eyes upon me, as if in question.

I stared at it when an idea came over me. What if it means to trade? A foolish idea, and probably my last, but what if this idea was Providence? What if this beast is of the Lord, like Jonah's whale? Sent to me to facilitate His work upon the land?

Lord, please guide me. Tomorrow, I return.

April 25, 1823

Today I traded a mouse for a spider's gold. My Lord, how you amaze me!

I caught a small mouse this morning, and once in the mines, its small cries called the great beast to again appear. I took the mouse from my bag and held it aloft, the spider unlaced its back maw, a gold nugget dropping free.

I released the mouse, the spider seized upon it instantly, crushing the poor squealing creature in its fangs, then it hurried down a tunnel hidden behind a fall of rocks. I felt a pull of pity for the mouse, but then I looked down to the gift the spider had left at my feet. A gold nugget the size of a coin.

Lord, truly, is this your will?

May 7, 1823

It has now been two weeks since the Lord led me to the mine. I have continued to trade with the great spider He has deemed fit to give me, for I know now, in truth, she is a gift from Him. She grows larger by the day, as does the gold she brings. I am astounded by her cleverness.

I believe, by God's grace and blessings, I have enough gold to secure the rightful deed to this land. To this bounty—a town grounded in God's law. A place where justice, morality, and equality for all may thrive in His name.

This week I travel to the county seat to remit payment for the deed and have the tract recorded in my name.

I shall leave a supply of rodents and vermin for my companion, lest she think I have forsaken her. I think I shall call her Arachne. It suits her.

June 4, 1823

Deed in hand, I have returned from the county seat. This land is now rightfully yours, Lord, and I shall build upon it the town you have called me to create.

June 5, 1823

It seems Arachne has fared my absence well; the pile of vermin I left for her was replaced by a mound of glistening nuggets. I smiled as I saw it, then reached down to retrieve the bounty when I saw her.

She came not from her tunnel, but she crawled to me down the cavern's wall. She was nearly atop me before I saw her form so perfectly blended to the wall.

She has grown larger still.

October 22, 1824

Met the most extraordinary woman at the market today. A beauty like no other, dark of skin with eyes the color of the sun itself, but it was her grace, her nobility which had me undone.

I must have been gawking at her because she turned to me—those eyes—and said, "Sir, I am not for sale. I am a freewoman, and I would that you keep your eyes to yourself."

I fumbled an apology and tried to offer her an apple. She refused but seemed to soften when I complimented her dress, which she said she made herself. I asked if she would consider helping me with the house—decorating, furnishing, things which are a woman's touch. She agreed. She said she's expensive. I'd say I'd gladly pay her worth.

Mary Beth Freeman.

I think I'm in trouble.

Mustn't forget a rabbit for Arachne.

December 24, 1824

I have confessed my love to Mary Beth Freeman. Her kiss left me undone.

February 14, 1825

By the Lord's bounty, how Aditville grows!

Shopkeepers, tradesmen, and farmers are opening businesses one after another. I forgo rent and they agree to abide by the laws the Lord has placed on my heart. This town will not have unfair treatment – neither for color nor creed. God does not tolerate such hatred and nor shall I. Not in this place, built in His name.

I have told Mary Beth about Arachne. Why did I hide this from her for so long? She wasn't frightened. Her spirit is fire, and I find myself drawn to it.

Mary Beth designed a window of stained-glass; it is mounted so when light passes through, it marks the floorboards of Arachne's hidden door.

The mines, the wealth, and most of all, Arachne, are all secrets that must remain hidden. They are too precious. Discovery of the wealth will no doubt lead to rebellion. But it is Arachne's safety I worry about most. Her size still grows. Townsfolk will see only a monster, a creature from the devil, not a gift from the Lord.

June 10, 1825

Oh, Lord, how you continue to bless me! Mary Beth is with child.

She is frightened about the townsfolk learning of our union. But I am not afraid. We shall bring in an accoucheuse of her choosing to attend to her here at the estate.

I will see to her and the child's every need. Whatever comfort or safety she requires, I will make it so. I still can scarcely believe it.

By God above—I am going to be a father!

November 17, 1825

Ada Marie Burrow Freeman.

She is perfect.

God's miracle.

March 4, 1826

The months since Ada came into this world have been the most joyful of my life. She is already crawling. Our girl is strong and spirited—so like her mother.

It fills me with unending pain that I cannot proclaim my love and my family from the mountaintops. God, you commanded me to create this town in your name, and yet still I cannot walk freely with my family without fear?

I pray God touches the hearts of this town and this country soon. My Ada deserves life and love without shame or fear. Mary Beth and I deserve to walk the streets of our home hand-in-hand.

It has been weeks since I have been down to the mines to tend to Arachne. Last I saw, she was the size of a wild hog. She must be hungry, I hope she knows I have not forgotten her. She is family, too. Tomorrow I shall go by the market and fetch something special for her.

March 24, 1826

My world feels as though it has collapsed into shadow—consumed by a darkness and despair I have never known.

Two weeks ago, I returned from the market to Mary Beth in a state of panic. I ran to her, and saw Ada's crib on its side, dirt scattered all over the floor, and the armoire I had built atop Arachne's hidden door standing open.

I could not believe what my mind began to tell me. It had been weeks since I fed Arachne, yes, but could she? Would she? The thought, nay the vision, of sweet Ada being pulled down into that tunnel, down into the dark, by the very creature who helped give us this life?

I rushed into the mines, I searched from end to end, my ears straining for the faintest sounds, hoping to hear Ada's cries. I saw movement along the far wall and there she was—Arachne.

I stepped forward, holding aloft the chicken I bought for her at market. Arachne did not move, save for her eyes following my every step. I laid the chicken on the ground and stepped back—my God, she was bigger than a wolf.

She crept forward, then opened the fanged maw inside her rear. Inside, my God, inside was Ada. Pale. Eyes closed.

I cried out, ran toward her in blind terror. Arachne reared up, her two front legs raised high as she hissed. In desperation, I pulled my musket and leveled it at her. I screamed, she took a step back, clicking.

For a moment, all was still. I prayed. Then, she reached with her two hind legs and placed Ada gently upon the ground. I kicked the chicken across the chamber with all my strength, then ran to my daughter.

Her tiny body was limp. Her white nursing gown soiled with dirt and something I—I dare not name. I placed my ear to her chest—a heartbeat. Faint, weak, but there.

I carried my miracle out of the mines and placed her into her mother's arms. The sound Mary Beth made when she saw Ada, I never knew a sound could shatter my soul.

I barricaded the trapdoor—chairs, dressers, statues, anything I could find to block the entrance. I will not risk Arachne returning. I no longer care who sees Mary Beth and I together. Let the town gossip. Let them hate. I'll face it all to save Ada.

We sent for a doctor. Oh, Lord, guide him here on eagles' wings. Lord, have mercy on Ada. Please, God, save my daughter.

March 28, 1826

I feel as though my soul is trapped in a nightmare—one from which there is no waking, only the endless stirring of darkness in my heart.

We haven't rested since I brought Ada up from the mines. Doctor Evans arrived from Knoxville a few days ago, he believes some manner of poison has taken hold in Ada, most likely through the now blackened wound upon her cheek. She has been unable to take any nourishment; Mary Beth's milk will not sustain her. She withers, growing frailer by the day.

Doctor Evans confided to me he has never seen the likes of this sickness before. He tells me to hope, yet his eyes hold none. "I fear her life is now in God's hands," he told me. He said to make peace and say our goodbyes.

Lord, do not take my angel from me. She has yet to know the sweetness of Your creation. She has yet to even say Your name. Lord, do not rob the world of her light. Take me instead. Please, Lord.

March 30, 1826

Ada passed in the quiet hours of the morning. She slipped away as I held her in my arms, her breath gone with a whisper. Mary Beth and I sat in shattered silence, clutching our world's brightest light, now extinguished.

We buried her beneath the great oak on the hill at the edge of town—the sky feels so close there. I asked the carpenter to make a casket before sundown, I couldn't bear the thought of keeping her another night. A good man and a father himself, he showed us great kindness, creating a casket for Ada within hours. He carved tiny flowers along the box's tiny sides. I am broken. He promised me he will etch her name into a silver plate and place it upon her grave.

The townsfolk came to the hill. No one asked questions. Some laid flowers. Some prayed. Alexandria let go of Mary Beth's hand to sing *Amazing Grace*, her voice calling those gathered to join.

Lord, I could not bear it. I knelt, took up the shovel, and dug as fast as I could, the hymn cutting my soul like blades. I buried my daughter with my own two hands. I screamed when it was done.

Mary Beth held me. The preacher and the townsfolk departed. The two of us stayed at our daughter's side until the sun left us as well.

The town knows. They know about Mary Beth. About Ada. About me. They may come. Let them. My body remains, but my soul is buried with Ada.

We returned to our empty house and I told Mary Beth what had to be done—Arachne must be destroyed before she harms another, whether killed or sealed away forever. Mary Beth held me.

I don't know if I shall return from the mines. These words may be my last. God, I devoted my life to Your purpose. I heard your voice. I went where You led me. I built a town in your name. In return, You take my only child. I curse You.

Mary Beth, if these pages reach your hands, know that loving you has been the greatest joy of my life. I would choose you again and again, in every lifetime. No law, no wrath, not even Heaven and its angels could stop me. If I do not return to you, forgive me. Forgive me for Ada's death, for I know my choices are to blame.

Forgive me for leaving you to carry this weight alone. I will always love you, Mary Beth, forever and always.

John Burrow

Chapter Thirty-Three
Louisville Slugger

John's journal trembles in my hands as a rush of conflicting emotions flood my already exhausted mind. His intentions were so pure, I could feel the depth of his love he had for Mary Beth and Ada in his writing. I felt his heartbreak at losing his daughter, the betrayal he felt by what he considered a family pet, and his commitment to the town as he went down to the mines to save their lives. It is tragic. Heartbreaking. But also terrifying.

Then it clicks.

When Mary Beth showed me her last day alive, there was an explosion, a rumble beneath her feet in the manor... it was John. He was in the mines, facing off with the monster that took his daughter's life. And when he couldn't kill it, he detonated the exits, trapping himself with the eight-legged beast, sacrificing himself for the town, only for the townsfolk to murder the love of his life. If only they knew what John did to save them! Though with their deep-rooted hatred, fueled by the fiend of a man Wyatt Ashford, I doubt the knowledge would have changed anything.

But now…I lift my head from the journal, my eyes fixed on the large armoire as a haunting chill fills the room with my realization.

Arachne survived—and has managed to break through at least one exit: the armoire. She must have associated this entry point with food, as John only ever used it to bring her meals from the estate.

Now she lurks within the mines, waiting patiently for something, *anything,* to move in. And when they do, she snatches her prey, dragging them down into the darkness to be devoured. And because none of the missing cases were investigated, her existence remains hidden in the shadows, allowing her to kill again and again.

Arachne is alive. And she is hungry. The Burrow Estate, her hunting grounds. And now—she has Emelia.

My heart pumps blood in chaotic waves, and my breathing struggles to keep up. A static rings in my ears as the room begins to spin. My mind unravels in layers like a psychedelic onion. Even now, I'm questioning if any of this is real, or if it's all just a bad trip.

Maybe the doctor was right—maybe the medication causes hallucinations. And now that I willingly took one, my mind is playing along in the charade. I mean… time travel? Death? I just so happened to find a journal over a century old? An ancient spider-like monster feeding on children— children who go missing but are never investigated?

It all sounds absurd.

Maybe I *am* going crazy… I mean, how could any of this possibly be true?

An overwhelming sense of clarity wraps around me like a heavy blanket. My eyes widen in determination as my face hardens. No—it *has* to be true. It's the only explanation that makes sense. Why I'm the only one seeing the ghosts. Why the town doesn't have many children. Why the underground map of the mines stops right beneath the Burrow Estate. Why the sheriff didn't want me going near the hill. Why Mr. Gilbert found all those unreported missing children cases. What took my daughter.

The answers are all here. And now, it's up to me to save my daughter from Arachne before it's too late. But damn, why does it have to be a spider?!

I squeeze my eyes shut, inhaling and exhaling deeply, trying to gather the courage to stand. I need to get ready. I *have* to go into the mines. I can't wait— Emelia needs me.

Just as I begin to rise, a mechanical voice cuts through the tension—"I love you!"

My heart skips a beat and I let out a startled squeal. The floorboard where I found the journal is at the edge of the bed—I must've triggered the Furby's motion sensor when I stood up.

I storm over to the toy, grabbing the furry purple robotic creature and lifting it to eye level as I storm out of the grand room.

"I *hate* you," I grunt as I hurl it onto the foyer floor before turning and marching up the spiral staircase to prepare for battle. Just before reaching the staircase, I glance at the counter. My purse sits there, and inside it— my cigarettes.

A cigarette while getting ready would really help calm the nerves...

Fuck it.

I jog over, grab the pack and lighter, flip it open, and snag one. Lighting it with a quick flick, I shove the lighter into my pocket and head back to the stairs, cigarette dangling from my lips.

Up in the master bedroom I switch on the lamp on my nightstand, then go straight for the large box labeled *Shoes*. I start digging through it, tossing out heels, sneakers, sandals, scattering them all across the floor like a bomb went off. Until finally, at the very bottom, I find them: green combat boots from that G.I. Jane costume I wore a few Halloweens ago. Kyle always calls me a packrat, but right now I'm thankful for my hoarding behavior.

Okay, now socks.

I toss the boots on the bed and rummage through a pile of laundry I've been meaning to put away for a couple of days. I find a bunch of long socks, but none of them match. Of course. Matching socks are never around when I actually need them.

I don't have time for this.

I grab a green one and a white one—same length, good enough. Sitting on the edge of the bed, I yank them on while scanning the room for my Louisville Slugger. I meant to look for it after Emelia had that nightmare... though, thinking back now, I'm not even sure it *was* a nightmare. A shiver runs through me as I tighten the laces on my boots. The thought that it might've actually been a monstrous spider in Emelia's room that night—I can't go there.

Not now.

I need to focus.

I need to get down there.

I need to save her.

I shove my feet into the combat boots, pulling the laces tight.

Now to find a flashlight.

I open my nightstand drawer and shift things around until I find a small, red flashlight.

"I guess this will have to do." I sigh as I shove the flashlight in one of my cargo pockets. Just then, a robotic voice pierces the still manor:

"Woah, woah!"

The Furby. Its motion sensor must've gone off again.

My heart drops.

I must've left the front doors open.

Someone's here.

I freeze, barely breathing. Then, metallic footsteps echo from the staircase. Each one lands heavy and deliberate, reverberating through the estate. Whatever is here is getting closer. I quickly put out my cigarette against the nightstand. I lock my eyes onto the top of the stairs as I scramble for something, anything, to defend myself.

My hand lands on a sandal.

Really? Out of all the shoes I own, I grab the flimsiest one? Not one of my spiked heels? Not even a tennis shoe?! Fuck.

The footsteps grow louder, closer.

THUD.

THUD.

THUD.

My heart is sprinting, thudding against my ribs. I raise the sandal high over my head, bracing myself.

Then—I see movement.

Without hesitation, I launch the sandal.

A familiar voice yelps.

"*Ow!* What was that for?!" Rubbing the side of his head, Kyle glares at me as he reaches the top of the staircase and wobbles into the room.

I release a breath I didn't realize I was holding. "Oh, thank god you're here, Kyle! Emmie is—"

"When Billy said you'd gone off the deep end, I thought he was exaggerating," Kyle interrupts with a mocking laugh as he surveys the chaos of the room, his words slightly slurring. "But this... this is better than I could've ever hoped."

His eyes gleam with something twisted. His smile spreads wide with an unsettling delight.

What?

Billy? Does he mean William Ashford?

And what does he mean, *everything he hoped for?* I sniff the air. Alcohol. More specifically, whiskey. Kyles go-to beverage.

I shake it off. *Focus. Emelia is still out there.*

"Kyle, Emelia is missing—"

He cuts me off again. "You know, I got the most wonderful news at the post office today."

He pulls a folded letter from the pocket of the same ripped jeans he wore the day he left. Unfolding it like it's some grand proclamation, he reads aloud.

"Dear Mrs. Gallo, we regret to inform you that your father has passed. His funeral is to take place in the

316

following weeks. We will contact you in the near future to discuss his belongings and his last will and testament."

Kyle's grin spreads unnaturally wide, almost feral. I've never seen this side of him before. It reminds me of Wyatt Ashford when Mary Beth was murdered.

I stare at him, confused and heartbroken. The news hits like a slow-moving storm, one I knew was coming, but still wasn't ready for.

Before I can get a word out, Kyle boasts, "Don't you see, Sarah? We're rich!" His eyes go cold. "Well... *I'm* rich."

I narrow my eyes at him, heat rising in my chest. "What do you mean *you're* rich? That's my father's inheritance." I growl, gripping the edge of the bedspread with white-knuckled fists.

Kyle shrugs and stuffs the letter back into his pocket like it's a used gum wrapper. He replies smugly. "You see babe, *you* get the inheritance... then you get committed to the loony bin... *then* I'm left in charge of it. Don't you get it? It's all very simple, Sarah!" He stumbles a bit, reaching out to steady himself on the dresser.

My mind begins to spin, puzzle pieces snapping violently into place.

Why he married me.

Why he was always so curious about my father's health.

Why he chose to work as a pharmaceutical rep.

Why he switched out my medication for hallucinogens.

He wanted me to unravel. To lose control. To be declared unstable. To be locked away.

So he could take *everything* my father left behind. It was never about love. Never about family. It was always about the money. What a sick bastard.

Hot fury now floods my chest. My jaw clenches so hard it aches.

"I *knew* you were up to something, you bastard," I snarl through gritted teeth. "But no one's going to believe you. I have a doctor's expert opinion that the medication *you* gave me was Nurotrexilm. You don't get to rewrite reality."

Kyle feigns a pout, then sneers.

"Oh Sarah, do you really think I'm that dumb? His expression shifts into something mocking, cold and calculated.

"You see, when I came down here to scout the place out to make sure it was the *perfect* little corner of nowhere for you to lose your damn mind—I met William. Sweet, charming, Sheriff William Ashford. And he is *more than happy* to testify to your supposed 'manic episodes' in exchange for a slice of the inheritance."

He laughs maniacally. "I didn't even have to *push* him. He basically begged for it!" He paces now, drunk on his own theatrics. "And then… Emelia goes missing. Under your watch." He pauses, tilts his head, and suddenly mocks a woman's voice in a cruel, high-pitched tone. "*Hi, I'm Sarah. I'm seeing things, and I can't handle taking care of my useless crippled daughter anymore!*"

My heart cracks, but the rage keeps it from breaking. Kyle laughs again, sharp and hollow, like a villain from a bad movie. Then, he stops. His face hardens.

"And Sheriff Ashford?" he says coldly. "He'll back up the story. That you couldn't take the pressures of motherhood anymore and you snapped. That you murdered your child. That it's all true." He leans against the dresser. "Medication or not, you'll rot in jail while I, the loving and supportive husband that I am, maintain control over the assets." He wipes away an invisible tear with mocking delicacy. "It really is... *quite beautiful.*"

My body quivers with pure, unfiltered rage. Even still, I manage an amused, defiant laugh.

"You forgot one thing" I say, a sharp smile curling on my lips, "not everyone is as selfish as you."

Kyle's brow twitches, confusion flickering across his face. I keep going.

"I had a feeling you were up to something... even before we moved. That's why," I rise to my feet, slow and deliberate, "I sent my father a letter. I asked him to name *Emelia* as the sole beneficiary of his estate. It's locked in her name, non-transferable, only accessible when she turns twenty-six."

I step right up to him, standing toe-to-toe.

"So if Emelia is missing—or as you so delicately put it, *murdered*—" I jab my finger into his chest. "*You* get nothing."

Kyle's eyes flash with fury. Red creeps up his neck to his face like a pot about to boil over. His body tightens. He slurs with smug venom.

"Well... then I guess I'll just have to keep her case open. Get power of attorney."

I glare at him and growl. "Over. My. Dead. Body."

Still staring down at me, Kyle reaches behind the dresser, his eyes never leaving mine, and pulls out the Louisville Slugger. His grin returns, twisted and full of hatred.

"That," he says coldly, "can be arranged."

With his free hand, he shoves me hard, then takes a wild swing with the bat, laughing hysterically as he sways with the motion.

I fling my body backward, spine folding in on itself. The bat misses me by inches.

He comes charging after me, each step fueled by drunken rage. The bat slices through the air with every swing barely missing my face. If he weren't drunk, I'd already be dead.

I scramble onto the bed.

He's right behind me. Laughing. High and shrill and dripping of pure evil.

"Oh, come on, Sarah! Why are you running?" he mocks between heavy grunts. "Don't you wanna have a little *fun*?!"

I can't even feel my heartbeat.

I'm barely breathing.

Panic has infected every nerve ending in my body. I leap off the bed and bolt for the staircase—

But he grabs me.

Fist tangled in my hair, he yanks me backward, slamming me against his chest. The bat presses hard against my throat. He drags me backward toward the upstairs railing.

I claw at the bat, desperate to loosen the pressure crushing my windpipe, the smooth, unforgiving wood digging into my neck. I gasp, choke, grunt—anything for air.

My vision begins to fade.

My head swells like it's filling with helium, ready to burst.

My heartbeat slows—almost as if it's given up, ready to let go of all the pain it's been carrying. I close my eyes.

Is this how it ends?

Kyle laughs in dark victory.

"You wanna hear another little secret?" he whispers, lips right against my ear. The stench of alcohol makes my nausea double. "I was the one who crashed the car last year."

My mind instantly flashes to a forgotten memory. Emelia's ballet recital. Kyle getting upset about Dan talking to me. Kyle screaming in the Mercedes. Kyle pressing the gas pedal. The car speeding up, faster and faster, until Kyle runs the red light… and my waking up in the hospital being told by doctors that *I* was driving the car.

He is the reason I lost my memories.

My license.

He is the reason Emelia is paraplegic.

And he allowed me—no, he *made* me—take his actions as my own. Blamed me for the crash and let me believe I was the reason for our daughter's suffering.

Fuck him.

No.

I can't go out like this!

My eyes flash open as I gasp, clinging desperately to life. My vision whizzing around the room—until I see it. The broken railing behind us.

With the last ounce of strength in my trembling body, I shove myself hard against Kyle, driving him backward.

The laughter stops. His eyes dart behind him, down toward the open floor below.

"What are you doing?!" He screams, panic in his voice. "If you push us over, we're both going to die!"

Good. I let out a guttural warrior's cry and slam into him one final time. Tripping over himself, Kyle stumbles, his back slamming into the railing.

The metal creaks.

Then—

SNAP.

The railing gives.

We topple backward into the void.

His scream echoes throughout the manor as we free-fall. For a moment, time slows. The stale air weaves through my hair, flying upward and tickling my cheeks. I close my eyes and smile. For the first time in a long while, I'm at peace.

Until the ride ends.

I feel Kyle's cracking body slam into mine as he hits the wood floor. But just as quickly, a loud, sharp crunch rings in my ear as I land on top of him.

CRACK.

Groaning from the aches radiating through my body, I glance over at Kyle's face. A wooden stake protrudes from Kyle's eye socket—his split eyeball pierced at the tip, its jelly-like fluid oozing down the wood and sliding down with pieces of brain matter onto the feet on the upside-down crucifix. I wrinkle my nose. The mix of brain matter and eyeball ooze seeping into the wood gives off a sickening aroma, a metallic hardwood with a sharp hint of pungency.

I roll off Kyle's body and slowly rise to my feet. For a moment, I just look down at him.

Fear still lives in his frozen eyes. A growing puddle of blood spreads beneath his head, soaking into the floorboards where the crucifix pierced through his skull.

But I don't feel anger. I don't feel sadness. I feel *nothing*.

I pick up the Louisville Slugger, now cracked at the base, and stagger with a slight limp toward the great room. Halfway there, I pause, glance back, and let out a sarcastic, light-hearted chuckle.

"Till death do us part, motherfucker."

Chapter Thirty-Four

The Mines

A bead of sweat trails down my temple as I drag the heavy rope toward the front door. I lean into it, using my bodyweight to push it until the door creaks shut with a thud. My eyes lock onto the ring on the back of the doorknocker. Memories flicker—John standing there the first time I saw him... then the day it started knocking on its own. I shake my head. I should've known something was off with that doorknocker. But it doesn't matter now. I need to get down to the mines—fast.

Hands shaking, I lift the end of the rope and try to loop it through the ring. It's like threading a needle—and coordination has never exactly been my strong suit.

After a few tries, I finally get it through the loop and frantically begin tying several knots. I don't know any fancy ones, I just hope whatever I'm doing holds out long enough for me to get down there. And back up. From what the journal said, it's a far drop to the bottom. And if the rope breaks before I can reach the bottom...

I swallow hard, shoving the thought into the timeout corner of my already overwhelmed mind. As I walk backward, unwinding and dragging the rope toward the great room, the Furby's motion sensor triggers again.

"Goodnight!"

"Ha-ha. Very funny," I grunt through labored breaths, as I hobble backward.

Every step sends a dull ache through my body, and my legs feel like they could give out at any second. Both my mind and soul are exhausted, hurting in more ways than one. The fall from the railing onto Kyle really did a number on me. My ribs throb, my head is foggy, and every movement takes effort. It's taking sheer willpower to keep going.

Finally, I reach the armoire. There's still plenty of rope left. I drop it to the ground with a heavy thud and place both hands on the armoire doors, pausing before opening them. I close my eyes for a moment, trying to still my pounding heart.

After a few deep breaths, I grip the handles and swing the doors open. My eyes scan the floor of the armoire—nothing seems out of the ordinary. I squat down, running my hand across the scratched wood.

Then—

I feel it.

Hidden within a knot in the wood, my finger finds an indented lip. I try to lift it, but it's stuck, like something's holding it down. I wedge my hand beneath the edge, pulling hard, breath held tight as heat pulses down to my burning fingertips.

I exhale sharply and pause, then try again—this time using all the strength I can muster. With a sudden crack, it lifts, slamming against the armoire's inner panels. Trails of thin, stringy brown residue sway from the trapdoor before falling and sticking to its underside, like webs of grotesque silly string. Cautiously, I peek over the edge—pure darkness. Cold. Unnerving.

Dead, frigid air rises up to meet my face, sending a chill rippling through my veins. I start to tremble. It's so dark, it feels like I'm staring into a black void—a sinister, endless hole into the unknown.

I slowly back away and sink to the ground, rocking myself gently. I'm terrified. Petrified. I've always been afraid of heights. Of spiders. Of the unknown. And now, I'm about to climb down into a deep hole, not knowing what's waiting for me at the bottom—all to save my daughter from a giant, alien-like spider monster.

"Come on, get yourself together. You have to. For Emmie," I whisper, my lips quivering as I reach for the rope. My hands still tremble as I chuck the rope down the hole. I pause and wait for the sound of it hitting the ground. I don't hear anything.

Great.

I tuck the bat between my belt and cargo pants like a makeshift holster and then wrap the rope around my calf and grip it tightly as I hobble backward toward the trapdoor. My heartbeat pulses in my throat, and my face is clammy with sweat.

My heels touch the edge—the dark abyss yawning below.

I haven't climbed a rope since junior high. God, I really hope I can do this.

With my free hand, I pull out the small flashlight. I flick it on and wedge it between my teeth. I take a deep breath in. And as I exhale, I begin my descent into the hole.

The darkness is overwhelming—claustrophobic, even. The dim moonlight fades the farther down I go, making it feel like I'm being swallowed whole.

My arms are burning. My hands feel like they're on fire, the rough rope scraping my skin raw as I cling to it with everything I have. Foot over foot, I descend, intermittently pressing the wrapped rope against the tops of my boots, the pressure driving the laces deep into my ankles.

The beams from my flashlight reveal a glimpse of the horror to come. The walls around me are coated in layers of brown webs—years of Arachne's passage, weaving her path to steal sleeping children.

Every time I falter and brush the sides of the hole, the sticky strands cling to me. They stretch and hum with tension, vibrating eerily with each release as I sway in the center of this endless black abyss.

Drool drips down my chin from holding the flashlight in my mouth, and my jaw aches from the constant pressure of keeping it in place. It feels like I've been climbing down forever—and my body agrees. Every muscle is trembling, every joint burning with the weight of the descent. When am I going to reach the bottom?

Then, I feel the rope loosening.

Oh no, the knots must be unraveling.

I scramble to climb down quicker, but it's far too late.

SNAP.

The rope falls down into the hole—myself with it. The fall is surprisingly quick; I must've only had about five feet left. But when I hit the ground, I land on something sharp, I feel it under my cargo pocket, jabbing into my thigh.

I wince, trying not to make a sound. I don't know how far into the mines Emmie is—or Arachne.

I pull the flashlight out of my mouth, my jaw feeling instant relief. I flash the light down to see what I landed on—it's an old, broken bone. Possibly a femur. I dig into the cargo pocket that took the hit. It stabbed my cell phone. I try to turn it on, but it's no use—the bone pierced straight through the keypad.

I sigh. Not like I could've called 911 anyway. Sheriff Ashford would've been the one to respond to the call, and with an upside-down crucifix lodged in Kyle's skull... yeah, that wouldn't exactly go over well for me.

At least I didn't land on the bat. I glance over at the Louisville Slugger lying a foot away. Groaning, I stretch out and grab it. Using it for support, I push myself up to my feet. With one hand, I rest the bat on my shoulder in a ready stance, with the other, I raise the flashlight in front of me.

The tunnel walls are caked in brown webs, cross-weaving in all directions, draping the passage like curtains made of cobwebs. The weaves blend in with the dirt tunnel walls and floors, almost camouflaged—if not for the glint of dead bugs, carcasses, and yellow-stained bone fragments catching in the beam of my flashlight, I might not have seen them at all. The air in the tunnel is musty, a scent similar to that of damp earth mixed sun-dried roadkill. My boots stick slightly with each step, the webs clinging to the soles like partially dried tacky glue. If it weren't for the thick layer of dust on the ground, I might've been trapped.

Using the bat, I gently push aside the webbed curtains as I inch forward through the tunnel. The deeper I go, the more remnants I see of the abandoned mine. Old torches wedged into the web-caked walls, and barrel fragments scattered along the tunnel floor, growing more frequent with every step—but so do the rocks.

I start to feel the rocks pressing through the soles of my costume combat boots, each step rougher than the last. The stones grow larger until I reach a rockfall barricade—boulders and jagged rubble crammed against every side of the tunnel.

Except at the top.

There, a wide opening gapes just beneath the ceiling, with rocks pushed outward from it, forming a slight incline against the steep barricade.

This must be the exit John sealed off.

But she got through.

I slide the bat back into my belt and begin to climb—until I feel one of my pant legs snag. I glance down. Webs.

They're stretched across the rocks— except these aren't caked with bugs or dust. Just smooth, sticky strands pulled tight between the debris, nearly invisible against the jagged stone. Perfect for trapping unsuspecting prey happening to wander into a spider's den.

I tug at my pant leg as quietly as I can, but it won't budge. I pull harder—still nothing. Sweat beads on my forehead and drips down my neck as I scan the tunnel with my flashlight, heart hammering.

There.

A sharp-looking rock catches my eye. I grab it and start sawing at the web, but the moment I touch it, the strands vibrate, snapping the signal up through the rocks.

If I remember right, spiders use vibrations to sense prey in their webs...Shit, I'm triggering the trap!

Panic surges through me. I turn the rock on my pants and start cutting, seam by seam, inch by inch. My hands burn, raw and scraped against the jagged edge, but I keep going, desperate to break free before I'm discovered.

Finally, the last seam is cut, and I slowly slide my foot free from the pant leg, careful not to trigger the web. I shove the rock into one of my cargo pockets and put the flashlight back in my teeth's grip, my jaw still aching from the repeated abuse. My heart is thumping in my chest as I start back up again, but this time, slow and deliberate in my every step.

My every grasp.

My every breath.

I got lucky that it was my pants. I might not be so lucky the next time I fuck up.

My breath grows heavier as I climb, my body is so drained I'm shocked it's still moving. Adrenaline pumps through my veins like engine oil, forcing me forward, pushing me through the pain. Until at last, I reach the top.

Carefully, quietly, I take the flashlight from my mouth and shine it through the opening, scanning the area. I move the beam slowly, starting on the far right and sweeping across. Bracing myself for whatever I might see. *Terrified* of what I might see.

Beyond the rockfall is a vast chamber, the ceiling stretching so high it vanishes into darkness. To the right, there are rusty metal mining carts. Some overturned, some piled together, and a few still holding old supplies, all buried in layers of dust and cobwebs. I keep moving the flashlight to the left, slowly scanning the pitch-black cavern. The ground glitters faintly in the beam as I inch the light farther…then—I see it.

In the center of the chamber stands a massive rock column, its base buried beneath a mound of gold nuggets of every size and shape. It looks like a miner's twisted Christmas tree—presents of gold wrapped in brown webs, decorated with swollen web sacs and human skeletons draped like broken ornaments. And there, near the base on the left side of the pile—

"Emelia!"

Her hair hangs forward, spilling over her face as her head droops, her body slightly suspended in webbing. I quickly and quietly climb down the rocks, still watching for webs as pebbles cascade down the rockfall and echo throughout the cavern. Reaching the ground, I move at a light jog until I'm standing in front of my daughter, her limp body tightly wound in webbing and secured to the mound of gold.

I pat her face gently but urgently, whispering, "Emmie… you've got to wake up, sweetheart."

She groans faintly, "Mom?" Her eyes flutter open, her voice barely a whisper.

Tears spring to my eyes. "Yes, my sweet, beautiful girl," I breathe, smiling through the emotion tightening my throat. "I'm here. I'm going to cut you free."

I wedge the flashlight in my armpit and reach for the jagged rock in my pocket.

Emelia lifts her head. "Mom..." she wheezes, "I don't feel good."

"I know, sweetheart. I'm gonna get you out of here." I find the rock and start sawing at the webbing. "We're gonna be out of here in no time."

"Mom...it's dark."

I look up at her—she's staring blankly past me, her eyes wide, like she can't see me at all. My heart cracks. Tears stream down my face as I start cutting faster, panic choking my throat.

"It's okay, hon. We're gonna get out of here, and—"

"Mom..." Emelia's tears begin to fall. "I don't think I'm going to make it—"

"Don't you dare give up on me now, Emmie. I almost got you—"

Just then—a small, brown spider crawls from her tear duct and slides down a tendril of silk to the ground.

Then another slips from her ear.

Then another.

And another.

I watch in horror.

No. I can't lose my baby girl. Not like this. She doesn't deserve this. I have to save her. This can't be the end! I cry as I whisper "no" over and over, my voice shaking. I keep cutting.

Faster.

And faster.

I can't lose her.

No.

No!

My chest collapses in on itself—the pain in my heart replaced by a pressure so sharp it feels like it's splitting me in two.

Emelia smiles faintly and whispers, "Mom after a storm, there is…"

"No. No, Emmie. I can't. I won't. I refuse—"

"Mom, please."

Her voice is soft. Her eyes begin to roll back as baby spiders crawl from every crevice of her body. Her cheeks split as they spill over—eating her from the inside out.

My vision blurs. All I can see is her face through the torrent of tears pouring from my eyes. I lean forward, press my forehead to hers, not caring if the spiders fall on me as I whisper.

"*Sun.*"

Emelia laughs faintly—and then I feel it. Her spirit leaving her body. I lift my head and kiss the top of hers. Then take a step back.

Her body is nearly swallowed in brown spiders. The sounds of quiet crunching as they chew through her, consuming what's left of my daughter from the inside out.

I collapse to the ground on all fours, dropping my flashlight, my limbs giving out beneath the weight of my grief. A blood-curdling cry rips out from my chest—raw, primal, and soul-shattering.

It isn't just a scream. It's every ounce of love, agony, and helplessness erupting out of my essence into the darkness. My chest heaves as the cry breaks into sobs, my fingers clawing at the cold, unfeeling earth beneath me.

She's gone.

My baby is gone.

And I couldn't save her.

As the light inside me fades into darkness, a pebble skips down the wall behind me, ricocheting off the cavern walls with a hollow clatter. Then—a clicking noise. Sharp. Rhythmic. Sinister.

I slowly rise to my feet, my body heavy with sorrow, and turn—hesitantly.

There's a shape. Faint, clinging to the dirt wall. But it's too dark to make out. I reach down, fingers trembling, and pick up the flashlight. Lifting it slowly, I guide the beam from the ground up the wall, inch by inch.

Then I see it.

Not a spider.

A child. There, hanging on the wall, is a little boy—no more than ten, his long black hair draped over his face. His skin is gray and tight over his bones, his sunken cheeks and hollow eyes fixed in a lifeless stare. His mouth hangs open, jaw slack and silent. It takes a moment to register—it's a corpse. A little boy's corpse.

But why is it on the wall?

Wait—the wall… is moving.

Barely at first. A subtle shifting. Then scraping. Grinding.

The space around the boy twitches—jerks.

Something massive begins to unfold. That's not the wall.

It's legs.

Eight of them.

Slowly, a shape peels away from the earth, like the shadows themselves are shedding skin. Legs bend and rise from a flat, still position. The dirt around the child morphs—revealing coarse, bristling hair and glistening brown patches.

Then I see her.

Arachne.

A dozen unblinking, obsidian eyes lock onto mine as her massive frame unfolds from its hiding place.

She lifts from the wall, enormous and grotesque. Her bloated body, the size of a large but narrow bear, slightly sways as flakes of dried human flesh drift off her stretched skin. Her long, hairy legs, at least twenty feet outstretched, grip the dirt with blood-stained talons as she creeps down the wall. Tar-colored drool strings down from her large fangs, which curl inward around a gaping mouth lined with jagged teeth, clicking in a rhythmic pattern.

She is awake.

And she's hungry.

Arachne's body distorts and cracks in unnatural ways as she descends slowly down the wall. The boy's corpse dangles from her second maw, held upright by thin, nearly invisible fangs tucked behind his limp, broken body. She clicks at me again. Sharp, deliberate. Like a twisted attempt at speech.

With a sickening jerk, she shakes the boy at me—his lifeless limbs flop like a marionette made of bones, held together by thin, sagging pale leather.

She's testing me. Luring me. Watching to see if I'll fall for her trickery. A true corpse puppet master.

I stare at the eight-legged beast that stole my baby and an unspeakable, silent rage ignites inside me, scorching through every vein. Every nerve. It burns hotter than hellfire—hot enough to make the Devil flinch. It doesn't just consume me. It *possesses* me. Grief has gutted me, scraping out whatever happiness remained in my soul. And now, that emptiness is filled with something ancient.

Something feral.

A wrath that feels older than God Himself. It coils in my marrow, a phoenix rising from the ashes of my broken soul, and erupts—not as a scream, but as a storm raining hails of fire and brimstone. My fury is no longer human. It's a living inferno, and I swear—I don't care how big she is. I don't care how many legs she has or how many of her black eyes watch me. I'm going to burn this cunt to the fucking ground.

Arachne opens her back maw, and the boy's body slides out. His brittle bones clatter against the stone like a witch doctor's windchime as he hits the ground. She raises her two front legs high and unleashes a roaring hiss, saliva spraying from her fanged mouth, her warm, sour breath washing over me in a wave of rot and decay.

But I don't flinch. I stare right back into her sinister eyes, my voice cold.

"All right, bitch."

I pick up the splintered Louisville Slugger and rest it on my shoulder. Cocking my head, a smug grin tugs at the corner of my lips. My eyes burning with hellfire.

"Let's dance."

Chapter Thirty-Five
Arachne

Arachne watches me as she lifts her legs in sinister coordination, crawling sideways like a crab. It's like she's studying me—waiting for me to make the first move.

I don't dare blink. She must know I can hurt her with the bat. She's smart, but that's to be expected. She's over a hundred years old—and you don't survive that long by being stupid.

With a low, deep click, she crawls backwards, fading into the shadows. She's gone.

Punching the flashlight out in front of me, I shine its light across the mine, desperately trying to find her. I catch a glimpse, her legs skittering just outside the beam before disappearing into the darkness. Clicking echoes off the walls with each movement.

She's taunting me.

If I can't find her soon, I'm as good as dead. My eyes dart around until they land on the mound of rough gold nuggets. That's when an idea hits. *Maybe the gold can light up the mines?*

I turn my flashlight on the pile. The light bounces and scatters off the uneven surfaces, casting golden beams across the mine, acting like dozens of tiny mirrors, creating a disco ball of light shimmering across the large open cavity.

That should do it—

A deep, sinister click resonates in the air behind me.

CLICK.

Chills run down my spine. I hesitantly turn around. She's right behind me.

Before I can react, her mandibles wrap around me, hoisting me off the ground and slamming me into her front fangs. I manage to keep hold of the bat, but I drop the flashlight.

It hits the floor and spins, the beam landing on the gold pile, light bursting across the room in scattered rays, casting jagged shadows. Our silhouettes, shadowy shapes against the mine walls as I fight for my life.

The fangs curl inward, wrapping around my torso and arms, squeezing me toward her mouth—toward those jagged, gnashing teeth, trying to eat me alive.

I shove the bat up between us, pressing it between her sharp teeth as she roars in vexation. Her fangs tighten, pressing me harder against her face, trying to crush me and force me into her snarling mouth. I grit my teeth and push with everything I've got, muscles shaking under the pressure. Then, pain explodes in my arm. One of her massive fangs curls and pierces straight through my bicep.

I scream. The venom from the fang burns, hot and cold all at once, spreading through the gaping hole her fang has made.

With my free hand, I dig into my pocket. My fingers close around the rock. A guttural warrior cry escapes my throat as I stab it into one of her beady black eyes.

It pops.

Yellowish-green puss-like slime oozes out as Arachne shrieks in ferocious pain. She releases me. My body slams against the hard, cold earth.

Arachne screeches, throwing the bat across the other side of the mine and clawing madly at the rock embedded in her eye with her clawed mandibles, her limbs twitching in frustrated pain—this is my chance.

Clutching my bicep, I force myself to my feet, gasping, wincing through the pain. I stagger toward the nearest mining cart, half-limping, half-running, and duck behind it.

I press my back against the cold metal, trying to steady my breath. I slide my elbow brace up to squeeze around my gaping bicep, using it as a makeshift bandage. It won't last long, but it will have to do for now.

Carefully, I turn slightly to peek over the edge of the cart. Arachne's thrashing wildly. Her massive body slamming into the walls, legs skittering in every direction, the rock still lodged deep in her eye socket. She screeches and clicks, each sound sharper, more unhinged than the last. The mine quakes with every impact as she slams into the wall.

Again.

And again.

Until—one of the blocked exits shifts. The pile of rocks vibrates, and a stone at the top breaks free, tumbling down with a sharp clatter that echoes through the cavern.

Then I feel it on my face—a rush of cool air flowing in through the opening. Fresh air. From the outside.

And Arachne feels it, too. She stops. Holding her stance in an eerie stillness. Her fangs twitch with curiosity. Bit by bit, her legs turn toward the shifting barricade. She knows.

A memory flashes—my first visit with Mr. Gilbert, standing in front of the old map of the mines on his office wall. His words ring clear in my head:

"No miner was ever able to access that area because it's blocked off by rock and debris... John Burrow must've set off gunpowder in the mines to block the area. I wonder what John was trying to hide..."

But John wasn't hiding the mines. He was hiding the *town* from Arachne. John died sealing these tunnels to protect the people above. And now one of those exits is opening.

I glance toward my daughter, or what's left of her. Her small, broken body now fully engulfed by Arachne's writhing, twitching babies.

If Arachne gets through, she and her spawn will run rampant through the town, devouring anything and everything in their path. And they won't stop there.

They'll spread.

Across the state.

Across the country.

They will *consume* the world.

Arachne lets out a low, gruff hiss, her legs twitching with anticipation. Then she charges it, like a wasp to rotten meat. Barreling to the exit, she begins clawing at the rubble, frantically digging, shrieking. Trying to get through. Dust and stone fly as her massive limbs tear at the blockade John Burrow died to create. Each swing of her clawed legs bringing her closer to the world above.

I can't let her out.

I *won't* let her out.

But how?

I anxiously scan the cavern, desperate for anything—*anything*—that can help. Then something catches my eye. In the old mining cart in front of me, buried under layers of dust, is a pile of black powder and long fuses. I snatch the fuse. It's old, but it's intact.

What if... my eyes flick to the thick stone column in the center of the cavern—it looks like it's the only thing holding this entire place up. But this won't be enough to bring it down. I glance across the chamber. On the far side—those old mining carts I saw when I first got here. I remember seeing more supplies. *There might be more gun powder and—*

I press the outside of my cargo pocket, feeling the lighter still there from my last cigarette.

I've got my lighter. I guess it pays to be a smoker.

I grit my teeth and move, half-limping, half-running across the uneven cavern floor. Arachne is still clawing at the exit, too consumed by her frenzy to notice me.

I reach the other carts. One of them is packed with long fuses and small barrels. Black powder seeping out of the cracked wood. These must be gunpowder kegs. *Jackpot.*

I look at my arm as blackened blood oozes down from the soaked brace. I don't have much time left, and there is too much here to carry back and forth.

I'll have to push it.

I look toward the column. Toward the mound of gold. Toward where my daughter's mostly eaten body still lies. I take a deep breath. Hands on the edge, I press my weight into the cart. The rusted wheels shriek in protest... then groan, slowly giving way. Inch by inch, I push it toward the column, my heart screaming in my chest as I drive my body past its breaking point.

Blood streams down the brace squeezing my bicep. The venom spreads like wildfire, crawling up into my shoulder. My throat tightens as I hold back screams.

I turn around. I grit my teeth and press my back into the cart. My thighs and calves burn with each step as I dig my feet into the earth, forcing the weight forward. Pain bursts through me like firecrackers, sharp and constant. My body begs to give up. But I won't let it. I can't.

I have to finish this.

For Emelia.

Arachne's clicks and roars resonate off the mine walls. Rubble skips across the ground with each swipe of her clawed legs.

I need to keep going.

I'm almost there. I can feel it. With a final push, the cart's wheels hit gold. I quickly start grabbing the gunpowder kegs, sticking them into the webs that wrap around the mound of gold nuggets and the column.

Pain shoots through my body. My sound of my heartbeat is growing stronger in my ears… but slowing down with each passing moment. My hands are numb. Grabbing a fist full of fuses, I stick them inside the barrels, twisting them together to create one fuse.

My body collapses to the ground. The mine starts to dim. A sharp ache pulses in my throat, shooting up to my temples. I look at my shoulder—blackened veins crawl up past the strap of my tank top, spreading like roots under the skin. Arachne's venom is moving fast. I don't have much time left. I'm dying.

I pull myself up, leaning my back against the pile of gold. My arm aches and trembles as I reach into my pocket. Wincing through the pain, I pull out the lighter.

Barely holding the fuse with my injured arm, I try to light the string—but my trembling thumb keeps slipping off the spark wheel.

"Come on…" I grunt through clenched teeth, forcing pressure through my shaking hand. But it's no use.

My thumb keeps missing.

My strength is fading.

My body's failing.

A sob cracks in my throat as a tear rolls down my cheek.

"I'm so sorry, Emmie…" My voice is barely a whisper. "Momma's sorry…"

I look down at the lighter, useless in my trembling grip. My whole body starts to convulse—not from the venom now, but from grief.

I failed my baby girl.

I failed her with Kyle.

I failed her when she was taken by Arachne.

And I am failing her now. I couldn't save her. I couldn't protect her. And now... now I can't even kill the monster that did it. I was supposed to end this. But I can't even light the damn fuse!

I let my head fall back against the mound of gold and close my eyes. My chest rises and falls, slower... and slower. My body is shutting down, and I don't fight it. My arms go limp. The lighter slips slightly in my grasp. The mine grows darker around me, the sounds of Arachne's screeching fading into a distant echo.

I smile, welcoming Death into my dying heart. I just want to be with my daughter again. Then—

CLAP. CLAP.

Two sharp, familiar claps break through my thoughts. My eyes slowly flutter open. First blurry... then finally clear.

Standing about twenty feet in front of me is the spirit of John Burrow, cradling a small baby in his arms. Beside him, the O'Brien family, and in front of them, a crowd of children standing together in the dim, golden light.

I recognize them. The little boy from the car, now smiling, hand-in-hand with the shirtless boy from the tub. A little girl in worker's jeans and an oversized beret, her face unfamiliar, but her hands unmistakable as she claps a steady rhythm, smiling to her own beat.

The giggling girls in white dresses who were playing jump rope are now playing patty-cake, their laughter light and warm, while the older ginger boy stands watch nearby, smiling and tapping his foot to the beat of their game.

The group of boys and girls from the kitchen sits crisscross in the dust, drawing pictures with their fingers, calm and at peace.

Even the boy from the chandelier stands off to the side—arms crossed, gaze turned away like a rebellious teenager but present still.

John and the O'Briens glance at one another and share a soft chuckle. Elizabeth perches on her daddy's shoulders, her hands cupping gently around his head, while Laura looks up at her daughter with glowing, motherly love. John leans down, eyes full of warmth, as baby Ada reaches up, her little fingers grasping the curled tip of his handlebar mustache. John smiles tenderly as he glances back up at me. And so do the others.

But—*Where is Mary Beth?*

Just as the thought escapes my mind, a gentle, spirited hand rests on my shoulder. I turn my head, my neck cracks in agonizing soreness as I look over.

Mary Beth is crouched beside me on the ground, calm and radiant. She gazes into my eyes with a gentle, knowing smile—as if to say, *everything's going to be okay.*

My eyes fill with tears, not from grief, but from a release of guilt. From the comfort of knowing I am not alone. From inner peace.

I gaze over at Arachne. She's almost through the exit. An internal inferno sears through every dead cell in my body. The spirit I thought had died with Emelia has risen. And it's stronger than ever. I can't give up. Not just for Emelia...But for John, Mary Beth, the O'Briens, and all the children. They deserve justice. And I'm going to give it to them.

"Arachne!" I scream, my voice thundering against the mine walls.

She doesn't stop but claws even faster at the rubble. I growl through my teeth.

"You've lived in the dark, stealing the lives of innocent children. For over a hundred years, you've gotten away with it. But this time, you made a mistake." My arms tremble as I lift the fuse and tighten my grip on my lighter. "You took the wrong girl. *My* baby girl. And now you'll pay for every soul you've devoured." I grin with callous coldness. "Because *I* am the storm that's about to show you the sun."

A sudden tingling sparks across my scalp. Then crawls. I see them. Tiny legs.

Arachne's babies cascade down in front of my face. Tiny fangs pierce my cheeks, gnawing, chewing their way in. I laugh manically. My mind is slipping, insanity filling the voids created by the tiny spiders slowly eating their way through my brain. Their whispers crawl inside my ears, my throat.

I try to flick the lighter, but my thumb is shaking too much. I keep trying. Over and over again, my thumb misses the wheel. It's no use.

My vision is becoming blotchy as the spiders start to crawl through my tear ducts. My hand feels weak, and I can't hold the lighter much longer. I feel it start to slide out of my palm until—

Mary Beth's catches it as she gently wraps her calm, steady hand around mine. She holds me still. This time, with one flick, the lighter flares to life.

I look at her. She smiles, fire blazing in her amber eyes. We nod—past and present united in perfect, blistering maternal rage as we both agree: The bitch and her spawn must die.

Madness takes the reins. Baby spiders burst from my scalp as I scream, their tiny legs skittering over my lips, "This is for every child you've snatched from their mothers." My breath catches. "This is for Ada... for Emelia."

I light the fuse. It hisses to life. Sparks race up the line toward the kegs pressed against my back and the mound of gold. My vision is gone, and I feel my spirit fading, flickering between the world of the living and the one beyond the veil.

Then suddenly—I can see.

I stand in a field filled with wildflowers of every color. Butterflies flutter in the warm sun, bouncing from bud to bud. I look up toward the clear blue sky, my face soaking in the light. I feel peace. Then, I hear giggling.

But not just any giggle.

"Emmie?"

I turn—and there, in the middle of the field, is Emelia.

Standing.

Dancing.

Twirling in her white tutu, her fingertips brushing gently across the flower tops. Her face glows radiant as she spins, laughing, dancing with the butterflies. My eyes begin to water with pure joy as I watch her pirouette in the field of wildflowers. As she spins faster, beautiful white feathered wings sprout from her back and lift her into the air. The butterflies follow. Her wings flutter gracefully, sunlight shining through the tips like stained glass. She twirls, weightless, the light passing through her curly hair like a halo.

I begin to cry. She is breathtaking—an angel.

Emelia smiles down at me. Her blue eyes filled with bliss. She reaches out her hand, inviting me to join her. As I reach out my hand toward her, my world flickers back to the present, where I sit leaning against the gunpowder kegs. Tears are streaming down my blind eyes as I hold my hand up, reaching for my daughter beyond the veil.

The fiery fuse sparks up my back. I can hear Arachne clawing at the rockfall, trying to escape while she can. I gasp, choking on spiders as they crawl down my throat one by one.

With one final breath, I yell in Arachne's direction, spiders flying out of my mouth with each word.

"Arachne! When you burn in hell," I scorn through bloody teeth, "give Kyle my regards."

My limbs grow heavy as my body sinks into the earth beneath me. The pain shooting through my nerve endings is now dull, numb. I can't feel anything anymore as my consciousness fades.

The darkness isn't scary now, it's beautiful. It embraces me, warm and gentle, welcoming me to the other side where my daughter's amazing laughter faintly waits... growing clearer with each step my spirit takes through the curtain that separates the living from the dead.

I lean my head back, one last single tear streaming down my partially eaten face. With a smile, I exhale for the last time.

Momma's coming, my beautiful songbird.

BOOM.

Epilogue

U.S. DEPARTMENT OF JUSTICE

FEDERAL BUREAU OF INVESTIGATION

CASE FILE: #0928-AE/ADITVILLE
Classification: TOP SECRET//SPECIAL ACCESS
REQUIRED-PROJECT WEBFALL

Report Title: *Post-Explosion Excavation & Discovery*
Prepared by: SA Vivian A. Foltz, SID
Location: [REDACTED]
Case Status: PENDING

SUMMARY OF EVENT

Date of Incident: July 30, 2000
Location: Burrow Estate, Aditville, TN
Event Type: Structural Collapse / Seismic Event / Criminal Discovery

At approximately 3:17 AM on July 30, 2000, a powerful underground explosion occurred beneath the Burrow Estate in Aditville, Tennessee. The blast, originating from a sealed and abandoned mine shaft beneath the property, triggered a town-wide seismic shock. The estate collapsed entirely into a newly formed sinkhole, and a thick plume of smoke and debris blanketed the surrounding area.

Significantly, local resident Gilbert Hickok had contacted law enforcement in the neighboring county on July 29, 2000, expressing concern over strange activity near the estate and unreported cases in the Aditville Sheriff's Office. His report was critical in prompting inter-county cooperation. Due to long-standing corruption allegations against Aditville authorities, jurisdiction was swiftly elevated to the Tennessee Bureau of Investigation and the FBI.

INITIAL ARREST AND SEARCH

Subject: Sheriff William Ashford
Arrest Date: July 31st, 2000
Charges Filed (Initial): Obstruction of Justice,
Tampering with Evidence, Deprivation of Civil Rights.

Sheriff William Ashford was arrested the day following
the explosion. During the execution of a federal search
warrant, the following were recovered from the Aditville
Sheriff's Office:

- 12 unreported missing children case files, some
  dating back to the 1800s.
- A century-old collection of Ashford family journals.

The journals contained:

- Confessions to the planned murders of the O'Brien
  family and Mary Beth Freeman, buried on the
  town's north hill.
- Records of the Ashfords' illegal seizure of the
  O'Brien store after the murders.
- Instructions passed down through the Ashford
  bloodline to protect the family's reputation and
  holdings by any means necessary.

One journal entry recorded an Ashford descendant's
attempt to remove Ada's gravestone to further conceal
the truth. Townspeople objected, deeming it "a sin
against God to disturb the grave of an innocent." The
gravestone remained, enabling investigators to locate the
burial site with minimal delay. The journal also noted
that the Ashfords threatened parents of missing children,
warning that any contact with outside agencies would
prompt an investigation implicating the parents in the
disappearances and suspected murders.

EXCAVATION & DISCOVERY REPORT

Timeline: July 2000 – August 2001
Agencies Involved: SBI Forensic Archaeology Unit, FBI Forensic Anthropology Division.

Key Discoveries:

- Over a dozen remains were recovered, including the Gallo family, 12 juveniles that matched to the missing persons cases, and one unidentified adult male pending forensic analysis.

- A burial site directly behind Ada Marie Burrow Freeman's grave marker was excavated, confirming the presence of the O'Brien family, Mary Beth Freeman, and Ada herself, consistent with locations described in the Ashford journals.

- Gold nuggets were collected during the excavation. Approximate value 250 million U.S. dollars.

- An unidentifiable biological entity, non-human in form, was recovered during the excavation of the Burrow Estate. The specimen has been secured and transported to Facility 51 under CIA directive for classified biological analysis.

All confirmed victim families have been contacted. The Bureau of Victim Assistance is coordinating federal resources for funeral coverage, mental health services, and civil legal support.

DOCKET SUMMARY

CASE NAME: *The People v. Ashford et al.*
CASE NO. 00-CR-1849-FED-ADTV
JUDGE: Hon. Christopher A. Douglas
STATUS: Active – Proceedings Ongoing

CRIMINAL CHARGES FILED:

Count 1: Obstruction of State or local law enforcement (18 U.S. Code § 1511)
Count 2: Tampering with Evidence (18 U.S.C. § 1519 and 18 U.S.C. § 1512.)
Count 3: Deprivation of Rights (18 U.S.C. § 242)
Count 4: Misprision of Felony (18 U.S.C. § 4)
Count 5: Criminal Negligence Resulting in Death (T. C.A § 39-13-212)
Count 6: Abuse of Power by Public Official (T.C.A. § 39-16-402)

CIVIL LEGAL REPERCUSSIONS:

Multiple civil actions were initiated by the victims' families. Unable to meet its financial obligations, the town of Aditville was declared insolvent and subsequently unincorporated. Its land and assets were transferred to federal oversight and listed for public auction, where they remain unsold.

Sheriff William Ashford and six co-conspirators were federally indicted on charges including but not limited to conspiracy to obstruct justice, deprivation of civil rights, and falsification of public records.

UNUSUAL FINDINGS: ADA MARIE BURROW FREEMAN

Case Note ID: 0928-AE-BIO1
Subject: Ada M. Burrow Freeman
Exhumation Date: December 12, 2000
Original Cause of Death: UNKNOWN

Autopsy of Ada's remains revealed:
* A previously undocumented neurotoxin present within skin tissue.
* A foreign organic mass, believed to be a biological egg sac, is embedded near the spinal column. The structure exhibited characteristics consistent with arachnid reproductive material, though it does not match any known species.

The egg sac organism and an unidentified species recovered from the Burrow Estate were secured under federal containment and transferred to Facility 51 for classified research under CIA directive. Preliminary analysis suggests both possess advanced regenerative properties. Scientists are actively working to revive the egg sac organism, believing that if brought to life, it could significantly accelerate breakthroughs in regenerative medicine, neural repair, and experimental defense technologies.

NOTE: Knowledge of these specimens is classified for public safety. Access is restricted to TOP SECRET personnel under PROJECT WEBFALL. Unauthorized disclosure violates federal law and national security.

—**End of Report**—

The End?

Acknowledgments

To my husband: Thank you for supporting me as I pursued writing a novel. Your long days of taking care of the home and family to give me the time I needed did not go unnoticed. I love you.

To Mott: Thank you for being the most patient and supportive editor I could ever ask for. Your kindness and flexibility mean the world to me, and I cannot wait to work with you again.

To Christy: Thank you for always having my back. Your support, allowing me to mind vomit ideas, helping me with accepting edits, and pep talks kept me going when I wanted to give up. I'm so lucky to have you in my life.

To Kenna: Thank you for being the best writing buddy a girl could hope for! Without you starting the journey with me and putting a fire under my ass, I don't believe I would have written this book.

To Shantelle: Thank you for being my cheerleader. Your beauty, strength, and fiery spirit were a huge inspiration for Mary Beth. Never change; no one could ever be you.

To my mother: Thank you for encouraging me to write my novel and pursue what makes me happy.

To those not directly mentioned but who still supported me: Thank you for your encouragement, support, and love. It takes a village. Thank you for being a part of it.

To those who thought I couldn't do it: Thank you for making this accomplishment that much *sweeter*.

ARC Team Acknowledgement

To my ARC Team: Thank you for the opportunity to share my story with you. Your sharp eye for typos, thoughtful trigger list, plot insights, and honest feedback were invaluable in helping me polish this tale to shine in its dark, twisted world. You are rock stars. All @'s refer to the team members' Instagram tag if they chose to provide it.

Alyssa Kunz (@My_readersheaven), Alyssa Riddle (@Lyssas.literary.lounge), Amanda Higdon, Courtney Galante (@Darkmoonreadsx3), Dr. Voss (@kylevauthor), Emily Tinsley (@Emilytinsley1), Jane Stiers (@Jasperspieceofmind), Jen (@SmutSpiceEverythingNice), Jen Sands (@Bookish._.banter), Jess (@Jessmcix_reads), Jennifer F. (@J3nn._.0), JoJo (@The_real_htxharley), Josh White (@Joshwhitebooks), Jules Geraci (@Kindledghouls), Kelsey Pierce (@Kelsey_reading_realm), Kristina (@Kristinas_book_Reviews), La'rina S. (@Ooolala.reads), Leanna Flores (@smallnightmares_), Lisa D. (@Xlisaxmarie), Lynsey Williams (@Busymommiesbookclub), Melissa D. Mejia, Ney Hamel (@Horromantasybookmom), Regina Doran, Ricardo Vazquez Berrios (@Anon_flcl), S. L. McGee (@Sl_mcgee_author), Sammy Herr (@Pagewanderer87), Scarlett Nicole Fravel, Spring L. (@Infinite_Ink_Society),

Content Warning List

The following is a general list of content warnings for the novel. Most, if not all, of these triggers are not caused by the main character, Sarah. Please note: the following list contains potential spoilers and may not include all possible triggers present in the novel.

1800s Horror
Ableism
Abuse (General)
Abuse of Power
Animal Death
Arachnophobia
Binding
Blood
Blood Drinking
Body Horror
Bullying
Buried Alive
Burned Alive
Cannibalism
Car Accident
Cheating / Infidelity
Child Abduction
Child Endangerment
Claustrophobia
Confinement
Corpse Mutilation
Corpses
Corrosion
Crude Language
Cult Activity

Dead Infants / Children
Death of Child
Death of Mother
Death of Parent
Death of Pet
Death of Spouse
Desperation
Disabled Child
Disabled Main
Character
Disappearance
Disfigurement
Dismemberment
Display of Human
Remains
Disturbing Imagery
Disturbing Smells
Domestic Abuse /
Violence
Domestic Assault /
Battery
Elder Abuse
Emotional Abuse
Entrapment
Explosives

False Reports
Fatal Fall
Fatal Illness
Fear of Dark
Forced Marriage
Forced Oral Act (Not
Sexual).
Funeral Imagery
Gagging
Gaslighting
Ghosts
Gore (Graphic)
Grave Desecration
Grief
Hallucinations
Hanging / Lynching
Home Invasion
Implied Incest
Infanticide
Injury (Severe)
Injustice
Insects
Loss of Limb
Macabre Imagery
Maggots
Mangled Bodies
Manipulation
Mass Grave
Medical Trauma
Mental Health
Missing Children
Monsters (Human &
Supernatural)
Murder

Narcissism
On-page Death
Panic Attacks
Paranoia
Paranormal Activity
Parental Neglect
Pest Infestation
Poisoning
Police Corruption
Predatory Behavior
Psychological Abuse /
Distress
Public Shaming
Racism
Religious Abuse
Religious Sacrifice
Rotting Corpses / Flesh
Self-Harm
Sexism
Sexual Harassment
Shadow Figures
Sick Parent
Skeletons
Strangulation
Suffocation
Suicide
Threats to Child
Torture
Toxic Marriage
Unexplained Noises
Verbal Abuse
Victim Blaming
Violence

About the Author

M. A. Robinson is a United States Marine Corps veteran who served as a military police officer stationed at Camp Lejeune, North Carolina. She is a Campbell University alumna who holds a Bachelor of Applied Science in Criminal Justice and is currently pursuing her Juris Doctor. When she isn't writing, she enjoys spending time with her family, relaxing with a good horror movie, and cuddling with her beloved fur babies.